# WHERE DARKNESS RESIDES

DANIEL MENDOZA THRILLERS
BOOK 4

DANIEL MALDONADO

This book is dedicated to those attorneys at the firms I worked at over the last twenty-five years who inspired me to be the best attorney I could be.

Thanks for all of your support and encouragement.

# 1  ISABELA

Isabela, Puerto Rico
Present Day

As the innumerable trees swayed with the Caribbean winds, the Regal Isabela Resort seemed ominous. The spectacular views of the Atlantic were unmatched because the resort was located high above the ocean floor. A unique hideaway in Puerto Rico, the Regal Isabela was well known for its championship golf course hugging the rocky promontory cliffs lining the island's northern shore. Nature lovers also enjoyed the innumerable local birds who nested there. But what drew high-end customers to the resort was its Spanish architecture framed in palm trees and colorful tropical flowers. Every building and casita was constructed with brownish-grey stones and topped with clay roof tiles imported from Spain.

It felt like home, inviting and relaxing. For Daniel Mendoza, the resort would be his home away from home for the next week as he attended the resort's tenth anniversary celebrations. After exiting the black limousine, Daniel strolled toward the main building to check-in.

"*Buenos dias, Caballero.* Welcome to the Regal Isabela," the male attendant beamed during his greeting. "How may I help you, Mr. Mendoza?"

Although initially shocked he was instantly recognized because he'd never patronized the resort before, Daniel remembered Gerald Ravan, the resort's corporate attorney, must have informed the staff of his imminent arrival because the corporation was paying his tab. The Regal Isabela was owned by the international hotel chain, The Regal Wisteria, headquartered in Tokyo. Mr. Ravan, a long-time client of the Mendoza law firm, arranged for the resort to pay for Daniel's flight to the island from Arizona, the stretch limo that greeted him at the Luis Munoz Marin International Airport in San Juan, and, of course, the luxurious accommodations as well as all meals and activities throughout his stay. Daniel was relieved he could finally relax after his recent, grueling royalty litigation where several witnesses, attorneys, and even the federal judge were murdered to hide his client's poor financial condition. Even Daniel could have been a potential victim but escaped with his life.

Now, the tragedy was all behind him. Daniel only wanted to get away from the dreary reminders in Arizona and focus on a lackadaisical vacation where all festivities were planned for him and he only needed to relax, soak in the sun, and enjoy five-star-rated meals. Regretting his new-found relationship with Corina wasn't as close where she would have accepted an invitation to accompany him on this trip, Daniel traveled to his homeland alone somewhat forlornly. It wasn't the first time he vacationed in Puerto Rico alone. It probably wouldn't be the last.

"I'm checking in by...by myself," he reluctantly responded to the attendant with a half-hearted smile.

After all, he was appreciative of the resort's hospitality and didn't want to seem ungrateful.

"Understood. We have you booked for casita number seven. It has an exquisite, ocean view and is located in the front row of the resort." The attendant handed Daniel a magnetic key card and a cerulean blue wristband. "Put that on. You'll need it around the premises, so security knows you're our guest. It will also allow you to attend the celebrations."

Daniel complied.

"Your luggage will be waiting for you in the casita," he continued while double-checking his computer to ensure the key card was active. The attendant pointed towards the door to his right. "A golf cart is waiting to drive you to the casita. Just let us know if you need anything during your stay. We'd be happy to arrange any special activities just for you at the resort's expense, of course."

"Thank you. I'm very pleased to be here," Daniel said as he walked to the door with a kick in his step.

The driver handed him a refreshment as Daniel scooted into the golf cart. The whirl of its electric motor propelled the golf cart along the pathway through the first set of casitas. It then rounded the corner away from the pool area on a larger pathway in front of the second set of casitas facing the ocean until the golf cart reached the third casita from the right, nestled lower into the mountain than the surrounding ones. Daniel tried to hand the driver a tip which was politely declined.

"No, thank you," the driver said with a strong Puerto Rican accent. "Mr. Ravan has taken care of everything. There's no need."

As the golf cart headed back to the main building, Daniel walked into the casita, relieved the long journey was finally over. The dark wood flooring matched the two sturdy bookcases to the entrance of the bedroom as well as the heavy wood doors and the king-sized poster bed. Daniel was used to lavish rooms at the various hotels he'd stayed in owned by the Regal Wisteria throughout the world. But the Regal Isabela was the first posh hotel on the island owned by the corporation. He was pleasantly surprised at its grandeur and elegant design.

Daniel took another sip of his refreshment before setting the glass on a wooden table. He walked to the closet to pull out his luggage only to find out all of his formal clothes were hung up and his casual clothes were neatly placed in the dresser drawers. After finding his swim trunks, Daniel changed, grabbed a beach towel, and walked outside to the terrace so he could dip into the plunge pool. Placing his towel on the chaise lounge, Daniel was startled when he heard the female voice of the private investigator his law firm regularly retained.

"Look at you. It's about time you arrived. I've been waiting for you," Pamela Williams said as she waded in the plunge pool, her long blonde hair tied into a ponytail.

"Not again!! I can't believe you're here," Daniel declared as he briefly clenched his teeth wondering how Corina would feel if she learned another woman was with him on vacation.

He finally relaxed after realizing it wasn't as dire

as he originally thought. Pamela was a lovely woman, two decades his junior, but they worked well together professionally.

*Corina would understand it's just business*, he reassured himself.

"Don't give me that. I know you'd rather not be alone in this lovely casita."

Pamela splashed some refreshing pool water on Daniel in a playful way, hoping to ease the tension.

He joined her in the plunge pool and sat beside her. He took a deep breath and soaked in the views as the sun began to set.

"To be honest, I know I need time alone to decompress but after...you know... after all that's happened, I'm not sure being alone will make things better." Daniel was worried his mind would relive the experiences again and again if he wasn't distracted. "I'm really glad you're here, Pam."

A beaming smile graced Daniel's lips. He looked around because he wanted to make a toast but forgot he didn't bring his glass with him.

"I knew you wanted me," she chuckled. "We can order some champagne if you like. Room service should be here any moment. I ordered you the chew...chew...."

"*Chuletas fritas*," Daniel interrupted.

"Yeah, the fried pork chops. You know what I meant," she explained. "Rumor has it you wanted to order them when you got here."

Initially pleased Pamela was thinking ahead, it suddenly dawned on him, "How did you know what I was.... Never mind."

With an even bigger grin, Pamela simply ignored Daniel's question and gazed over the rolling hills toward the azure waters of the Atlantic. She knew Daniel would one day figure it out. Just not today. She only wanted to enjoy their brief quiet time together before the food arrived and Daniel's mind was distracted with sustenance and daily living. Daniel got the hint and drew closer to the edge of the plunge pool facing the ocean. He temporarily dipped his head underwater to cool himself down from the Caribbean's warm climate and shook his head as he arose, spraying water in the air. Daniel was accustomed to the tropical humidity having vacationed in Puerto Rico every year for the past decade.

Being here made him feel exhilarated. Pamela could see it in his eyes and his demeanor. Gone were the deep contemplative thoughts about legal strategy and worries about an opponent's nefarious machinations to obtain an advantage. Gone were the endless meetings with clients, new and old, both in person and over the computer to address some new-fangled issue. Gone were the interpersonal squabbles with staff and attorneys where Daniel played interference to resolve any disputes and keep the cog of his boutique defense firm going without a hitch. Right now, it was just the two of them together. Not in a romantic way. At least not yet. It was good for this duo who worked closely over the years to just hang out and relax without any expectations.

Disturbing the serenity of the moment, an attendant approached from the side of the terrace pushing a cart. Two stainless steel plate covers protected their meals.

'*Buenos noches, Señor y Señora Mendoza*," the attendant said while placing their food on the patio table opposite the plunge pool. He also set down a bottle of champagne, utensils, and linen napkins.

Pamela and Daniel slowly eased out of the pool.

"*Gracias,*" Daniel expressed while drying himself with the towel.

Pamela raised the plate cover. "Looks delicious." The aroma of shrimp and dorado wafted in the air. "My dinner smells good. I'm sure you're jealous," Pamela cajoled as she watched the water drip down his body. She resisted expressing her thoughts.

"*Bueno provecho,*" the attendant declared while exiting the terrace and walking along the outside of the casita.

Daniel sat down to eat. Pamela joined him. As Pamela expected, Daniel was focused on eating the meal and enjoying the lush surroundings. After eating several slices of pork, Daniel broke the silence.

"Isn't your job going to miss you while you're here?" he asked while scooping up a hefty morsel of mashed *malanga* which was reminiscent of mashed potatoes but made with a local root vegetable instead.

"Virginia and George are holding down the fort. They're used to it now that I'm not working as much. You know...I'm spending more time with my dad."

"How is your dad?" Daniel wondered.

"He has his good days and his bad days. But over-all, he's doing better."

Pamela wanted to change the topic but was appreciative of Daniel expressing his concerns about her father's well-being.

"Who's holding down the law firm while you're on vacation?" Pamela inquired. She knew the answer already but also enjoyed the lighter conversation...

"John and Marissa as usual. After all, they are the

senior associates at the firm. They're in court today for a wrongful death trial. l should be there with them since I'm the partner on the case and the client is expecting me to try it." Daniel became worried but then it clicked. "Who am I fooling? The client is Regal Wisteria. They're paying for all this and know I'm here instead of in court on their behalf."

Daniel relaxed even further at the self-revelation.

"Nice!" Pamela exclaimed although she was already aware of the arrangement. Daniel told her before the trip but had apparently forgotten. Other things were obviously on his mind. "How are you and Corina doing?"

"We're...well, we're..."

Before Daniel could finish, loud yelling came from the adjacent casita, startling both of them. The sound of smashing dishes followed.

## 2 RESTRAINED

### Isabela, Puerto Rico
### Moments Later

The lights at the adjacent casita, number eight, were quickly dimmed shortly after the commotion. The casita's occupants did not want to bring any further attention to themselves from the other guests at the resort or worse yet, hotel security. Pretending the casita was unoccupied was a naive but workable ruse. After the door to the terrace was quickly closed, the older of two casually dressed men grabbed his cell phone and answered an unexpected call.

"Yes, *Chango*. We got him," he excitedly proclaimed while wiping the sweat from his brow.

The younger man was restraining a third Puerto Rican male in a chair when the call came in. He forcefully tied a knot in the rope wrapped around the male's waist while inconspicuously listening to the conversation.

"I don't want you harming my son," *Chango* demanded. "If anything happens to him...You don't want to know what I'll do to the two of you and to your...."

Nervous at the implication, the man hesitantly replied, "Yes, boss. We...we will make sure he's well taken care of. No need to worry."

The older male gestured to his companion to ensure the captive was comfortable. He complied as best as he could while ensuring the restraints were secure. The last thing needed was an escape.

"Where are you? I'm coming over," *Chango* inquired, anxious to finally see his son after a long time apart.

Jose *"Chango"* Quintana was the head of *La Familia*, a local Puerto Rican mafia. He was otherwise known as *El Gran* as were all the previous heads of the family. *Chango* had been *El Gran* for over two decades after his father was brutally murdered by a rival mafia during a turf war over drug routes in the Caribbean. *Chango's* oldest son was groomed to eventually take over the family business, but greed and ambition overcame him. The son was banished to the States and charged with expanding the family business as punishment for secretly warring with some of the factions in *La Familia*. The meted punishment wasn't what most of the faction's members wanted. They wanted blood. However, *Chango* couldn't betray his eldest son despite his despicable behavior.

While living in the States, drug sales steadily increased which also meant increasing the family's wealth and influence in Puerto Rico. *Chango* became very proud of his son and hoped this would ease the tensions created by his son's betrayal. It did not. Rival mafias were envious of his success. So were some of the family members who longed for a bigger piece of

*La Familia's* pie and influence, both politically and personally over the locals in their territory. But *Chango* wasn't willing to cede any control to his *copas*. At least not yet. He was waiting for his son to return in triumph. Instead, *Chango* learned his son secretly returned to the island after additional disgraces of the family he had recently learned about.

"Boss, it's too busy here. More than normal. The resort must be celebrating or something. I'm not sure it's a good idea for you to come. Not yet anyway," the older man who apparently was a long-time soldier of the family explained.

"Dammit. How long do you think the celebrations will last?" *Chango* inquired.

The older male shrugged, not knowing what to tell his boss. He looked over to his companion for some insight.

"The banners said the celebrations last all week," the companion clarified. He became concerned about changes to their original assignment.

"It doesn't look like it's going to die down anytime soon, boss. We'll wait here until it's dark and then sneak away," the older male stammered. He wasn't sure if the idea was acceptable, but it was all he could come up with at the time.

"Alright...alright. I'll meet you at the office later tonight. Bring my boy with you."

*Chango* abruptly hung up the phone, furious at the development, but happy his son was finally located.

Walking closer to his captive, the older male became more frustrated. He hadn't planned on finding the son at the Regal Isabela resort amidst the celebrations but at a more private place where they could easily slip away. He also hadn't planned on his boss finding out they had captured his son so quickly. He wasn't sure if it was his partner who tipped the boss off or if they were being secretly followed by another member of the mafia. Giving *Chango* back his son was the original plan but when the other *copas* secretly offered him money to bring the son to them instead, things changed. He needed to figure out how to lose any tail or determine whether his younger partner would object if he was going to follow through with his promise to deliver *Chango's* son to the *copas* and get paid a lucrative amount of money.

*Maybe I should cut him in on the action*, he thought. Eyeing his companion filled the man with disgust. *I don't want to share my take. But I may have to*, he conceded.

Reluctantly, he motioned the younger man to follow him out to the terrace.

"What's up? What do you need?" the younger companion asked inquisitively. He too was confused as to the new predicament and whether they were going to escape unseen from the resort with an unwilling captive in tow.

"Look, I know this is a unique assignment to say the least, but we...," he walked further into the terrace to ensure his captive was not in earshot. "We can make a lot of money. You're willing to make some money, aren't you?"

"What do you mean money? This isn't a paid gig."

"Well, that's what I'm talking about. You know *Chango* wants his son back. But others in the family want *Chango's* son first if you know what I mean."

He sighed at his comment knowing the weight of

his secret mission was now in the open and he no longer had to hide it from his partner.

"I...I'm new to all this. I don't know about it. I don't want to get in trouble."

"You've heard he stole a lot of money and family heirlooms from some of the family members years ago. They're still not happy about that. They want their money back. They're willing to pay us if they can have first crack at him to see where he hid the money. What do you say? Are you in?"

After a long pause, the younger partner eagerly answered, "I'm in. But how are we getting out of here?"

"Leave that to me," the older male said as he walked back into the casita.

## 3   VOIR DIRE

### Phoenix, Arizona
### Same Day

"Ladies and gentlemen," Judge Jessica Furman said as she dismissed the attorneys from the bench after a conference to discuss the next stage in the trial. The attorneys headed back to their respective tables. "We are now going to do *voir dire*. It's a fancy word, I know, but it's one of the few legal phrases not in Latin. It's Anglo-Norman for the phrase 'to tell the truth.' This is when the attorneys decide which of you in the jury pool will sit as jurors in this case. I will first ask the jury some background questions. Then each side will have the opportunity to ask the entire panel questions to delve deeper into your background and any potential biases. It's important to answer the questions truthfully. If there is a question you think is too personal to answer before the entire panel, please let the bailiff know and we can let you answer in private without the other members present."

The sixteen jurors in the jury box as well as those

in the gallery became even more attentive when they realized the trial was now focused on them. Several jurors' smiles brightened. Others turned their attention from the judge to the attorneys seated at the counsel tables to prepare themselves for the questioning. A younger juror who was of college age was dozing off possibly due to all-night partying.

Judge Furman continued.

"The parties have prepared a brief statement I will read to you to give you a background of the case," Judge Furman announced. She then faced the jury while holding the statement in the air with her right hand. "This case arises from a traffic collision that occurred west of 68th Street on Camelback Road in Scottsdale, Arizona, on May 2nd at approximately 1:15 p.m., between a car driven by Carlos Hernandez and a shuttle bus driven by Martin Weaver. Mr. Weaver was driving a shuttle bus owned by the Regal Phoenix Resort and Spa in the inside lane of westbound traffic on Camelback Road. Mr. Hernandez was driving his Lexus LC convertible in the middle lane of westbound traffic on Camelback Road. A collision occurred between the two vehicles and Mr. Hernandez was ejected from the vehicle and fatally injured. Mr. Hernandez's estate contends Mr. Weaver's vehicle encroached into Mr. Hernandez's lane of traffic and struck his vehicle. Mr. Weaver contends Mr. Hernandez's vehicle encroached into his lane of traffic and struck his vehicle."

After reading the statement, the judge asked the jury questions regarding whether they were acquainted with the plaintiffs, the defendants, the attorneys assigned to the case, and the numerous witnesses who were going to testify during the trial. She then proceeded to ask them about their employment history, educational background, their age, and marital status and whether any jurors would have a hardship if they were assigned to a two-week jury trial.

The attorneys feverishly took notes as each of the jurors gave their answers to the judge's questions. The attorneys for the Weavers and the resort, John Davis and Marissa Robles, each drew sixteen squares on a legal pad with each of the jurors' numbers at the left corner of the square. They then wrote notes for each question answered by the juror so they could evaluate each juror at the end of *voir dire* and decide whether to strike or pass the juror. It was standard practice for attorneys to grid out the jury like this.

"Thank you, jurors. I am done with my questions. Mr. Clarkson, are you ready to ask questions on behalf of the plaintiffs?" the judge inquired.

"Yes, your honor," the older attorney said as he stood up.

His silver hair was slick and professional despite his hometown drawl. When he approached the lectern, he dragged it across the floor so it would be centered to the juror box. His partner rushed over to assist him given its size.

"Thank you," he said to his partner with a pleasant smile as he then faced the jury.

"My name is Doug Clarkson. My partner and I, Danica Bridgers, represent the Hernandez family. Unfortunately, Carlos Hernandez is no longer with us, but he would want an objective jury to resolve this case. So we, his wife, Selinda, and their two children want you to honestly answer our questions. If your answer is yes to the question, just raise your hand and

I can follow up with additional questions if needed. Thank you."

The jurors shook their heads in agreement.

"If you are selected to sit on this case, will you be able to render a verdict solely on the evidence presented at trial and in the context of the law as the judge will give in the jury instructions disregarding any other ideas, notions, or beliefs about the law you may have?"

Doug scanned the jury box as the jurors one by one slowly raised their hands indicating an affirmative answer. He nodded to each juror to acknowledge their response. One lonely juror failed to raise his hand. Doug eyed the juror to determine why he was the exception. "Juror number...."

"Number four," the male said after double-checking his juror badge before answering.

"Yes, juror number four. Why do you feel you will be unable to follow the law as instructed by the court?"

"I don't agree with the law. The laws are unjust and allow plaintiffs to recover loads of money like that woman suing McDonald's for spilled coffee." The juror was proud of his answer while the other jurors listened attentively to see how the attorneys reacted.

Doug proceeded to ask the juror questions to elicit answers about why he felt verdicts were high and if the juror could be fair and award the plaintiffs the millions of dollars they were requesting in this wrongful death case.

"Well, this case is different. I mean someone died. It's not like they just scraped a knee or just got whiplash," the juror explained.

"I appreciate you acknowledging the severity of

this case. Do you think you are able to award the Hernandez family the money they deserve if you find the defendants caused the crash and my client did not?" Doug asked.

"Yes. Yes, I can," the juror said reassuring himself.

The juror also hoped he reassured the plaintiffs' counsel of his sincere objectivity. After being questioned, he was more personally invested in the case and wanted to be seated on the jury after all.

Doug asked the next question on his *voir dire* list.

———

During the break from questioning the jurors, John and Marissa were outside the courtroom in the hallway while watching the jurors file into the elevators in groups to head down to the first floor to patronize the courthouse's restaurant. Once all of the jurors were no longer in the hallway, the two discussed the case.

"I can't believe Daniel isn't here right now," Marissa remarked. "It's not like him to miss a trial."

"Didn't he tell you he's vacationing in Puerto Rico?" John asked.

"No. I...I'm shocked."

"We'll be okay. We've second chaired many trials. We can do this ourselves and make Daniel and our client proud. I'm sure Daniel's confident in your skill level. I know I am."

John didn't want to appear patronizing, but both attorneys had been practicing for over seven years, most of that at the Mendoza law firm.

"Yeah, you're right," Marissa said as she took a deep breath, steadying herself for the long week ahead. "He deserves a vacation after everything he's been through."

"I'm sure he's going to check in on us every day for an update," John added although he had his own doubts about that.

He hoped Daniel would instead focus on enjoying himself in Puerto Rico. Upon his return, Marissa and John would announce their surprising victory. John could dream after all.

Mr. Weaver walked out of the courtroom and approached his attorneys.

"I wanted to thank you for representing us. You guys are doing an excellent job," he declared.

"Thank you, Mr. Weaver," Marissa replied.

"How is Rose doing?" John asked.

"She's feeling better. She's with our son right now," Mr. Weaver explained.

"I'm glad the jurors met her before *voir dire*. A trial can be very stressful," Marissa explained.

"Do you think the plaintiffs' counsel will call her as a witness?" Mr. Weaver asked. "This is too much for her with her Alzheimer's."

"They won't. They didn't list your wife as a witness," John said. "They can always change their minds, but plaintiffs' counsel is aware of your wife's Alzheimer's, and they're concerned about it tainting the jury with sympathy for you. They've filed a motion we've yet to argue with the judge."

"Good." Mr. Weaver was relieved.

"Are you taking notes too?" Marissa asked Mr. Weaver. "We'll want your input on how you feel about the jurors and if there are any you have concerns about."

"Oh yes, I am. Copious notes. I have a few concerns," he added with a smile.

Before he could discuss them, the elevator doors opened, and the jurors filled the hallway again.

"Looks like the jurors are back. Remember the judge's admonition. We can't speak to the jurors. Just be polite and smile," John reminded them both as he stood at attention and nodded to the jurors while they entered the courtroom.

————

When it was the defendants' turn to question the potential jurors, Ms. Robles stood up and walked the well of the court - that area of the courtroom between the bench, the jury box, and counsel's tables. She smiled at each of the jurors in the jury box.

"Mr. Clarkson asked you a lot of questions which makes my part really easy. I'm not going to repeat any questions already asked. I did have a few questions and I'll be quick about it. First, if you were my clients would you have any issue with you being on the jury?"

The jurors seemed stumped by the question and pondered whether they could be fair and impartial. Several of the jurors immediately raised their hands affirming they would be good prospective jurors. One juror contacted the bailiff and whispered something to her. Marissa watched as the bailiff approached the judge. Summoning the attorneys to the bench, the judge then turned on the white noise generator to drown out their voices so the jury and anyone else in the courtroom couldn't hear their discussion.

"We have an issue with juror number nine," the

judge explained. "Juror number nine would like to discuss his answer in private. We can discuss it in my chambers. Is that acceptable to counsel?"

"That's fine, your honor," Mr. Clarkson responded.

"I'm fine with that also," Marissa said.

The judge, the juror, the court reporter, and the attorneys walked into the judge's chambers for privacy without having to dismiss the entire courtroom. Once the court reporter was situated with her portable stenograph, the judge proceeded.

"Juror number nine, I understand you wanted to discuss your answer to Ms. Robles' latest question in private," the judge asked.

The juror was nervous but felt compelled to disclose his beliefs.

"Yes, your honor. I am sure Mr. Clarkson's clients will want to know this but given my experience, I would be biased."

"Why is that?" the judge inquired.

She, as well as the attorneys, were perplexed by the juror's revelation given the positive answers the juror gave during the questioning so far. The juror appeared to be neutral, and a likely candidate selected by either party to be seated as a juror.

"Well, I could not find in favor of Hispanics. In my experience, they are reckless drivers and cause accidents."

The juror was not embarrassed by his statement which he firmly believed.

"Thank you," the judge said. "Can you wait outside with the bailiff while I discuss with the attorneys?"

The juror rose from his chair and walked to the

hallway outside the judge's chambers, closing the door behind him.

"Mr. Clarkson, I take it you will have no problem dismissing the juror for cause," the judge declared.

"No, your honor. We appreciate the juror's truthfulness in this matter. It's better we learn it now before trial."

"Agreed," the judge replied. "Ms. Robles?"

"I have no objections to that, your honor."

"It's settled then. We will thank and dismiss juror number nine."

## 4 TOSSED

### Isabela, Puerto Rico
### Later That Evening

After eating flan for dessert, Pamela wiped her mouth with a linen napkin, placed it on the table, and leaned back on her chair.

"I'm full," she announced.

Bursts of cool Caribbean wind refreshed her. Daniel was also pleased and not just with the meal. Dinner went better than expected. The small talk was pleasant and unrelated to either of their jobs. It was focused mainly on Puerto Rico and its rich culture and diversity. Daniel welcomed the discussion because it refreshed his soul and helped him reminisce about his previous visits to the island.

"What's on the agenda tonight?" Daniel asked with a gleaming smile.

The anniversary celebrations had already started, but Daniel wasn't sure if they should participate in the hotel festivities or just relax in the casita after his long flight. He hoped Pamela had an idea or two which would make the evening even more special. A part of him, however, wished he could have shared these moments with Corina instead. He unexpectedly imagined what she was doing. Images of her beautiful smile overtook him. Shaking these thoughts, he instead focused on enjoying the time with Pamela. She was here and deserved his undivided attention.

"Well," he added after composing himself.

"I don't know. You know me. I'm always up for some fun. Real fun, but...."

Pamela's eyes widened as if her mind was working overtime. She hesitated in sharing her thoughts with Daniel out of concern for ruining their lovely evening.

"What is it? I know you, Pam. Something's ruminating in that crazy head of yours. Don't pretend it isn't?"

He laughed.

Daniel didn't expect her response.

"It's just that...you know...after all the loud noise we heard from the casita next to us, I thought maybe someone may be hurt. I'm concerned," Pamela explained.

"Why didn't you mention that before? We could have done something earlier." Daniel stood up and looked across the bushes into the neighboring casita's terrace. "Looks like all the lights are off."

Pamela walked closer in hopes of seeing something revealing. She didn't. Like Daniel said, the terrace was completely empty. There were no signs of broken dishes or that anyone had actually been on the terrace. Nevertheless, something made Pamela eerily suspicious.

"I'm going to change really quickly and walk next door if you don't mind. You're welcome to come."

She walked into the casita, fully expecting Daniel to follow without looking back. When she heard his footsteps behind her, she smiled. They both changed into casual resort wear skipping a shower so they could check the next casita without further delay.

"I smell like chlorine," Daniel said as he sniffed his arm. He sprayed cologne to mask the smell.

"They won't mind," Pamela responded as she exited the casita and walked the few steps to the next one.

"Hello."

Knocking on the door, Pamela couldn't hear anything from inside. She pressed her ear to the door but still nothing. The noise from the celebration drowned out even the sound of her voice when she repeated her greeting.

Daniel tried to look inside the casita.

"It's hard to tell if anyone's home," he said after moving his head in every direction of the window to inside the casita as best he could. "Are you sure we even heard anything coming from their terrace? Maybe it was just the sounds of celebration? That's all."

He double-checked in anticipation of Pamela instructing him to do so. When she noticed him doing it, she quickly stopped herself from admonishing him.

"I'm going inside," she declared.

"Wait. You can't do that. What if there are people inside, you know...?"

She glared at him with a strange look.

"You know what I mean. Making love. They wouldn't want us barging in the middle of that. We could get in trouble," he declared.

25

Daniel looked around for resort security in case but saw none.

"I'm used to awkward situations," she explained. "It won't be a big deal. I'll talk myself out of it. You're an attorney. You can talk yourself out of a paper bag."

Pamela laughed as she worked her magic on the casita door lock. She opened it slowly to avoid startling any guests.

"Is anyone home?" Pamela asked as she walked deeper into the dark casita.

The lights were off. She found the light switch and turned it on. The casita was a mess.

"Looks like someone ransacked it," Daniel said as he stood next to her. "Drawers are open. Clothes are haphazardly strewn everywhere. I wonder what they were looking for?"

Daniel walked towards the dresser for any clue.

"That's exactly what I was thinking," Pamela added.

She too searched the casita to determine the nature of things.

"I only see male clothes," Daniel announced as he tossed something aside to look further into the drawer.

He then picked up some clothes from the floor and returned them to their place in the dresser. He hoped clearing the mess might reveal something. It did. He saw an airline ticket on the floor, picked it up, and read the name on it - "C. Quintana."

*I wonder who that is*, he thought.

Meanwhile, Pamela searched the wooden desk on the opposite side of the casita.

"Looks like there was a laptop here," she said.

The laptop power cord was still plugged into the outlet, but it lay lifeless on the desk as if the laptop was suddenly pulled away without any regard for what it was connected to. Pamela read the papers and booklets scattered on the desk for any clues. They were mainly local travel information for guests unfamiliar with the area. Nothing was helpful or suggested anything about the occupant or what was on the laptop.

Daniel found a chair in the middle of the casita's living room. He could smell sweat and blood emanating from the rope still loosely wrapped around the bottom of the chair. The back legs appeared slightly bent as if an individual restrained in the chair was beaten or even tortured. Daniel wondered if it was just his imagination getting the best of him.

"Pamela, I think you'll want to see this," Daniel excitedly uttered. His heart was racing.

She came rushing towards him.

"What did you find? Oh my!!"

She carefully examined the chair without touching it or removing anything attached to it.

"Now, I told you something strange happened here," Pamela said.

She wanted to add she regretted not coming sooner. Her mind imagined stopping the culprit or possibly preventing the escape.

Daniel knew all too well what Pamela was thinking and any regret she felt.

"Don't blame yourself, Pam. We don't know how many people were here. We could have walked into a hornet's nest."

Nothing Daniel could say would assuage Pamela's conscience.

# 5 INQUIRY

## Isabela, Puerto Rico
## The Next Day

Walking towards the main building of the Regal Isabela resort, Pamela and Daniel were mystified after searching casita number eight. Daniel showed Pamela the airline ticket he found on the floor. He believed it was a clue but what it meant or who it referred to, they didn't know.

"It could have been left by a guest from a previous stay," Pamela mused. "Who knows how long it's been there?"

"I've stayed at numerous Regal Wisteria resorts. I know they are meticulous in cleaning their suites. They're proud of their impeccable customer service. I don't think they would have allowed another guest to stay in the casita with belongings from the previous guest, especially with their anniversary celebration looming."

"You may be right, but everyone makes a mistake. No one is perfect. Not even the cleaning crew."

Pamela was stern in her conviction but didn't

want to upset Daniel. Obviously, he was very proud of his client and may have been blinded by loyalty. Or perhaps a fanciful desire to see something where in reality there was nothing. She was the investigator and had experience with searching hotel rooms and homes. Pamela was aware that not everything added up. Sometimes things were false leads and meant nothing at all.

"I admit. I may be making more about the ticket than what it is. I have a feeling this means something and is important. But I'll let it go," Daniel said.

He wouldn't bring it up again to her, but he filed it away in his memory in case new information arose.

As they approached the main building, the fireworks were even louder. In the distance, they could see the open-air circular restaurant with guests seated around its circumference, enjoying good food, the night sky, and conversation. A string quartet was playing classical music for the guests. The resort's event coordinator and staff were entertaining groups of guests, both young and old, with various festivities. Upon seeing the other guests enjoying themselves, Daniel wondered if it was worth pursuing some unexplained event where the participants could be long gone. However, Daniel didn't want to disappoint Pamela. He also knew he saw fresh blood in that casita. He wouldn't be able to forgive himself if he did nothing and it turned out a person was seriously injured or, worse yet, murdered.

"Looks like the festivities are well underway," he said sheepishly. "Once this is all over, we'll have to listen to some Puerto Rican music. I hear they have *bomba* dancers coming later this week. I think you'll like that."

Pamela wasn't impressed. She was too focused on getting to the bottom of the mystery.

"Yeah, maybe later," she reluctantly responded, barely acknowledging the comment.

Her eyes were steadfastly staring at the main building while she watched for anyone entering or exiting it or anything suspicious.

"Let me open the door," Daniel said as he rushed to do so.

"I guess chivalry isn't dead after all," she joked as she turned aside to let Daniel pass her and open the oversized wooden door.

"After you."

Daniel bowed slightly, pretending to be the resort's doorman.

"*Gracias, Caballero*," Pamela mocked in broken Spanish.

Shaking his head, Daniel decided to give Pamela a pass.

*At least she tried speaking Spanish*, he thought.

With dogged determination, Pamela headed straight to the nearest attendant.

"Excuse me, sir," she said knowing better than to speak in a language she wasn't strongly conversant in. "Can you assist me?"

She smiled the way she normally does when subtly convincing someone to provide information they're not supposed to disclose.

"What do you need, *Señora*?" the attendant asked with an equally amazing smile.

"Well...I'm staying in casita number seven and the neighboring casita is...is being disruptive," she explained.

"I'm so sorry. I can have security speak to them if you'd like," the attendant suggested.

"I don't want to get them in trouble, actually. In fact, I just want to speak to them myself."

"You are welcome to speak with the guests in the adjacent casita. But I would advise against it. You never know how guests will respond and your safety is, of course, paramount."

Pamela wasn't concerned about any confrontation given her extensive training in Aikido since she was a child. Explaining that to the attendant was definitely out of the question. Daniel watched the whole ordeal. He was amused but remained silent. He wanted to see how Pamela wormed her way out of this predicament.

"Oh, I understand. I'm not trying to be difficult. I just would like to know who is staying in casita number eight. It will make things easier if I know their names." Pamela continued smiling in a flirtatious way to disarm the attendant. "That way...you know...I can use a personal touch and assure them everything is okay, and we won't make a big deal about it. We just want the disruptions to stop."

"I certainly can't tell you their names. The resort respects its guests' privacy."

"Sir, the last thing I want you to do is to violate a guest's privacy. I don't want you to get in trouble. No, not at all."

"Sorry, I can't help you."

"Well, what can you do for me? Can you at least let me know if they are staying the entire week?" Pamela asked implying she was concerned the disruptions would continue.

Worried she might become a disgruntled guest,

the attendant responded, "Let me check." He clicked the mouse a few times to check the appropriate reservation. "That's strange."

He called the general manager to double-check his reservation system.

"Ok. That's good to know."

The attendant never relayed to his boss why he needed the information.

"Well, *Señora*. I don't know what to tell you or how to explain it, but casita number eight has been vacant for the past few weeks. There shouldn't be anyone using the casita now. Are you sure you heard something from that casita?"

Pamela was taken aback at the revelation.

"Maybe you're right. Maybe I've got it all wrong. Thank you," she professed as she gently stroked the attendant's hand resting on the countertop. Pamela turned to Daniel and said, "Let's go, honey."

She suddenly grabbed Daniel's hand and dragged him towards the door.

Daniel shook his head in disbelief. He opened his mouth to admonish Pamela but knew better.

———

After barely walking outside the main building, Daniel stopped. "Wait a minute. I need to check in with the firm and their trial today."

Daniel looked at his watch to confirm the local time in Arizona which was four hours behind Puerto Rico at that time of the year. He grabbed his phone, walked a few feet away from Pamela, and dialed Marissa's cell phone number. Pamela impatiently waited.

"Hey, Marissa. It's me, Daniel."

"Hi, boss. It's good to hear from you. How's your vacation?"

Her voice was somewhat perturbed.

Realizing he'd only told John he was leaving, Daniel confessed, "Oh, I'm sorry. I should have told you, but I was running late for the flight. I take it John told you where I am."

"He did."

By the sound of Marissa's voice, Daniel knew she wasn't concerned he was on vacation, but that he wasn't at the trial. The strategy had always been that Daniel would first chair the trial with both Marissa and John working together as second chairs.

"I have confidence in you, Marissa. The both of you. You'll do well in the trial. There's nothing more my presence could have added that you and John aren't capable of handling."

Daniel's reassurance was what Marissa needed although she would have performed excellently even without it.

"Thank you, Daniel."

It was one of those rare moments where Marissa or anyone else in the firm called him by his first name besides Daniel's secretary, Lydia. Daniel understood the significance of Marissa's response. He was inwardly pleased with the development of their relationship.

"Tell me about the trial. How's it going?" Daniel asked.

"*Voir dire* took a lot longer than expected."

Daniel heartily laughed at the disclosure.

"Doug Clarkson is a talker. He's thorough and a little disingenuous at times. Be on the lookout for his shenanigans. Don't trust anything he says. He will stab you in the back the first chance he gets and will lie... I mean will shade the truth to the judge about his actions or the facts."

Daniel realized he should have sat down with John and Marissa and had these discussions before he left Puerto Rico, but he was preoccupied with personal things at the time.

"That's good to know," Marissa remarked while mentally taking notes to advise John about Mr. Clarkson.

"Did the judge at least impanel the jury today?" Daniel asked.

"Yes, she did. The parties selected eight jurors and two alternates," she explained.

"Good. Good. And how many jurors are required to reach a jury verdict?"

"Both sides ultimately agreed to six out of the eight. Doug originally wanted seven, but the judge said that wasn't required. He relented after he realized the judge wasn't going to budge."

"I told you how he is. And what about the alternates?"

"The judge said she'll let the parties decide at the end of the trial whether the alternates will deliberate along with the rest of the jury."

Melissa seemed unsure about the judge's decision to put it off. Daniel wisely caught on to her concerns.

"I always let the alternates deliberate. They've earned that right because they sat through the entire trial. Besides, if for some reason, a juror is disqualified, then the alternates don't have to get up to speed with deliberations. There isn't any delay in coming to a verdict. At least, not in my experience."

Marissa listened attentively. She suddenly remembered Daniel making the same choice in previous trials. She was about to ask Daniel a question but hesitated. Before Marissa could reconsider asking, Pamela beckoned Daniel to come back to her. She mouthed the words, "We need to go."

Daniel nodded toward Pamela and said to Marissa, "I have to go. I'll call you tomorrow."

The call abruptly ended as Daniel headed back to Pamela.

———

Daniel and Pamela walked on the starlit pathway back to their casita. A Puerto Rican male watched them intently. By the way he was dressed, he didn't appear to be a guest. As the two rounded the corner, the male made a cell phone call.

# 6  OPENING STATEMENTS

Phoenix, Arizona
The Same Day

"And we're going to be asking you to award a large sum of money, in the tens of millions, for the tragic wrongful death of Carlos because of the defendants' recklessness when they caused this crash. His family has suffered enough from the loss of their husband, father, and close friend. Unfortunately, we can't bring Carlos back, but we can hold the defendants accountable for this needless crash. They don't want to accept responsibility for it and haven't so far. But we need you, the jury, to hold them accountable. We thank you, ladies and gentlemen, in advance for your service."

Doug Clarkson smiled soberly towards the jury as he grabbed his yellow legal pad with his handwritten statement and walked away from the lectern back to the plaintiffs' counsel's table. His partner, Danica, had been observing the jury the entire time for their reactions to Doug's opening statement. Some jurors listened attentively while others crossed their arms -

body language which jury consultants claim are a sign those jurors were closed off to Doug's comments. Surprisingly, the college student was selected as a juror. He periodically dozed off while Doug spoke. Shaking his head occasionally helped him stay awake, but not always. The student needed coffee or an energy drink as a pick-me-up.

Forgetting he'd placed an oversized photo of Carlos Hernandez on the easel stand in front of the jury to emphasize during his opening statement, Doug walked back to the well of the court. He moved the stand toward the back of the courtroom but still facing the jury. He wanted the jury to see Carlos' handsome, smiling face while the defense counsel gave their opening statement. It was a subliminal reminder of the tragic loss the jury was dealing with. And of course, a subtle way to undermine the defense counsel.

When Doug finally sat down, the judge spoke. "Thank you, Mr. Clarkson. Ms. Robles. You're opening statement."

Marissa recalled Daniel's advice: "Remember to drink some water before you speak because the nervousness causes your throat to parch." The long sip of water she took not only quenched her thirst but also calmed her nerves. Marissa walked to the lectern with a printout of her opening statement. She scanned the jury and was pleased. The jury was evenly split and consisted of five males and five females of various ages. It was not the typical older jury impaneled in the Phoenix area as she had in past trials. The older jurors were generally more conservative and less likely to award ridiculous amounts of money. Younger jurors were not as frugal. But a wrongful death case was different and preconceived notions were not always applicable. Marissa tried not to worry about those things and focused instead on her opening statement.

"May it please the court, counsel, ladies and gentlemen of the jury, my name is Marissa Robles. I am an attorney who represents Mr. and Mrs. Weaver and their employer, the Regal Phoenix Resort and Spa. Martin Weaver is here today and will be here for the entire trial. His wife, Rose, is unable to attend the trial because of health reasons. You met her briefly yesterday. They have been married for over thirty years and have lived in their home in Cave Creek, Arizona for nearly two decades. They have a son, Nicholas, who graduated from Arizona State University, and also a daughter, Margaret, who is a pharmacist."

Marissa wasn't sure if the entire jury panel could hear her, so she raised her voice when continuing.

"You've heard from plaintiffs' counsel but he only described a part of this case. He failed to mention everything that happened on that Tuesday afternoon of May 2nd. You'll hear from Martin and experts about how this accident occurred. It's up to you to decide what happened after listening to all of the evidence. Plaintiffs have the burden of proof, which means they have to prove to you that it was more likely so than not that their version of events is true. We don't have that burden.

"You're going to hear that Martin Weaver is very familiar with that road. The Regal Phoenix Resort and Spa is just a few blocks from the site of the accident. Mr. Weaver is going to testify he has taken this route many times when he's driving the company's shuttle bus for work multiple times per day for the past twenty years. Martin is going to testify he was traveling westbound on Camelback Road in the far left lane and noticed a car and a motorcycle merging onto Camelback Road into the two right lanes from Goldwater Boulevard. He is going to testify that he remained in his lane of travel when Mr. Hernandez collided with his vehicle. Mr. Hernandez drifted into Martin Weaver's lane and collided with his vehicle."

Feeling her throat becoming a little parched, Marissa took another sip of water and then looked at the jury to gauge their response so far. The entire jury panel was mesmerized by her and focused on every word she was saying. A rookie attorney would mistakenly believe this meant the jurors were on Marissa's side. But an experienced attorney realized jurors always took defendants to task and wanted to know what excuses and defenses were offered. So jurors were more attentive during defense counsel's opening statement.

"During the trial, you will also hear from the motorcyclist who will testify that Mr. Hernandez never turned his head to the left before entering Mr. Weaver's lane and he was looking straight ahead the entire time even right before the accident. Mr. Weaver will testify that he saw Mr. Hernandez making his right turn and that he was aware of the presence of Mr. Hernandez's vehicle to his right the whole time. It is unknown why Mr. Hernandez didn't look to his left before entering the lane and why he did not perceive Mr. Weaver's shuttle bus.

"You're going to hear from the plaintiffs' own traffic engineering expert that there is no physical evidence Mr. Weaver drifted into Mr. Hernandez's lane. Although he observed drifting by other vehicles, that was in an area beyond where the accident occurred. You're also going to hear from our accident reconstructionist, Hank Richardson. He will discuss the scrapes and gouge in the road surface that plaintiff's expert located. Their own expert's measurements placed the gouge one foot into the left lane, the lane that Martin was traveling in, and between the first two stripes north of the concrete and asphalt transition. Mr. Richardson is going to testify that the damage to the right side of Mr. Weaver's shuttle bus and the left side of Mr. Hernandez's convertible provide insight into the interactions between them. Based on the physical evidence, there is no possible way Mr. Weaver entered the lane to his right. If he had, this would have resulted in an immediate impact that would have caused the convertible to steer to the right.

"Mr. Richardson will tell you that, because the convertible did not steer to the right but steered to the left, the contact did not occur with Mr. Weaver's vehicle in the center lane. In addition, the large shuttle bus would have acted like a fence, making it unlikely that the convertible would have been struck in the center lane and the gouge mark was in the left lane. Mr. Richardson is going to tell you that, based upon the physical evidence, the accident occurred in Mr. Weaver's lane when Mr. Hernandez, who wasn't aware of the shuttle bus' presence, entered the left lane."

The jury seemed pleased that there was going to be a "battle of the experts" in the trial. This would make things more interesting and distract them from the gruesomeness of the tragic accident. Marissa continued.

"That's what happened in this case. It is unfortunate that Mr. Hernandez was fatally injured when he was ejected from the convertible because he failed to wear a seat belt. However, his fatal injuries are not our fault. Mr. Hernandez is responsible for entering Martin's lane and causing this accident. Based on the evidence, we will ask that you return a verdict that finds in favor of the defendants, Martin and Rose Weaver and the Regal Phoenix Resort and Spa, and against the plaintiffs. Thank you."

The courtroom was completely silent as Marissa walked back to the defense counsel's table.

# 7 MOTIONS

Phoenix, Arizona
The Same Day

"Is it okay if I put you on speaker? Robin's also in the room," Carl asked.

"That's fine," Marissa said. "I'm calling because the plaintiffs' counsel filed a couple of trial memorandums this morning and the judge wants us to file our responses later today so we can argue them after the jury is dismissed. I need you guys to draft the responses. Lydia has copies of the trial memos and can get them to you."

Carl checked his computer and noticed Lydia had already emailed him the trial memos.

"We've got them," he told Marissa while letting Robin know she was also copied on the email.

"Good. The most important trial memo is the motion to exclude Hank Richardson's testimony. He's both an accident reconstructionist and a biomechanical expert. They're not challenging his testimony as an accident reconstructionist. Only his testimony as a biomechanical engineer. They claim he's not a doctor and cannot testify as to the mechanism of action, causation, and the likelihood Mr. Hernandez would not have been fatally injured if he was wearing a seat belt. Without Hank's testimony, we won't be able to argue that Mr. Hernandez was responsible for his injuries even if he didn't cause the accident. It's important for us to win this."

Carl and Robin both skimmed the trial memo as Marissa spoke.

"Can you work with Hank in drafting a response?" Marissa instructed.

"We're on it," Carl replied.

"Thanks," Marissa said as she ended the call and went back into the courtroom to resume the trial with John.

The call was taken in the war room - a special room designated in the Mendoza law firm where preparations for trials are made. It was filled with binders related to the Hernandez lawsuit, dedicated computers, and workspace. The binders contained various things, including the trial exhibits designated by the plaintiffs and defendants, deposition transcripts of every witness deposed including the experts, all expert reports and photos taken of the accident, and all of the pleadings filed and disclosures made in the case. The purpose of the war room was to make everything readily accessible to the attorneys working on the litigation. Attorneys like Carl and Robin were assigned to the war room for moments like these when opposing counsel filed last-minute pleadings or some fact or legal position needed researching.

Robin grabbed the binder containing all of the pre-trial motions filed by the parties. She quickly glanced through it and saw various motions to exclude the testimony of certain witnesses and experts.

"There's nothing filed by the plaintiffs' counsel to exclude Hank's testimony before the motion deadline last month," she affirmed.

"It makes sense," Carl added. "Otherwise, the judge would have ruled on this issue at the final trial management conference." He was checking the binder with all of the court's rulings. "The minute entry order for that day doesn't mention any motion about Hank. Just the motion involving Dr. Easterman." He flipped a few more pages in case a page from the order was out of place.

"We need to argue they failed to timely file this motion and request a *Daubert* hearing challenging whether such testimony from a biomechanical expert is admissible," Robin explained. "I've drafted those motions before at my last job. I'm not sure why the plaintiffs' counsel waited until trial to file this motion. Seems like some last-minute desperate attempt."

"Agreed. This morning, I heard Marissa tell John that Doug Clarkson is a shyster. This seems like something he would do," Carl explained.

"I hope you weren't like this when you were a plaintiff's attorney," Robin said unsure she had overstepped her bounds.

"I can't say I was always above board, but you have to understand. Plaintiff's attorneys are under a lot of pressure. Our caseloads are way more than the caseload for defense counsel. We're assigned roughly three hundred litigation and pre-litigation cases."

Carl wasn't trying to garner sympathy. He only wanted Robin to understand his previous predicament. "Most attorneys who worked for the defense have no idea of the overwhelming amount of work we have to do. All they see are the large sums of money we make compared to them."

"Wow, that's insane. I'm surprised you guys don't get burnt out sooner. I could never imagine having that many cases. We only have thirty to fifty cases depending on their complexity. I was overwhelmed at times even with just those numbers."

Wanting to switch the conversation back to the trial memo, Carl asked, "Did they even depose Hank?"

"Let me check."

Robin pulled out the binders filled with the deposition transcripts. She skipped the transcripts of Mrs. Hernandez and the kids and flipped through some of the transcripts of witnesses to the accident. She pulled out another binder filled with transcripts. The second binder contained the depositions of the experts.

"Hmm, that's strange. I don't see any transcript for Hank. All of the other experts were deposed. Maybe they forgot to depose Hank," Robin said.

"I'm sure Daniel wasn't going to remind Doug to depose Hank. It's not his place," Carl mused.

Robin agreed. She walked back to the computer in the war room to review the trial memo in depth. Carl followed her.

"I can't believe this," Robin huffed. "They're not even citing the applicable rule of evidence to exclude Hank's testimony. The trial memo superficially focuses only on Hank's education and not on his knowledge, skill, experience, and training in forming his opinion as a biomechanical expert. That's allowed under the evidentiary rule to qualify as an expert."

"They probably didn't cite the rule because, if they did, it would undermine their position," Carl added. He scrolled down to a different page. "The trial memo cites case law from Wyoming and Florida rather than any applicable Arizona case law."

"The judge doesn't have to follow those out-of-state cases. I can't believe there isn't any Arizona law on this issue. We need to research Arizona cases addressing the exclusion of expert testimony," Robin suggested.

"I'll research that," Carl volunteered.

Legal research wasn't his forte, but he needed more opportunities to expand his skill set in that area.

*This trial memo is the perfect way for me to prove I'm a valuable member of the team*, he thought.

"Thanks. I'll call Hank and let him know about this trial memo and if he has any insights on how we can defeat it."

Robin dialed his office number.

"Collision Safety Consultants. How may I help you?" the receptionist asked.

"My name is Robin Blake with Mendoza and Associates. I'm calling for Hank Richardson."

"Please hold."

The receptionist flipped over to a different line to call Hank's office. She then flipped back to the call with Robin.

"I'm sorry. He's not in today. His calendar indicates he's at an inspection right now. Would you like me to leave a message?"

"Yes, please. Can you let Hank know that the plaintiffs' counsel in *Hernandez v. Weaver* filed a trial memo to exclude his trial testimony and we need to file a response today? Can you have him call me back as soon as possible?"

"Oh, most certainly. The inspection should be over within the next thirty minutes or so. I'll have him call your office as soon as he's done."

"Thank you."

Robin became anxious at the delay, but she reassured herself things would be okay, and they would draft an appropriate responsive motion before the judge's deadline with or without Hank's assistance. Carl noticed her increased anxiety. He felt it too. Most attorneys welcomed trial for the adrenaline. These were some of those moments even though it did not occur in the courtroom.

"So how's your husband doing?" Carl asked to distract from the situation and lighten the mood.

"He's fine. He's getting used to me not having to work late hours like I used to at my old job. He loves it. They worked us to death there. We needed to be available to respond to emails and client questions at all hours of the day and night every day, even on the weekends. Sometimes, I would get emails at eleven p.m. or later. Sometimes, as early as four in the morning. It was crazy. My boss was a workaholic. She didn't do anything besides work other than jogging twice a day. She expected everyone to be the same way. I'm so glad I'm no longer there."

"I can imagine. Plaintiffs' attorneys may have a lot of cases but were done by five p.m. every day and didn't need to work at night or on the weekends unless we were in trial."

"That's why I like it here at the firm. My quality of life is a lot better now," Robin acknowledged.

"Speaking of quality of life, how's your relationship with Samantha coming along?"

Carl was puzzled. He'd tried to keep his renewed relationship with his ex-wife a secret from co-workers. Other than Marissa, his long-time friend from law school, Carl hadn't spoken with anyone at the firm about Samantha. Not even Cheryl, the office gossip. He suddenly remembered he brought Samantha to the firm's Christmas party last year. He was relieved. No one was spying on him like he instantly imagined when Robin brought her name up. But he definitely was going to watch out for Cheryl. As the receptionist, Cheryl was privy to a lot of personal information not available to other co-workers.

"We're doing fine. A lot better than we thought." Carl decided not to disclose that the two were going to couple's counseling. *That's a little too much information,* he thought.

"I'm glad to hear it. You guys make a lovely couple. I hear your daughter, Senovia, is a cutie." Robin's beaming smile was out of this world.

The speakerphone in the war room interrupted their conversation.

"Robin, I have Mr. Richardson on the line for you," Cheryl announced.

"Thanks. Can you transfer him?"

"Sure."

The line clicked over, and the sound of rushing wind filled the war room.

"Robin, I'm driving back from Tucson, so I have you on speakerphone. I apologize for the noise. You know how windy the drive back to Phoenix can be. Tell me about the trial memo."

"Thanks for calling me back so soon, Hank. They're saying you don't have the educational background to testify as a biomechanical expert," Robin explained.

"That's rubbish. There's no such thing as a biomechanical degree. So there's that. You gain knowledge about biomechanics from experience. I have a bachelor's in mechanical engineering. I've also performed biomechanical engineering analysis for at least two decades when working for biomechanical firms, including my own firm, Collision Safety Consultants. All of that is in my CV."

A whipping sound screeched over the speaker. Hank paused until the noise subsided.

"I...I've also conducted research in occupant dynamics and have conducted various presentations and authored numerous publications in various areas. Like I said, that should be in my CV."

"We will certainly attach it to our response," Robin reassured Hank, knowing he was concerned the judge may exclude his testimony at trial.

All experts dreaded a ruling preventing them from testifying as an expert. It affected their livelihood because attorneys would learn about the ruling and file similar motions to preclude Hank from testifying ultimately affecting his ability to be retained as an expert either by a plaintiff's counsel or defense counsel.

"I've also testified as a biomechanical expert numerous times, including in a number of superior courts throughout the state of Arizona and the United States District Court for the District of Arizona. I've testified in state courts in New Mexico as well as California. If you don't have my trial testimony list, let me know. I can have my wife send it over to you."

"Thanks, Hank. I appreciate that. I'll let you go so you can have a safe drive home. We certainly don't want you to get into an accident."

Hank chuckled before hanging up the phone.

As soon as Robin ended the conversation, Carl motioned to her to come to his desk in the war room.

"I found this Arizona case called *Lohmeier v. Hammer*. The Arizona Court of Appeals held quote under Arizona law, it is not necessary that an expert witness be a medical doctor in order to offer testimony regarding the causation of physical injuries so long as the trial court has properly determined that the expert has specialized knowledge that will assist the jury in its resolution of that issue unquote. The best part is that the *Lohmeier* case involved a biomechanical engineer, coincidentally, Hank's old boss. The court held that an expert's degree of qualification goes to the weight given the testimony, not its admissibility at trial."

"That's great work, Carl."

He was very proud of himself for tackling the research task.

"But wait, there's more. I found a recent court of appeals decision specifically addressing Hank Richardson as an expert. The plaintiffs in that case also filed a similar motion. The court of appeals held that it was not an abuse of the trial judge's discretion in admitting Hank's biomechanical engineering testimony at trial."

"Awesome!!" Robin exclaimed.

"It's an unpublished decision though," Carl reluctantly acknowledged.

"It may be unpublished and not binding but if we attach a copy of the opinion with our motion it will definitely sway Judge Furman to rule in our favor. I just know it will."

The two attorneys started drafting responses to the trial memos.

# 8 NEEDS

### Scottsdale, Arizona
### The Same Day

"Mr. Williams, I've told you many times not to overexert yourself. You need to minimize your fatigue," the nurse admonished while directing him back to his recliner in the living room.

He tried to resist and turn back to the jumble of stuff he was working on to entertain himself and prevent him from being bored.

"I...I..." he gasped.

Noticing his shortness of breath, the nurse quickly interrupted him, "Just relax. You need to regain your strength."

Realizing he was weaker than he thought, he relented and allowed her to continue her efforts. Once he was seated, the nurse went into the kitchen to bring his dinner.

"You need to eat this," she said as she placed the plate on the tray table and scooted it in front of him. "You need to eat your nutritional requirements each day like the dietician said to prevent unnecessary weight loss. A well-balanced diet is important for your illness. It'll strengthen your immune system to help you fight any infections. The meals also help with the fatigue."

"You need...you need. I know what I need," he muttered as his eyes burned with frustration.

Although obstinate as always, Gavin Williams reluctantly ate his meal. Dinner consisted of lemon-glazed salmon, fresh broccoli, a hefty scoop of rice, a slice of avocado, some fresh fruit, and chocolate pudding for dessert. It wasn't the fast food he was used to eating over the years, but he endured it, nonetheless. The nurse then placed a tall glass of milk on the tray table.

"I hope you didn't add dry milk powder into the milk again," Gavin sneered as he hesitantly took a sip. "Yuck! You did."

His facial expression couldn't hide his disgust.

"You know I need to do that, so you get the necessary calories to maintain your weight. It's what..."

"I need. I know. I know."

He continued angrily eating his meal. Luckily, he had no difficulties swallowing. After a few hearty bites of food, he could sense his strength returning. But he knew the nurse would make him take a late afternoon nap before calling his daughter, Pamela.

———

Once he was completely finished with his nap, Gavin called his oldest daughter.

"Hey, sunshine," he beamed as if speaking with his middle child brought back the joy and vigor of his youth.

"Hi, Dad," Pamela said as she walked to the terrace for some privacy. "How are you feeling today?"

"Same as usual. Strong as an ox," he declared while flexing his biceps as if his daughter could see him.

"And stubborn as one too," she rejoined. "Your nurses have been texting me while I'm here in Puerto Rico. I hear you're not listening to them."

"Why those...."

"Dad, please calm down. They're only looking out for your best interest. You have gotten a lot better with...."

She didn't want to mention Gerald Ravan or Regal Wisteria and their assistance with her father's health. Pamela was concerned Daniel might hear her and find out about her family's long-standing association with the company.

"You need to just follow your doctor's advice and the dietitian's guidelines and you'll be fine. You've been doing great, Dad. I'm so proud of you."

"Not you too with my needs,'" Gavin replied. This time he didn't let his anger exasperate him. He stayed calm for his daughter's sake. "Let's not discuss this anymore. You're in the Caribbean to have fun and not to worry about your father."

She sighed deeply but agreed for her father's sake. She knew stressing him out would only cause him fatigue and make things worse. That was the last thing she wanted.

*Patience*, she reminded herself.

She breathed in and out like her *sensei* taught her so long ago as a child while learning Aikido. "Ok, Dad."

"Thank you. Now, how's Puerto Rico? I want to know everything about it." he asked.

"It's lovely here. It's so green and lush. The waters are so warm and aqua blue, not like the dull, cool waters of the Pacific. And the locals are so friendly. Oh, the food...the food is so...um...delicious. Wish you were here. I'm sure you'd enjoy it."

"Oh, I know I would. It sounds marvelous. I can't wait to go there someday myself," he admitted.

Gavin, however, knew he didn't have the strength for the long flight to the Caribbean. It was only a fanciful dream albeit a comforting one. Holding on to dreams like this was a way for him to keep hope alive. There was no cure for his illness, at least not yet, and he knew that. But he didn't allow that reality to affect him; otherwise, he could succumb to depression or other mental issues. His doctors warned him of the possibility. With the help of the medical staff and his daughter, he was grateful to have avoided it so far.

Hearing fireworks coming from the phone, Gavin stated, "Sounds like the festivities have started. What have you guys done for fun?"

"Well, we haven't attended any celebrations yet. Something else came up."

"Don't tell me you're working instead of enjoying your vacation? You're supposed to be on what they call...respite...I think. Don't overwork yourself. You need to rest and relax," Gavin insisted.

He was happy to play the fatherly role again.

"Now look who's making demands," Pamela giggled to downplay her response. Her voice became serious. "This is important. We think someone's been kidnapped and tortured."

"Really?" Gavin became more interested in the conversation because it wasn't like the typical dull and tedious investigation Pamela sometimes conducted which normally involved her trying to catch a cheating spouse and prove infidelity. "Why do you think that?"

"It's a long story. I'll tell you once I get back."

He could tell she was anxious to get back to her investigation.

"Okay, sunshine. Enjoy yourself. One last thing before I go. I heard from Milagros that Cameron's in town. He's staying at a local hotel. He hasn't dropped by to visit me. I figure it's because he hasn't forgiven me after all this time. He's your brother. Maybe he's willing to speak to you about it. We're family and we're all we've got. We can't keep avoiding each other."

Gavin coughed a few times as a sign of his impending shortness of breath. The conversation was unexpectedly causing him added stress.

"Dad, are you okay?"

A long pause made Pamela even more concerned for her father's well-being.

"I'm doing fine. It was just a temporary issue."

"You really need to see the doctor again and get evaluated. It's been a long time since you've had an appointment. Promise me you will."

# 9 INTERVIEWS

Isabela, Puerto Rico
Later That Night

Pamela received a text message while enjoying the *bomba* dancers. She quickly glanced at the message but continued watching. The lead female dancer was holding onto her traditional white skirt with both hands, thrusting her arms in a series of unique gestures based upon her spiritual connection with the Afro-Puerto Rican music. The drummer synchronized his beats on his *barrile* following the dancer's gestures. The lead female sang a chorus about a love triangle while the other two singers responded in turn. Pamela, however, was not well-versed in Spanish to understand the intricacies of the song's storyline. She was so enthralled with the rhythm of the dancers and the drums she almost forgot about the text message.

Soaking in one last glance of the performance before heading to a secluded area of the resort mentioned in the text message, Pamela first ensured Daniel was distracted and not looking for her. She saw him talking to a group of guests at the bar. He seemed happy and must have been regaling them with a story about a trial he recently had. The guests were mesmerized and appeared engaged.

*Good. He's too preoccupied,* she reassured herself and stealthily walked away.

As she approached the designated rendezvous point, Gerald Ravan appeared out of nowhere.

"It's good to see you, Pam," he declared as the two embraced. "How's your father?"

They discussed Gavin's progress and setbacks and the possibility of enrolling him into the latest clinical trial using a state-of-the-art medication recently developed in Japan.

"I'm really excited to know he'll get into the clinical trial with your assistance, Gerry. I don't know what to say. You've done so much for him."

Pamela became teary-eyed at the thought of her father's improved health and increased mobility and independence. She tempered her expectations. She didn't want to get ahead of herself and get her hopes up only to have them dashed as she had in the past.

"Anything for you and your father," Gerald asserted. He too was eager to see an old friend get back to normal if possible.

Once Pamela regained her composure, she told Gerald about her suspicions someone had been kidnapped or tortured at the resort.

"This isn't good. Not now of all things. We're in the middle of our ten-year celebration." The worry on his face was obvious. Gerald was also upset the resort's security personnel hadn't foiled the incident and two guests were aware of it before he was. "I'm glad you bought this to my attention, Pam. I'm concerned my security personnel might be in on it or have turned a blind eye. I'm not sure if I want to alert them about it yet. Maybe you can look into it and keep me up to speed with your investigation," he asked.

"Certainly. I just want to remind you that it could be nothing just a messy suite or some kind of sick prank or BDSM. I don't want to alarm you unnecessarily."

"I trust your instincts. If you say you think someone was kidnapped, I'm sure you have a good reason to think that. I understand you don't want to worry me, but we've been working too long together for any misunderstandings."

"Thanks, Gerry."

"Just let me know if there is anything you need."

He started walking off, expecting Pamela to get back to him later.

Instead, she approached him.

"I may need to interview a few employees - security personnel, housekeeping assigned to the casita, and anyone else who may come to mind," she explained.

"I'll make sure you're given the names and access to the personnel."

———

Sitting at the desk in the diminutive room designated for the maintenance engineer, Pamela asked the maintenance worker assigned to casita number eight to sit down on the chair opposite her. The younger, Puerto Rican female nervously stared at her but didn't move.

"*¿Qué quieres?*" she asked.

"I'm sorry. I don't speak Spanish," Pamela replied.

"I just asked 'what do you want?' Can you tell me?"

"Sit please," Pamela again pointed to the chair to coax the woman into relaxing.

She was obviously reluctant to speak although she'd been informed by management to cooperate with the investigation. The employee eventually sat down and stared at Pamela. She didn't say another word but waited anxiously. Pamela gave a confused look and then it dawned on her.

"I've seen you before. Haven't I? Isn't your name, Inez? You're assigned to clean my casita, number 'seven."

The woman smiled wistfully, unsure if she would be recognized.

"You are correct. We've met before. I'm assigned casitas seven, eight, nine, and ten," she admitted.

"Well, Inez. I'm told casita number eight has been vacant for several weeks now. Is that accurate?"

"Yes, it is," she firmly insisted.

"I don't believe you."

"What do you mean? Management hasn't booked the casita. You can check their reservation system."

"Well, I was recently inside of number eight. There were clothes and belongings everywhere as if someone had been staying in it for a while. Do you know anything about that?"

"I don't. I just do what I'm told."

"And what is that?"

"To clean, vacuum, empty the trash, switch out the sheets and towels. Stuff like that."

She almost cracked a smile but resisted her impulse. She didn't want to let her cockiness do her in.

"So you know nothing about anyone staying in casita number eight?"

"Exactly!"

"Well, the logs show for the past week or so, that you thoroughly cleaned casita numbers seven, nine, and ten every day."

"Yes, because guests have been staying in those casitas. It's my job."

"The logs also indicate that you've lightly dusted casita number eight on all of those occasions. Are you telling me you never noticed anyone staying in eight when you were there?"

"No, not at all."

She seemed incredulous at the revelation.

"I'm disappointed, Inez. You may not be aware of this, but the resort has cameras hidden outside of the living quarters to protect the guests. The videos show you talking with a man at the front door of casita number eight. He also gave you money. Either that was a tip for cleaning the casita or a payoff or both. So, I'm asking you again, was anyone staying in casita number eight?"

"If you already knew about it, why are you asking me?"

"We just wanted to confirm and see if you were going to be truthful. Apparently, you're not loyal to the company or to Mr. Ravan."

"I am loyal...," her voice was taut out of concern for her well-being. "I just needed the extra money for bills. They paid me twice as much just to clean that casita and not tell anyone. I won't do it again. I promise."

"Who's they?"

"The security guard, Jose. I don't know the name of the person actually staying in the casita. He never told me his name. Neither did Jose."

"Thanks, Inez. You can go now," Pamela said dismissively.

"But what about my job? I can't lose my job."

Her eyes pierced Pamela. They were searching for an ounce of compassion and guidance.

"It's not up to me. It's up to Mr. Ravan. All I can say is that you told me the truth finally, but you weren't originally going to. He may not like that."

She solemnly exited the maintenance room and returned to work. Daniel Mendoza watched her and then entered.

"Nice job. I heard what she said. If we have the video, then we should be able to figure out who the guest was," he declared.

"Not so fast. I lied to her. We don't have a video?"

"What? So how did you know she was involved?"

"It's not the first time a maintenance worker has secretly allowed a guest to stay at a hotel. I see it all the time in my line of work. I figured her reluctance to answer my questions meant she was doing something nefarious and didn't want to get caught. Claiming there was video proof only made it easier for her to admit it even if she never realized I was lying to her." Pamela smiled. "I'm surprised you don't use that trick in your profession."

"We can't. When deposing or cross-examining a witness at trial, if I falsely assert there was video proof, opposing counsel would demand access to the video. Without an actual video, I've lost all credibility, especially in front of a jury."

"That's the great thing about my job. When I question people, they never have legal representation. Most typically voluntarily talk to me. If they refuse to talk to me, then I can spy on them to see what they are up to. In the end, they can't hide the truth."

Daniel shook his head in disbelief. Before he could say a word, a security guard entered the room.

"I'm told to speak with a Pamela Williams," the guard said.

"Are you Jose?" Pamela asked, hoping it was a coincidence.

"No. No. Jose's gone for the day. I'm one of the security guards who was on duty the night you're asking about. Management sent me."

"Okay," Pamela said.

Daniel walked to the other side of the desk to observe the interview.

"How many security guards were working that night?" Pamela asked.

"Three. I worked in the main building. Another security guard was assigned to the parking lot. The third security roamed the resort to ensure the guests were safe. That's the procedure almost every night. On weekends, we may have a second guard roam the resort because there are a lot more people staying here."

"Who was the guard assigned to roam the resort?"

"Now that I think about it, it was Jose."

"Are there video cameras on the property?"

"A few. Some are in the parking lot. A couple inside and outside the main building and pro shop. And one or two near the tennis courts. We don't have any in the main area of the resort where the casitas are. We want to protect our guests' privacy."

"Can you take me to the security room so I can see the video for that night?"

"Of course. Follow me."

———

The security room had a bank of screens displaying the video feeds from the various cameras stationed throughout the resort. The security guard walked towards a monitor near the desk on the left side of the room. He sat down and said, "The videos from previous days are automatically stored in the cloud every day. Which night do you need?"

Pamela told him, and the guard clicked the necessary button on the computer mouse to open a folder for that day with videos saved from all of the cameras.

"Can we see the video for the parking lot?" Pamela inquired.

"Sure."

After a couple of clicks, the video came up, showing the parking lot near the front of the resort closest to the main street. The guard played the video at three times the speed to shorten the process of reviewing it.

When the video reached the end, Pamela declared, "No one comes in and out of the parking lot all night. Is there any other way to leave the resort?"

The guard became pensive.

"Wait. I saw something," Daniel said as he walked back to the video screens. "There." He pointed to the third screen on the top left. "Where is this? This looks like a maintenance road near the casitas. Where does it lead?"

"I think it leads to the other side of the golf course

and then there is another road that exits to another street. You can leave the resort from that street," the guard explained.

"Can you pull the video feed for that night?" Daniel asked.

The video played again at a faster rate until the guard slowed down the video when three individuals appeared. Two men were in between a third person who was hooded. They escorted the hooded person into a black Escalade and then drove off.

"Is Jose in this video?" Pamela asked the guard.

"No, he's not."

# 10  DARKNESS

An Unknown Location In Puerto Rico
Later That Night

The ringing in his ears was extremely painful and was giving him a throbbing headache. He could barely make out the words spoken by his two captors. Their voices seemed distant perhaps in another room on the opposite side of where he was seated. It sounded as if they were speaking both Spanish and English.

Turning his head toward their voices, he struggled to see them. It was darker than he expected. Pitch black. He tried focusing his eyes, but everything was blurry and dim. He couldn't make out any figures or anything at all. After a while, he realized he was blindfolded. He desperately tried to remove the blindfold, but his arms wouldn't move. They were restrained along with his legs and torso.

Sweat dripped down his forehead, more so from physical and emotional exhaustion than worry. The blindfold became increasingly soaked from sweat, stinging his eyes and making it harder to focus on what little light penetrated inside the blindfold.

Trying to move his body only increased his pain. He was battered and bruised everywhere and had difficulty breathing. As he took a deep breath to calm himself, his chest writhed in excruciating pain. His ribs were either cracked or severely bruised. No matter the reason, he was in a weakened state and unable to free himself. He sensed his mind was quickly fading. Before he collapsed from exhaustion, he made out a few words from the others. They must have gotten enraged because their voices bellowed louder than before.

"*Coño*!! The boss isn't going to like this. There's no coming back from this, man. We're dead," the younger male declared to the older one.

He anxiously paced back and forth in the room holding a gun in his hand and repeatedly pressing it against his forehead out of frustration.

"Stupid. Stupid. Stupid," he said every time the gun pressed against his head.

"Stop it! We need to focus and think," the older man insisted, staring at the other with intense disdain.

He was also worried the younger male would do something unexpected making the dire situation even worse.

"Nothing's working. He won't tell us where he hid the money. Maybe he doesn't know?" The younger male stopped pacing when the realization hit him hard.

"He knows. Believe me. He knows. We'll get it out of him. We have to."

The older male's cell phone rang. He eagerly answered it and listened to the caller's demands. The younger male anxiously looked on, hoping their fates hadn't been sealed.

"It's taking longer than expected but we'll break him," he reassured the caller.

Soberly nodding his head to the caller's instructions, he ended the conversation. He then stormed into the back room with the younger male at his heels.

"Listen, this time you're telling me where you hid the money!" he demanded. "I know you buried it here."

Noticing the restrained male was half-asleep, the older male grabbed the gun from the younger male. He was about to pistol whip their captive but instead slapped him with his open hand. The shocking blow quickly startled the captive, awakening him.

He grabbed the captive by the collar and shouted, "Where's the money?!! Where's the money."

"I...I don't know," the captive uttered in a half-crazed voice reminiscent of his earlier denials.

"You do know. Get me the pliers from the Escalade," the older male instructed the younger. "Now!!"

He scurried outside to get the tool.

"Here it is," the younger male said as he handed the pliers to his compatriot.

"I'm going to ask you one last time where you hid the money. If you don't tell me, then I'll have no choice but to take the next step," the older male declared.

"Go ahead. You can't do anything worse," the captive cajoled. "I can take whatever you can give. You'll pay for this once my father finds out."

He mustered all of his strength to appear invincible and unfazed, hoping it would dissuade his captors from any further violence. He didn't realize it had the opposite effect.

Holding his right hand, the older male gripped the captive's fingernail on his forefinger and yanked it out with the pliers.

"Where's the money?"

Gritting his teeth to dull the pain, the captive said nothing.

"Fine."

The older male gripped another of the captive's fingers and yanked out another fingernail.

This time the captive wailed in agony.

"I can do this all day if I have to. Tell me where you hid the money!!"

Still no answer.

Deciding to use a different tactic, the older male forcefully opened the captive's mouth. He then used the pliers to extract one of the captive's molars. The tooth's crown ripped apart, leaving the root still in the socket of the jawbone. Blood gushed out of the captive's mouth and onto the older male's face.

The captive's agony erupted like a volcano. Rather than succumb to the pain, the captive laughed maniacally. His eyes glazed in horror.

"Fuck you, *puto*! You'll never get the money. I'm going to kill you and your entire family," the captive threatened as if the murders were a foregone conclusion.

The older male panicked at the threat. Realizing no matter how many fingernails or teeth he pulled, the captive would never disclose where he hid the money, and his associates would be displeased. It was a no-win situation.

# 11  CROSS-EXAMINATION

Phoenix, Arizona
The Next Day

Judge Furman made her ruling on the trial memo to exclude Hank Richardson's expert testimony and announced it to the attorneys.

"I'm mindful of the *Lohmeier* case cited in the defendants' response. Mr. Richardson doesn't have to be a medical doctor to testify as to the causation of Mr. Hernandez's fatal injuries so long as he has the specialized knowledge to assist the jury in resolving that issue."

Doug's jaw dropped. He suddenly realized he may have made a fatal error by not getting the testimony excluded. It would be difficult to overcome but his team would come up with a new strategy in light of the judge's decision.

Judge Furman continued, "The record shows that Mr. Richardson has specialized knowledge to assist the jury in this case and his opinions fall within the scope of his education, knowledge, experience, and overall qualifications in accident reconstruction and injury biomechanics. He may testify consistent with his reports, including his reconstruction of the accident, calculations of the forces, and opinions on the capability of such forces to eject Mr. Hernandez from his vehicle if he had been wearing a seat belt, and whether those forces could have caused the fatal injuries. His testimony does not require a medical education or license, although weight and credibility of his opinions are, of course, matters for cross-examination and jury consideration."

Looking directly at the plaintiffs' counsel while delivering this part of her ruling, Judge Furman stated, "Challenging Mr. Richardson on evidentiary grounds would be untimely in any event because the motion deadline passed, and trial has commenced. In addition, on the merits and the current record, such objections would be overruled. Mr. Richardson may testify as disclosed."

"Thank you, your honor," Doug acknowledged even though he was obviously disappointed with the judge's ruling.

"Thank you, your honor," Marissa said.

She held back a smile, turned to John, and squeezed his arm in approval of the ruling. John smiled at Marissa disregarding courtroom etiquette.

"Now that this issue has been addressed, counsel who is the next witness?" the judge asked.

Danica stood up and answered, "Plaintiffs will be calling Michael McDowell. Mr. McDowell is the plaintiffs' accident reconstructionist."

"Thank you, Ms. Bridgers. Bailiff, can you bring the jury into the courtroom?" the judge instructed.

The bailiff exited the courtroom and walked to the jury room where the jury waited during breaks.

He escorted the jury back to the courtroom. When they entered, all of the participants in the courtroom were standing up out of respect for the jury.

Once all the jurors were seated, the judge requested that everyone else in the courtroom sit down. Mr. McDowell was already seated in the witness box having previously been sworn in. The plaintiffs' counsel proceeded to ask Mr. McDowell about his educational background, his previous work as a detective with the Scottsdale police department, his credentials as an accident reconstructionist, and how he worked as an expert mainly for insurance carriers rather than plaintiffs like the Hernandezes.

"Mr. McDowell, can you tell the jury what you did after you were retained in this case?" Danica asked.

"I first received and reviewed the police reports and photos of the accident scene. I also inspected Mr. Hernandez's convertible. It hadn't been repaired yet. I took photos of the vehicle which I believe were disclosed in this case."

"Did you go to the accident scene?"

"Yes, I did."

Mr. McDowell would look to the questioner and then turn to the jury every time he answered. It was a tactic professional witnesses used to connect to the jury. The jury appeared receptive to him given his willingness to address them directly.

"What did you do when you were there?"

"I looked for any signs of the accident. There was still some crash damage on the road like broken glass from the windows and also shattered plastic from what appears to be from the left-turn signal light based upon the damage to the convertible."

"Did you find any else?"

"I also found some skid marks and gouges on the far left lane."

"And you believe those skid marks and gouges are from this accident?"

"I do. I was out there only two weeks after the accident. It's possible there was another accident in that same area, but unlikely. I looked into any other accident reports for that area around the date of this accident and there were none. So I am confident that what I found there was from this accident."

Most of the jurors took notes during the testimony. Others were so enthralled with the expert testimony, they seemed fixated on the witness and nothing else. The college juror, who normally yawned during the previous witness testimonies, was uncharacteristically wide awake.

"Thank you. From your review of the police report and photos, an inspection of the Hernandez vehicle, and the crash scene, did you reconstruct the accident?"

"I did."

Mr. McDowell flipped open the binder he brought with him while testifying which contained his expert file. He pulled out his expert report. He quickly skimmed it to refresh his memory.

"What was your reconstruction of the accident?" Danica asked.

"Based upon my review of all of the evidence, Mr. Weaver was traveling faster than Mr. Hernandez. He was likely traveling over the speed limit. Mr. Weaver drifted into Mr. Hernandez's lane causing the collision. And then because of the speed differential, the convertible spun around, causing the skid marks and the gouges one foot west of the dashed line."

"And is it your expert opinion that Mr. Hernandez caused the accident?"

"Yes, yes he did."

"Are your opinions made to a reasonable degree of scientific probability?"

"Yes, they are."

"Thank you, Mr. McDowell. I have no further questions, your honor."

"Mr. Davis, your witness," the judge declared.

"Thank you, your honor," John said as he walked to the lectern. He opened up his binder and started questioning the expert.

"Mr. McDowell, you located a gouge mark in the lane that Mr. Weaver was traveling in, correct?"

"Yes."

The witness answered solemnly. He knew that during a cross-examination opposing counsel only asked questions designed to elicit a "yes" or "no" response and to minimize the witness's ability to elaborate on an answer. Because he was familiar with this technique, he was unfazed. The jury, however, had to see past this tactic to understand what the full testimony would be.

"The gouge mark was one foot left of the dashed line, correct?"

"Correct!"

"That means it was one foot into the lane that Mr. Weaver was traveling in, correct?"

"Correct."

"There's no physical evidence that Mr. Weaver was making a lane change?"

"No, there isn't," the expert nervously agreed.

"And there's no physical evidence that Mr. Weaver was drifting into the middle lane - the lane Mr. Hernandez was traveling in?"

"Well, no. There is no physical evidence."

"You're speculating he entered that lane, correct?"

"I don't believe I am," Mr. McDowell insisted.

"The motorcyclist traveling in the same lane behind Mr. Hernandez never saw Mr. Weaver drift into Mr. Hernandez's lane, correct?"

"No, he did not."

"The motorcyclist testified earlier on the witness stand that he was traveling at the speed limit and Mr. Hernandez was going about the same speed, correct?"

"Yes, he did."

"The speed limit is forty miles per hour in that area, correct?"

"Yes, it is."

John was pleased he got the witness to agree to these fundamental facts. A failure to do so would only undermine the expert's credibility.

"Your expert report claims Mr. Hernandez was traveling about twenty-eight or twenty-nine miles per hour. But there is no physical evidence that he was traveling that speed, correct?"

"Correct. There's no physical evidence."

"It's speculation, isn't it?"

"I disagree with that. I think based upon my..."

"And it conveniently helps your accident reconstruction if you ignore the motorcyclist's testimony and testify Mr. Hernandez isn't traveling the speed limit?"

"I don't believe so. I'm just relaying the facts as I saw them."

The jurors feverishly took notes when Mr. Mc-Dowell responded. Even Marissa noted to remind John of the jurors' reaction.

"There is no reason to believe that the motorcyclist was lying when he testified that he and Mr. Hernandez were traveling the speed limit, correct?"

"He just may have been mistaken."

"So you think he was lying?" John slyly asked, knowing the answer to the question helped his clients.

"Well, I can't say that."

John slightly smiled.

"When I deposed you last September, I asked you to calculate how further south would the initial impact be from the gouge. Do you remember me asking that question during your deposition?"

"I remember the deposition but not everything I testified to. It's been a long time."

"I can show you the deposition transcript if you'd like?"

"Please do."

John pointed to the paralegal seated next to Marissa which prompted her to put the relevant portion of Mr. McDowell's deposition transcript on the video screen. The transcript appeared on the individual monitors in front of the witness, counsel, and the judge as well as the two giant monitors in the courtroom - one facing the jury and one facing the gallery for the attendees of the trial.

"For counsel and your honor, this is page seventeen of Mr. McDowell's deposition at lines eleven through twenty-three."

John waited for the plaintiffs' counsel and the judge to review the physical copy of the deposition transcript before proceeding.

"According to your deposition testimony, you calculated that at forty miles per hour (or fifty-eight feet per second), it would take half a second for the collision until impact, correct?"

"Yes. Yes, I did."

"And that it would be an easy equation to calculate the distance from the gouge marks to the initial impact of the collision. You calculated fifty-eight feet divided by two, which was twenty-eight and half feet, correct?"

Mr. McDowell reviewed the transcript and double-checked the math before answering.

"Yes, that's correct."

"Our accident reconstructionist, Hank Richardson, calculated approximately twenty-nine feet between the gouge mark you found and the initial impact, correct?"

"Yes, that's what Hank calculated," Mr. McDowell testified.

Given the witness was familiar with Mr. Richardson and they were former co-workers, he used Hank's first name when referring to him. The jury took note of that.

"And your calculations are similar, correct?"

"Correct."

"When you did your site inspection of the accident scene, you looked at the initial contact area, correct?"

"Yes, I did. But only briefly."

"There was no physical evidence at that location, correct?"

"No, there was not."

"There was no physical evidence indicating that the impact occurred in the middle lane, correct?"

"That's correct."

"One of the issues, in this case, is that there is an offset which you and the traffic design engineer claim resulted in Mr. Weaver drifting into the middle lane where Mr. Hernandez was traveling, correct?"

"That's correct. Instead of the lane continuing straight going westbound, the lane lines shift to the left at some point. If the driver isn't paying attention to how the lane shifts, they continue driving straight into the middle lane. If the driver is paying attention, then they steer to the left and stay in their own lane."

Again, Mr. McDowell turned to the jury when testifying. This time he used both hands to demonstrate how the vehicle travels straight or veers to the left. The jury paid attention during this basic demonstration.

"Thank you for that description, Mr. McDowell. And it's your contention that Mr. Weaver wasn't paying attention and drifted into Mr. Hernandez's lane, correct?"

"That's correct. He drifted into Mr. Hernandez's lane because of the offset."

"You didn't measure the offset at the point of the initial impact, correct?"

"No, I did not."

John turned his head to again instruct the paralegal to switch to a different page in the deposition transcript. When she turned to the appropriate page, he continued.

"According to your deposition testimony, you have no disagreement with Mr. Richardson's finding that at the initial point of impact the lateral offset is only six inches, correct?"

"Correct."

"And you still have no disagreement with Mr. Richardson's calculation as you sit here today and testify before the jury, correct?"

"No, I do not."

"You failed to mention in your report that the offset was only six inches at the initial impact, correct?"

"Yes. I didn't think it was important to mention."

"So, it wasn't important to mention?"

Clearly taken aback by his previous answer, Mr. McDowell fumbled for an appropriate response. "It wasn't my job to measure the offset at the point of impact."

"Whose job was it?"

"The traffic design engineer retained by plaintiffs' counsel. I believe his name is Mr. Sineda. Robert Sineda."

"You've read Mr. Sineda's report, correct?"

"Yes, I did."

"His report discusses the lateral offset on Camelback Road, correct?"

"I believe it does."

"His report failed to mention that the offset is only six inches at the initial impact, correct?"

"I...I need to double-check his report to answer the question. Is it okay if I review it?"

"Please do."

Mr. McDowell checked his expert binder, found Mr. Sineda's report, and reviewed it. After flipping through the report several times, he answered, "No, it does not."

This time he did not look toward the jury while answering.

"Your opinion is that when the shuttle bus hits

the convertible, the convertible spins to the right, correct?"

"Yes, it is."

"You agree with Mr. Richardson that Mr. Weaver's shuttle bus acts as a fence, but you only agree that it acts like a fence only if Mr. Weaver's vehicle doesn't enter into the middle lane correct?"

"That's correct."

"Well, you can't have the shuttle bus at the same position on the roadway as the gouge mark. The shuttle bus would have to be further over because the convertible has to spin to the right before it goes into the left lane and makes the gouge mark. So the convertible would have to be in a position where it's further left of that gouge mark, correct?

"Correct."

"You believe Mr. Weaver's shuttle bus would have to be further left of the gouge mark in order for the convertible to make the gouge at that location if Mr. Hernandez enters his lane, correct?"

"Correct."

John asked the paralegal to display an aerial view of the accident scene before proceeding with the next questions. He used a laser pointer to highlight certain areas of the photo.

"How wide is the lane?"

"The lane is about eleven feet. That's the standard width of lanes throughout the country."

"How wide is the shuttle bus?

"It's about eight feet and four inches."

"How wide is Mr. Hernandez's convertible?"

"Six feet."

"If Mr. Weaver is traveling in the middle of his

lane, how much distance is between the shuttle bus and the dashed line?"

John walked to the large monitor facing the jury and pointed to the middle of the lane. The jurors took their eyes off Mr. McDowell and looked at John while he posed his questions.

"About one foot on each side," Mr. McDowell answered.

"If Mr. Weaver is traveling on the left side of his lane, how much distance is between the shuttle bus and the dashed line?"

"Almost three feet."

"So there is plenty of room between the shuttle bus and the Lexus?"

"Yes, there's room."

John walked back to the lectern.

"You're assuming that Mr. Weaver was hugging the right side of the left lane even though he was aware that Mr. Hernandez was in the middle lane, correct?

"That's the likely scenario."

"There wasn't any testimony from Mr. Weaver that he was hugging the right side of the lane, correct?"

"No, there wasn't."

"Mr. Hernandez could have purposefully entered the left lane and not know Mr. Weaver's shuttle bus was present?"

"That's a possibility."

"Mr. Weaver could be in his blind spot, correct?"

"That's a possibility."

"I have no further questions, your honor," John declared.

## 12 RETURN

### Isabela, Puerto Rico
### The Same Day

The hospitality phone in casita number seven rang and rang. Before it went to voicemail, Daniel Mendoza walked inside and answered it.

"Hello."

"*Buenos tardes*, Mr. Mendoza. This is the front desk. I would like to talk to Pamela Williams. Is she there?"

"Hold on. Let me get her."

Daniel walked to the terrace where Pamela lay on the chaise lounge. She was obviously deep in thought and not enjoying the lovely views of the Atlantic Ocean. Oblivious to his presence, Pamela began murmuring to herself. Not wanting to invade her private thoughts, Daniel quickly interrupted her.

"Hey, Pam."

She took a deep breath before turning towards him as if she suspected something was out of the ordinary. Daniel looked at her with an air of concern even though he had no idea of the purpose of the call. He kneeled beside her near the chaise lounge hoping this would disarm her.

"The front desk is on the phone. They are asking for you. I can tell them to call back later if that's what you want."

A part of him wanted it too.

"No. No. I'm okay."

Pamela walked inside the casita and grabbed the phone.

"Hello. Who am I speaking to?" she asked while watching Daniel through the open doors. He was relaxing and sipping a beverage. She was pleased he was distracted and not paying attention to her.

"Ms. Williams, Mr. Ravan would like to meet you as soon as possible. We have a golf cart waiting in front of your casita. Please go outside and the driver will take you to his location," the employee instructed and then hung up the phone.

She hesitated for a moment considering whether to go back to the terrace and let Daniel know she would be gone. Instead, she went outside and got into the golf cart. The driver didn't even acknowledge her. He simply drove to a remote location of the resort still overlooking the ocean. Pamela exited the golf cart and it drove off.

Gerald Ravan was in resort wear, unlike the business attire he normally wears. Shades covered his eyes. He obviously came from a recent, festive activity but he wasn't in a celebratory mood. His demeanor gave off a vibe of deep concern.

"I love this view," he softly declared, wanting to lighten his mood. He walked a little closer to the edge of the cliff, subtly beckoning Pamela to follow him. She did. "The Caribbean is a place I rarely visit." He closed his eyes and let the breeze engulf him. "It's refreshing. Isn't it?" He didn't wait for a response. "I should come here more often." Taking a few more steps, Gerald continued, "I have some bad news, Pam. I wanted to deliver it to you in person."

She looked intently at him half-expecting what he was going to say but also wondering if his presence had anything to do with her investigation of the kidnapped guest.

"Your father is in the ICU. The doctors think he may have had a heart attack, but they aren't sure. They're running tests now."

He glanced over at her. Silent tears tracked down her cheeks although she had a stoic reaction to his unsettling words. Knowing she would not outwardly express her concern, he walked toward her and embraced her. The tightness in Pamela's body released as if her worries dissipated with the strong winds and escaped into the vastness of the ocean.

"It will be okay," Gerald reassured her. "Gavin's been asking for you. He wants you with him. My private jet is at the airport and is ready to take you back to Arizona."

One of Gerald's personal bodyguards wearing a black suit and mirrored aviator glasses approached them.

"We are ready, Mr. Ravan," he said.

"Thank you," he told the bodyguard. Turning to Pamela, Gerald said, "Please go with my bodyguard. He will drive you to the airport."

Pamela looked up. She saw a black Escalade on the same road she'd seen earlier on the video feed in the security room. She climbed into the Escalade after the bodyguard opened the rear passenger door and then waived goodbye to Gerald.

Gerald watched as the Escalade drove away.

———

As the Escalade drove eastbound towards the airport, Pamela called Daniel's cell phone to let him know the situation.

"Hey. It's me."

He looked around the terrace, thinking she was playing some trick on him like she always did.

"Sorry, but I had to leave. Something came up," she explained.

"Is it about your father?" Daniel worriedly asked.

"Yes. He's in the hospital. I'm on my way there right now."

Daniel hadn't realized she had left the casita. He felt guilty for not personally seeing her off.

"I'm so sorry. I can be on the next flight back, but I have something to do tonight for the anniversary celebrations."

"No worries. Get here if you can, but if not, I understand. I know you are a guest at the request of the resort. I'm sure they have a lot of things planned for you. I'll still be here."

"I'll be there. I promise."

Pamela was pleased with his commitment. It was unexpected but needed given the circumstances. She hung up the phone and dialed Virginia at her private investigators' agency.

———

Although generally concerned about Pamela's father's well-being, Daniel was also worried for Pamela. The stress of the past year showed on her face. She denied it and pretended everything was okay. But Daniel knew better. He thought this week in Puerto Rico would be good for both of them. Not just to have a soirée at his client's expense but also to relax and get away from the stress of work. The kidnapping complicated things and returned Pamela to her investigatory mode rather than the vacation mode she desperately needed. Daniel couldn't deny he was also consumed by the investigation even though he desperately needed relaxation. Now that Pamela was gone and preoccupied with her father, he could drop the investigation and just relax.

*Well, not completely*, he thought. *If there is a new lead, I'll start the investigation again.*

His self-reassurance made the decision to focus on enjoying himself more palatable.

*I'm sure Pamela will understand.*

Daniel settled into the chaise lounge, took a sip of his beverage, closed his eyes, and allowed the smell of the ocean to sustain him.

---

An individual watched in his binoculars as Pamela drove off in the golf cart. He saw her enter the Escalade and then high-tailed it back to casita number eight. From that casita, he stealthily watched Daniel relaxing on the terrace. Startled by the ring of his cell phone, he quickly answered.

"Yes, boss. There's only one left. The male."

## 13  MEMORIES

Scottsdale, Arizona
Early The Next Day

Pamela sat in the ICU room watching her father sleep. He was exhausted and she didn't want to wake him, having arrived so early in the morning on the private flight from Puerto Rico. The call nurse informed her his doctor would be in but around eight a.m. She had plenty of rest on the flight and was now too anxious to sit and do nothing for the next few hours before the doctor arrived.

She wistfully smiled while staring at him. Memories of her father swirled in her head. The first time he took her to the *dojo* to learn Aikido as a child. Making pancakes for Mother's Day. An Aikido tournament in Tokyo where she witnessed her father win. His win inspired her all the more to train and become excellent. Funerals of his special ops buddies who he honored and missed. Times when he was drunk beyond measure and sulking in the corner with a bottle of booze and filled with self-pity. She never knew why and never bothered to find out. When her mother loaded the three kids into the car and drove away from the family home as her father watched and then slammed the door when he went back into the house. She assumed he binge drank all night and slept all day after a drunken stupor.

Pamela welcomed the memories but at the same time dreaded them because the pain resurfaced. She thought she had washed it all away with all of the endless nights of self-reflection and discipline through her martial arts. Apparently, she hadn't. Long ago, as a teenager, she'd forgiven her father. They renewed their relationship and were now closer than ever before.

She couldn't understand why she was angry at him now. He hadn't done anything to really upset her in a decade or more. Maybe it was the illness she was really angry at? Seeing him wasting away at times, and then mysteriously bouncing back was an emotional rollercoaster she was willing to endure for the sake of her father. She knew it was a fatal illness, but she hoped and prayed a miracle cure would come. These conflicting thoughts must have made her angry at him. She reassured herself it was a normal part of the grieving process.

Dr. Thamm warned her of the stages of the disease. She knew them very well. Perhaps too well and it was consuming her as she saw her father progress slowly but steadily from stage one to stage two. She feared the future stages and what it would mean for her father and their relationship. She was afraid of losing him like she lost her mother already. She realized if her father died, all she had left was her sister, Milagros. Her brother, Cameron, was estranged from the family. Nothing she did repaired her relationship with Cameron. So she stopped trying.

*He's dead to me,* she remembered saying the last time they fought, and he stormed off.

When she arrived at the hospital, she expected Cameron to be there even though she hadn't spoken to him about spending time with their father like she'd promised. Cameron wasn't at the hospital. She had mixed feelings about that. Avoiding any confrontation with him was welcomed. But realizing he was not by their father's side angered her. Where was he? She imagined him partying and avoiding responsibilities like he always did. Why was he back if not to see their father? Why wasn't he at the hospital like she was? The answers eluded her.

The door to the hospital room opened. Pamela expected Cameron to walk in. But it was Dr. Thamm.

"Good morning, Pam. It's nice to see you. I'm glad you could make it," he announced as he hugged her.

"Thank you, doctor."

"Gavin's been asking for you. He'll be happy to see you."

Dr. Thamm walked closer to the bed, checked the IV monitor, and glanced at his patient. Pamela quietly observed him. She'd seen the nurses do the same procedure throughout the hours she'd been in the hospital room. But knowing Dr. Thamm was there brought her comfort.

"He's doing a lot better," he added. "Heart attacks are an expected side effect of the disease. The good thing is that this was a mild one. He may need to be here for a few days before we can discharge him. We can also put him on an antiplatelet to reduce his chances of having a heart attack in the future. I've already written a prescription which he can take with him once he's discharged."

Pamela smiled and gently nodded in response. She wanted to say "thank you" but the words were caught in her throat. Dr. Thamm understood, squeezed her hand, and exited the room so she could be alone with her father.

———

When the nurses came in to attend to her father, Pamela walked out of the hospital room into the hallway and then into the foyer where she could make a call. She wanted to check in with Daniel to see what time his flight back to Arizona was. She wasn't sure if he was taking the company's private jet or if he was taking a commercial flight back. All she hoped was that he would arrive in Arizona soon. She didn't know exactly why she wanted him with her. Pamela was accustomed to handling things alone. Something about the past few days in Puerto Rico together made her feel more comfortable and relaxed with Daniel than before. She really desired his presence now.

She walked in circles in the foyer as the phone rang. One ring. Two rings. Three rings. It went straight to voicemail. It was unlike Daniel to not answer her calls. He oftentimes interrupted other calls to take hers.

*Perhaps, he's still enjoying the festivities*, she thought.

A part of her was happy for him. After his voicemail greeting ended, she said, "Hey, Daniel. I'm here in Scottsdale. Hope you're enjoying your time in Isabela. Did you book your flight yet? Let me know. Okay. See you soon."

Disappointed she had to leave a voicemail message, Pamela walked back to be by her father's bedside. She assumed the nurses would be done and he would now be awake. She was excited to finally talk to him about how he was feeling and the clinical trial he would be enrolled in once all of this was over.

*That should lift his spirits,* she gleamed.

## 14 PLAYA

Isabela, Puerto Rico
The Same Day

Daniel walked through the wooden gate at the Regal Isabela onto concrete steps that meandered down the lush hill into a dirt pathway ultimately leading to *El Pastillo* beach. The wide stretch of beach was lined with palm trees, some swept by strong winds while they were saplings, causing them to form unique shapes. The waves calmly lapped upon the shore making a lulling sound and bringing Daniel to a spiritual connection to the sea. He sauntered along the shore, eyeing the sapphire skies, and smiling inwardly.

Not knowing why he was there rather than at the festivities planned by the resort, Daniel could only think of what transpired over the past few days. Some of his memories were filled with joy like when he first saw Pamela in the plunge pool. He wondered why she came to Puerto Rico. Or their evening meal together when they laughed and discussed work and their social lives. He was always surprised by how much Pamela knew things about him he had never disclosed. Sometimes to no one at all. But he never dwelled on that. Instead, he simply enjoyed her company and the pleasantries between them.

The age difference was something he never considered a hurdle to their friendship. Pamela was twenty years his junior. Most middle-aged men like himself would be flattered to hang around such a lovely, younger woman. They would perhaps prefer to seek refuge in her arms in a romantic way rather than being platonic. But not Daniel. He saw them as friends and nothing more despite the subtle hints and overtures she made.

*Those were just playful comments to stroke his ego or to tease a lonely man,* Daniel rationalized.

He knew Pamela was strictly professional and would never cross the line. After all, what woman would genuinely speak to a man about his love interests if she was truly wanting a relationship with him? It made no sense to Daniel. Most things about women didn't. He was socially awkward in that way.

As he took a few more steps along the beach, he noticed several flat stones lying on the sand. Picking up a few, he tried skipping them on the ocean. Some skipped once or twice. One immediately sunk into the water. Daniel was pleased with his attempts. It reminded him of his childhood when he played at the beach in California. It was a simpler, innocent time when he lived on Chambers Lane.

Not like it was now. The stress of the past few years maybe even decades was finally catching up to him. Although his former marriage to Christine was a high point in his life bringing innumerable moments of joy, the divorce destroyed him in ways he could not fathom. Daniel had to dig deep inside himself to finally accept how he contributed to the failed relationship. After the divorce, he threw himself into work which only made things worse. When he became a partner at Williams Brown years later, he met his professional goal, but his social life was still in tatters. By then, Daniel thought he would have gotten remarried and would have started a family of his own. The son he raised during the marriage, Wisdom, was not his biological child, but Christine's son from a previous relationship. A part of him hoped he would have children of his own. But it wasn't meant to be.

Daniel pictured himself at the firm's Christmas party when it was announced he made partner. Mr. Brown spoke to the entire room of attorneys and their spouses and significant others and proudly lavished praise not only on Daniel's acumen as an attorney but also on his professional demeanor and sensitivity to all parties involved in any litigation he was a part of. In some ways, it rang hollow. Not because it wasn't true, but because he had no one to share his accomplishments with. The night when he became a partner, he was alone just as he was when walking along *El Pastillo* beach enjoying the view and the sand dunes ahead.

He suddenly stopped walking. Wondering why he couldn't find love over the years, he remembered Corina - the latest woman in his life. Her lovely smile. Her beautiful laugh brought him joy. Their relationship, however, never grew beyond just friends no matter how much he wanted to see it blossom. She was the type of woman Daniel would marry if they were both in love. Strong, independent, able to speak her mind without fear, and compassionate or stern toward him when appropriate. There were nights when he questioned why they were never able to take the next step. He surely wanted to, but Corina did not.

Reassuring himself about her choice, Daniel reasoned she was a woman who had so much pain from her past experiences that she wasn't willing to be tied down again. Her free spirit meant she pursued only those things she desired. Unlike Daniel, it was not her career but the little things that mattered - time with her extended family and friends, traveling abroad with her girlfriends, and taking care of those she loved. These things were more important than the uncertainties of a relationship or even marriage. No matter how many times Daniel tried to broach the subject of being more than just friends, Corina ignored him and avoided the conversation. He knew she cared, just not in the way he wanted her to or, even still, needed her to. At that moment, the thought brought sadness to his soul he had not felt since the divorce so long ago. He knew he needed to accept it once and for all and let her go.

Perhaps that's why he was here walking along the shore to release his expectations into the sea, to free himself of hope unattained, and to be renewed with a sense of purpose he could not at the moment fully understand. The thought brought some relief but not much. Staring off into the horizon, Daniel smiled and sighed. The horizon was endless, and he hoped to meet it there.

Amidst his thoughts, the sudden tugging of his arms felt uncomfortable. He instinctively resisted it.

DANIEL MALDONADO

His body uncontrollably collapsed as he was dragged by two men away to a mysterious place.

"No, no. What are you doing to me?" Daniel desperately asked as he became unconscious from something injected into his body.

## 15  DARKNESS TWOFOLD

An Unknown Location in Puerto Rico
Several Hours Later.

As Daniel became less groggy from the sedative, his senses slowly returned. He faintly smelled blood and sweat but it wasn't from his own body. The smell emanated from across the room. Turning his head in the direction of the pungent metallic and sour aroma, Daniel couldn't see where it was coming from. He was blindfolded. He wanted to stand but he was restrained in the chair he was seated on. He struggled to free himself but to no avail.

"Stop that," a male voice across the room demanded. "They'll hear you."

Daniel immediately froze especially after realizing he wasn't alone in the room.

"Who's there?" Daniel whispered.

He resisted making more noise. He wasn't sure if his captors could hear him or if the person speaking to him from across the room was a captive like himself.

"Shush," the person insisted with an air of frustration.

Listening intensely, Daniel could distinguish two muffled, male voices in the far distance. Their voices were even further away than the voice admonishing him to be still. He couldn't understand what the two voices were saying but they were definitely speaking Spanish. Suddenly, salsa music blared throughout the room. Daniel wasn't sure if the two males were partying. But the music was so loud, it seemed like the purpose was to disguise something the pair was doing rather than for a social gathering. Occasionally, the sound of metal clanging overcame the music.

"Where are we?" Daniel asked, knowing it would be more difficult for his captors to hear him speak over the loud noise.

There was no response from his fellow captive.

He slowly turned his head from side to side to determine if there was anything else he could discern from being there. No natural sunlight warmed his face or anywhere else his naked body was exposed.

*The windows must be covered, he presumed. Or we are in a windowless room? Think, Daniel. Think.*

He took a deeper breath to determine if he could smell anything else inside the room that would give him a clue. All he could smell besides sweat and blood was dampness in the air. It was the typical humidity in Puerto Rico after the torrential rains. But the room felt cooler than his accommodations at the resort even though it overlooked the ocean.

*We must be at a higher elevation on the island*, he thought as he accounted for the lower temperature.

Unfortunately, the entire island center was mountainous. Not being awake during his transport to this new location, Daniel did not know how far from the resort his captives drove or in which direction. He had no idea what part of the island he was being held against his will.

*It could have been ten minutes or an hour*, he surmised. *Who knows?*

The island wasn't that large and could be circumnavigated in a little more than two hours in a car. He was exasperated by his inability to ascertain his whereabouts. Because his arms were restrained, he couldn't flail his arms about in anger to release his frustration. He could only sit in an uncomfortable position waiting for the inevitable.

Desperate to get more information, Daniel asked, "What's your name? My name is Daniel Mendoza. I'm a U.S. citizen."

He waited in vain for an answer.

Wondering how long he had been there, Daniel surmised it had only been a few hours because he was still full from overindulging in breakfast that morning before heading out to the beach.

*But my companion? Was he the kidnapped man from the other casita? Or someone else?* Daniel pondered.

He had to know. Not only for his sake but because he knew his fellow captive's identity could be a clue to his freedom.

"What's your name? How long have you been here?" he asked.

Calculating in his mind, Daniel figured the answer should be two maybe three days. If longer than that, then the captive was someone other than the resort guest. This, of course, was based on getting an accurate answer from the other captive. Daniel had no idea if the other individual was also blindfolded and could tell how many days had actually passed. Just sitting there, it seemed like forever.

When no response was forthcoming, Daniel became even more frustrated.

*Calm down,* he chided himself. *You need to stay calm and level-headed. You need to come up with an escape plan with or without his help.*

Daniel wondered if Pamela called him once she arrived in Arizona. He could tell his cell phone was no longer on him.

*Even if she had called, my captors would have my cell phone and would intercept the call,* he thought. *Or maybe they ditched the phone somewhere along their route.*

He had no idea.

*She's probably too busy with her dad anyway,* he thought. *Surely, Gerry must notice I'm missing by now. He'll look for me.*

The thought of Gerald Ravan searching for him gave Daniel comfort. Gerald was a resourceful man with international connections. Having recently learned that Gerald also had extensive connections in Puerto Rico with the governor and numerous local officials, he hoped those resources could be a tool in rescuing him. He remembered Gerald saying he might leave Puerto Rico early before the end of the festivities to finish some business. Realizing no one else on the island would be missing him, Daniel sighed. The other captive took notice.

When Daniel heard the other captive move slightly, he said, "If we work together, we might be able to get out of this. What do you say?"

Daniel didn't expect a response. He continued probing the room with his unconscious mind to determine its size and shape and any possible exits. Perhaps, he was just occupying himself with meaningless tasks during a stressful situation. Or maybe he was accomplishing more than he understood. Whatever it was, he seemed more relaxed. And then it hit him?

*Why do they want me? What do I have that they want? Or do I know something I shouldn't?*

His mind raced. He wondered if they were aware of Pamela and grabbed her too before she made it to the airport. She obviously wasn't in the room with him.

*Could she be somewhere else? Could she be hurt? I have to get out of here!! I have to do something!!*

Remembering the blood and sweat in the casita, Daniel pondered whether he was next to be tortured. He braced his mind and body for that eventuality. Having never served in the military and having never learned any martial arts, Daniel knew he was unprepared for it. He was an attorney after all. Not a soldier. Not a hero.

*But who's that man with me? Why is he so important? What does he know that they needed to torture him to get the information? Did they break him? Are they looking for it now?*

Daniel exhausted himself with his myriad questions and concerns.

# 16 FORENSIC PATHOLOGIST

Phoenix, Arizona
The Same Day

"Good afternoon, Dr. Weimar. We've met before, haven't we?" Doug Clarkson asked as he approached the lectern to question the witness scheduled for the afternoon session for that trial day.

"Yes, we have. When your firm retained me last year," the doctor answered.

He smiled at the jury when responding so that they would feel comfortable about why the witness had a cordial relationship with the plaintiffs' counsel.

"And I have placed on your monitor what's been marked as plaintiffs' Exhibit Number 2. Can you identify that particular document, first of all?"

The doctor glanced at his monitor before answering.

"It's the report I prepared for this case."

"Can you tell the jury about your particular background?"

Turning towards the jury again, the doctor explained, "I am a physician specializing in anatomic, clinical, and forensic pathology. I am also licensed to practice medicine in the State of Arizona."

"Are you board certified?"

"I am board certified in the specialties I previously mentioned by the American Board of Pathology."

"Can you describe to the jury what your specialty in forensic pathology entails?"

The doctor beamed when posed the question. Testifying was his forte. He enjoyed explaining his chosen field, especially to those who were unfamiliar with it.

"Forensic pathology involves the study, evaluation, and analysis of sudden, suspicious, unexpected, unexplained, medically unattended deaths, primarily to determine the cause of death. It also includes the determination of the manner of death, the mechanism of death, and in some instances the time and place of death or the relationship between injury and disease. To a great extent, it's the kind of work that is associated with a medical examiner or a coroner's office. Although forensic pathologists like myself can also practice privately and are involved, as other medical specialists are, in writing, teaching, and research."

The jury was in awe at his explanation. Having an excellent witness made the trial more exciting in their eyes and made it easier to pass the long day.

"Thank you, Doctor. You have a fascinating profession. Can you tell the jury what your report, plaintiffs' Exhibit Number 2, addresses?"

"I've addressed the question of the injuries, the patterns, the instrumentality, the scene investigation, from a forensic pathology standpoint, and some observations about the autopsy."

"What do you do for a living?" Doug Clarkson asked.

He knew this question was critical to convincing the jury that the doctor was knowledgeable and unbiased.

"I am associated with the Phoenix County Hospital, where I'm the Director of Forensic Pathology. I previously was the coroner of Maricopa County for about twelve years. And I'm also a medical legal consultant on a private basis for attorneys, agencies, families, and companies."

Doug questioned Dr. Weimar regarding the last time he performed an autopsy and the number of autopsies he performed every year for the past decade.

After being questioned about his role as a medical legal consultant, Dr. Weimar responded, "I also participate as a secondary pathologist or observer on about one hundred or so autopsies done at the Maricopa County Coroner's Office. These are for the most part homicides, and other complex cases where we feel it is wise to have a second forensic pathologist involved in the case. However, in those cases, I do not actually perform the autopsy. I'm there, as I said, as a secondary person strictly to observe the autopsy."

"And does the coroner's office issue a report as to the manner and cause of death?"

'Yes, the primary report details the results of the internal and external examination of the body and includes any toxicology analysis conducted."

"Does the autopsy report include a coroner's verdict?"

"Well, we don't call it a coroner's verdict. We just refer to it as the coroner's statement which is the diagnosis as to the cause of death. It also includes checking off the box on the death certificate regarding the manner of death."

"Doctor, did you observe the autopsy of Carlos Hernandez as a medical legal consultant?"

"Yes, I did."

The jury looked intently at the doctor as they anticipated his testimony regarding the death of Mr. Hernandez.

"Was the examination of Mr. Hernandez complete and thorough?"

"It was to the best of the pathologist's ability to perform the autopsy. As I testified earlier, I did not perform the autopsy myself. My role was limited to observing the autopsy on behalf of the Hernandez family."

"Did you review every note, memorandum, and report prepared by the Maricopa County Coroner's office regarding Mr. Hernandez's autopsy?"

"Yes, I did."

"Did you review any reports prepared by the Scottsdale Police Department regarding the subject accident?"

"Yes, as well as all of the photos taken of the accident scene."

"And do you feel that you are qualified to make an opinion as to the findings of the Maricopa County Coroner's office as to whether or not you agree or disagree with those findings?"

"I have opinions and am sufficiently informed to be able to make opinions relative to the findings of the Maricopa County Coroner's office. I, in fact, agree with their findings."

"And in this case were you able to determine the cause of death?"

"Yes, I was."

"What was the cause of death?"

"The cause of death was blunt force trauma."

Mrs. Hernandez sobbed as she visualized her husband's lifeless body at the scene of the accident. Most of the jury turned their heads toward her when they heard the sobs. She was comforted by her two children and quickly muffled her sound so as not to disturb the trial. Doug Clarkson watched the jury and was pleased with the result. He continued once everything settled down.

"Is part of the job of a medical examiner to determine the manner of death?" he asked.

"Yes."

"Is that something you were able to determine?"

'Yes, I was."

"What was the manner of death?"

"Mr. Hernandez was ejected from his convertible and his head hit the ground causing a fatal head injury."

"Thank you. Nothing further, your honor."

The judge turned to the defense counsel's table and said, "Ms. Robles. Your witness."

"Good afternoon, Dr. Weimar," Marissa said after waiting until Mr. Clarkson sat down at counsel's table.

"Good afternoon," the witness responded.

He was used to vigorous cross-examinations by opposing counsel having testified many times before. His demeanor became more solemn and observant. He wanted to ensure he heard everything Marissa was going to ask him to ensure his response was appropriate and concise.

"Doctor, how much money have you been paid by

the plaintiffs for your involvement in this case at this time?"

"Including my testimony today, it would be approximately a hundred thousand dollars."

The jury was taken aback by the amount. Marissa knew this question painted the doctor as more of a paid witness rather than an objective one.

"When were you first involved in this case?"

"I was called by Mr. Clarkson within an hour of the accident."

"Within an hour?!" Her eyebrows furled to display her dismay.

It was unusual for a paid consultant to be retained so quickly after an accident. She wasn't sure how to convey this to the jury by questioning an adverse witness who would likely downplay it. As she was told many times in preparing for past trials, she needed to prove her case by questioning her own experts who would have a more favorable answer. She decided not to ask any more questions on the issue and noted on her legal pad to question her own expert about it.

"Did you go directly to the coroner's office upon being retained?"

"No, I went to the accident scene. Mr. Hernandez's body was still there, and I accompanied the body to the coroner's office."

"You testified earlier that you observed the autopsy, correct?"

"Yes, I did."

"But you did not perform the autopsy, correct?"

"No, I did not."

"When you perform autopsies, do you normally record the autopsy?"

"Yes, I do."

"What percentage of the time do you record autopsies?"

"One hundred percent of the time. It's standard procedure to record an autopsy."

"Is that true when you merely observe the autopsy?"

"It is."

"Do you know if Mr. Hernandez's autopsy was recorded?"

"I...I assumed it was."

When asked this last question, Dr. Weimar became concerned about where the line of questioning was going.

"Doctor, I will represent to you that his autopsy was not recorded. Were you aware of that?"

"No, I wasn't."

"Would you consider that a failure to meet the standard a professional medical examiner should use in performing an autopsy?"

"Yes, I do," he reluctantly admitted.

The jury listened attentively to his response. Some of the jurors' facial expressions showed their concerns about the revelation.

"Doctor, when you perform an autopsy, do you take photos during the examination?"

"Yes, I do. I take photos of both the external and internal examination because I want to be thorough."

"Did you take photos during the examination of Mr. Hernandez?" Marissa asked.

"No, I did not because, as I testified, I was not performing the autopsy. I was merely observing it. It is the job of the pathologist performing the autopsy to take photos."

"Were photos taken during the autopsy of Mr. Hernandez?"

"I seem to recall they were," he answered confidently.

"Did you review photos taken during the autopsy for purposes of preparing your report, plaintiffs' Exhibit Number 2, and for purposes of your testimony in court today?"

"Now that I think about it, no, I did not."

"Doctor, I will represent to you the photos that were allegedly taken during the autopsy are missing. Were you aware of that?"

"No, I was not until you mentioned it right now."

"Would you consider missing autopsy photos as a failure to meet the standard that a professional medical examiner should use in performing an autopsy?"

'Yes, I do."

Several jurors shook their heads in disapproval.

"Are you aware that the Weavers' forensic pathologist was not able to perform an independent autopsy of Mr. Hernandez?"

"Yes, I was."

"Can you tell the jury why the Weavers' forensic expert was unable to perform an independent autopsy?"

"Mr. Hernandez was cremated shortly after his autopsy. I believe it was within an hour or two at the most."

"Do you believe it's fair to the Weavers that they are unable to independently verify the cause and manner of death which you testified about today? No body. No photos. No recording of the autopsy."

Mr. Clarkson immediately stood up and stated,

"Objection, your honor. Irrelevant. Calls for speculation. It's also a compound question."

"Overruled. I want to hear what he has to say. I will allow the question," Judge Furman replied.

"No, I do not consider it fair to the Weavers to be in that position."

"Thank you for your honesty, doctor. I have no further questions," Marissa said as she walked back to the defense counsel's table.

# 17 DELIRIUM

An Undisclosed Location in Puerto Rico
The Same Day

T his *pendejo is going to get us killed*, the captive
thought after hearing Daniel Mendoza ask his
repeated questions. *Who is this guy?*

Thinking long and hard about his father's foot soldiers, the captive couldn't place the voice of the individual also in the room with him. He also thought of
childhood friends, distant relatives, and even co-
workers and associates who might be involved just the
same. He wasn't familiar enough with any of them to
determine if they also occupied the room. One person, in particular, flashed in his mind. At first, a
shadowy figure appeared, and then his face came into
focus.

*Nah, it can't be Victor. Victor's voice is nasally,* he
remembered.

The captive replayed his myriad interactions with
Victor to double-check whether it was in fact him. He
remembered the discontent Victor and the others
voiced when learning of his treachery. Beyond the ini-

tial outrage, every other interaction with Victor and the other family members was not only cordial but deferential. It could have been out of deference to his father or fear of the captive's retaliatory action should they confront him directly. The captive had no idea of the motivation for the members' fidelity. Given his present circumstances, obviously, for some, it was all a charade until the appropriate opportunity arose to seek revenge. And that was apparently now.

*If it's not Victor, then who could it be?*

At a loss, the captive suspected the other individual in the room was a plant designed to gain his favor so he would reveal the location of the stolen money.

*I'm not falling for it.*

But he wasn't sure. Searching his memories again, no one else came to mind. His thoughts, however, were periodically distracted due to flashes of excruciating pain throughout his body. He started breathing slowly as he almost succumbed to unconsciousness. Wanting to stave it off, the captive moved whatever part of his body was free from the restraints. Those slight movements increased his blood pressure and the blood flowing to his brain. He hoped it would be enough to prevent him from becoming unconscious. Feeling himself recovering gave him strength and made him more resolute.

Hearing another question coming from across the room, he remained silent. He dared not respond again in case the idiot in the room with him continued to speak and make things worse. The last thing he needed was for his captors to barge into the room angry and vindictive.

*Thankfully, the music is drowning out his voice.*

*Those two goons will be busy for a while,* he reassured himself.

He smiled at the thought but realized at some point they would be back for him and this time with a vengeance. They were obviously resolved in finding the money and were preoccupied with their greed. He thought about trying to escape like his companion suggested but the bindings were too tight, and his body too weakened from the repeated beatings and torture. He wondered what the other guy had in mind as an escape plan and if it would work.

*He probably has no idea anyway,* he chided himself when the faint hope arose. *I need to focus.*

———

"Dig a little deeper," the older captor said to the younger as he watched.

He sipped from a bottle of Medalla Light and wiped his brow as if he was the one doing the actual hard labor. He'd been watching the whole time without lending a hand. It was a perk for his long service to the family.

"There's nothing here," the younger male snapped while stomping harder on the spade, so it wedged deeper into the ground. Sweat dripped down his forehead. "I've been digging for hours."

Checking his watch, the older male corrected him. "It's only been forty minutes. Keep digging."

"We're not going to find anything. There's no money here. Why would he bury money in the ground? It makes no sense. That *pendejo* is lying to us. He wants to keep the money for himself."

The younger male glared at the other hoping to convince him to end the useless search.

"If we don't find that money we won't...."

"I know."

The younger male shoveled more dirt out of the hole and onto a large pile in the middle of the yard. Salsa music blared from the house into the backyard where the two were diligently working. It masked the noise from their activity and any attempt by their captives to call for help.

When it hit the one-hour mark, the older male tapped the younger one on the shoulder. "Follow me," he commanded as he stormed inside.

Relieved, the younger male complied.

———

When the door slammed open, the two males rushed into the room. Daniel could hear them panting out of anger and exhaustion. Rushing footsteps worried him until he realized they were headed to the other side of the room. He gasped in relief but worried about what was next.

"You think we're stupid. Don't you? You've been wasting our time trying to find the money in your safe house when you lied to us about where it's buried but we've got time to get it out of you. You're not going to be rescued," the older male confidently insisted.

*What money?* Daniel thought hoping more would be revealed which he could use to determine what was going on.

The captive laughed hysterically. He knew he was finally caught but couldn't care less whether he permanently outsmarted them. The deception gave him the time to think and scheme.

"It's not funny," the younger male exclaimed as he punched the captive in the stomach.

The male took the punch in his stride as if he was a prized fighter. The punch gave him inner strength.

"Is that all you've got? I'm never telling you where that money is," he maniacally declared.

The older male's eyes bulged in frustration. He frantically glanced around the room looking for something to hit the captive with to break his spirit. And then he saw him - Daniel strapped to another chair looking delirious. The older male tromped over to Daniel's chair and whaled on him repeatedly. Punch after punch after punch. Daniel cried out in despair for the beating to stop. It did not.

"You better tell me where that money is or I'm going to kill him," the older male fumed. His rage was getting the better of him.

"I don't know that *puto*!! Why would I care?!!" the captive retorted as he sat up in his chair with an air of defiance.

The older male kept pounding, punching, and slapping Daniel like an enraged wild animal. The screams continued. Nothing fazed the captive.

## 18 MOTION DAY

### Phoenix, Arizona
### The Same Day

"Why aren't you in court today?" one of the younger associates asked Marissa as she was walking to her office wearing business casual clothes rather than a skirt suit which she typically wore when in court.

Marissa glared at the newer associate and corrected the misunderstanding.

"It's Judge Furman's Motion Day. She doesn't have trials on Fridays. She spends the entire day addressing motions and other legal issues in other cases she's assigned because she's unable to address these issues earlier in the week because she's in trial. Does that answer your question? Is there anything else you need?"

Marissa was obviously perturbed. When the associate looked dumbfounded and quietly left, Marissa shrugged her shoulders and continued toward her office. John saw her in the hallway and followed her inside.

"How do you think the trial is going?" he asked. "It seems like we're connecting with the jury."

Marissa placed her briefcase on her desk and wished she had a cup of coffee before starting her day. She needed the pick-me-up.

"It's going to be a long day," she said aloud rather than to herself.

"Huh," John said.

"Never mind." Marissa sat down and scooted closer to her computer. "We need to prepare for Monday's trial testimony. Who's on the witness list for that day?"

Marissa looked for the witness schedule in her briefcase but before she could find it John replied, "It's Selinda."

"The wife?"

"Yes. I'm surprised they didn't put her on the stand first," John replied. He sat down after realizing Marissa wasn't objecting to his presence. "Probably, so the jury will have another emotional start to the second week of the trial. I've never seen that happen before. It's a first for me."

"Me too. Do you want to cross-examine her," Marissa asked as she slumped deeper into her chair. "To be honest, I'm a little overwhelmed with all the technical issues. I can do it if you don't have the time. I just need to have a relaxing weekend if you don't mind."

"I don't mind. It will be good for me to do it. How are you doing?"

John was concerned Marissa wasn't fully herself. He could see it in the shallowness of her eyes and hear it in the hoarseness of her voice.

"I'm fine."

"You don't seem fine. You looked fine yesterday when we were leaving the courthouse. Did something happen last night?"

Marissa didn't want to admit what was really going on, but she knew if she didn't tell John the truth or something near the truth, he would never let it go. He was relentless but in a gentle way. She also couldn't lie to him. He knew her too well.

"Okay. It's just last night some of my family came into town," she finally admitted.

"That's great. Isn't it?"

"My mom's pressuring me to spend time with them. I want to but I'm in the middle of a trial and can't just focus on familial obligations. I need to be at my best. Daniel's counting on me. The client is counting on me. I've explained it to them. They just don't understand. I don't know why they had to come this weekend."

"I totally know what you mean. Family doesn't understand how time-consuming trials are. Exhausting days...sleepless nights...endless worrying. But let me tell you, family is more important than working yourself to death. The job will always be here. Your family may not. It's important to spend time with your family while you can. They can only be so understanding."

John remembered the many times his ex-wife complained about his long hours and how his work was his mistress. His lips tightened at the thought and the feeling of regret.

"I know you're right. I just can't leave. Not now."

"We've got this, Marissa. I promise you. You have nothing to worry about. Take the rest of the day off, visit your family, and let me handle this. If you need to take Monday off, that'll be fine. I'll have Carl or Robin sit in on the trial. They'll love the opportunity to be in court again."

John's sincerity was too convincing.

"You're right. You're right."

Marissa stood up with added enthusiasm and wiped a budding tear from her eye as she gathered her things.

"Great!!" John walked closer to her door. "I'm going to prep for Selinda's cross-examination. Don't let me see you around the office. If you're still here, I'm calling security."

Marissa laughed after a relieving, deep sigh. John's smile as he exited gave her the comfort she needed.

———

Driving the short distance from her luxurious, uptown condominium to her mother's house near downtown Phoenix, Marissa parked in front of the older, brick home she was familiar with. It was the same home she grew up in and the one she lived in while in college, even in law school. Her parents hadn't moved in over forty years. She smiled at the thought but then became sober.

*Here's nothing*, she reassured herself.

Strolling from her car, she walked to the front door and entered the unlocked home.

"*Mamá*, I'm home," she blared as the iron security door slammed behind her.

The smell of roasted ancho chiles and vegetables filled her nostrils. She immediately knew her father was making homemade enchilada sauce. It was her aunt Carmen's favorite dish.

"Coming, *mija*," her mother said as she rushed to her side, hugged her tight, and kissed her on the cheek. "It's good to see you. I'm so happy you could make it. That Daniel Mendoza is a slave driver," she added.

Her aunt and uncle also rose from the kitchen table to greet Marissa. They both in turn hugged her and kissed her.

"Where's Gabriela?" Marissa shyly asked as she frantically looked around for the little girl.

"She's asleep. We need to be quiet before she wakes up," her mother admonished.

"Don't worry, *mija*. If she wakes, that's fine. She'll want to see you," Carmen said as the group walked closer to the kitchen. "You look so beautiful."

"Thank you."

Marissa wasn't feeling beautiful, but she didn't want to spoil the mood. After all, this was the time to enjoy her family and to enjoy Gabriela and not the time to dwell on her insecurities.

Marissa's father was removing the charred onions, tomatoes, garlic, and ancho chiles from the stove. He tore the stems off the chilies. Using his fingers, he split the chiles down the side to remove the seeds and the veins. He placed all of the vegetables and chiles into a pan, added some water, and let them simmer.

"*Mija*, I didn't know you were coming," her father exclaimed when he realized what all the ruckus was about.

He turned towards her so she could hug him.

"*Papi, te extraño mucho*!!" she exclaimed as if she

hadn't seen him in forever even though it had only been a week or two, perhaps a little longer.

Tears began to well up. She was always a daddy's girl. Seeing him brought back all of those feelings of love and security.

———

John sat in his office reviewing the deposition transcript of Selinda Hernandez and taking notes for questions he intended on asking her during the cross-examination. He remembered when Daniel took her deposition. Nearly nine months had passed since then. He was surprised at how quickly the time passed.

Remembering he had recently asked Marissa out on a date which she politely declined, John was pleased Daniel bowed out of the trial to attend the celebrations in Puerto Rico. It gave John the opportunity to spend more time with Marissa albeit in an official capacity rather than the personal, intimate time he preferred. He wasn't sure if the time together would only reinforce her platonic view of him. John hoped it wouldn't. Instead, John wanted the time together working on the trial to stir some romantic feelings in Marissa toward him like it did for him. He worked hard to conceal them from her but was concerned that his response to her, like his eagerness to take the lead on cross-examination and encouraging her to spend time with family, revealed he still liked her and hoped for more.

Whatever the future held, John knew he had no control over it. He tried again to focus on the trial preparation and to rid himself of his petty dreams.

Taking a yellow highlighter, John highlighted an answer in the transcript where Mrs. Hernandez admitted she hadn't seen her husband after the accident because he was taken away by ambulance and later cremated. She even testified she wasn't given the opportunity to identify her husband's remains before the cremation. John found this odd.

He continued skimming the deposition transcript when a notification popped up on his computer screen. It was a message from a dating app indicating he had matched with several women on the site.

*I didn't set up a dating profile*, he thought.

John opened the email to check if it was authentic. It was.

## 19 OFFICE

### Phoenix, Arizona
### The Same Day

When the door opened to the Mendoza law firm, Pamela Williams entered as if she was the owner of the company - confident, sublime, and eager to start her day even if she wasn't there for an assignment. It was unusual for her to actually come to the firm. Her assignments were usually emailed to her or conveyed over the phone. Once in a while, she met with an attorney. It was usually Daniel and often-times outside the firm for privacy reasons. Today, however, Pamela came to see Daniel before she headed back to the hospital to spend more time with her father.

The receptionist looked up, startled at the way the door suddenly opened and quickly slammed closed. She hadn't expected anyone to arrive. It was supposed to be a slow day. According to her Outlook calendar, no appointments were scheduled with any of the attorneys or paralegals.

"Hey, Cheryl," Pamela said as she leaned towards

the pass-through window mistakenly thinking Cheryl could hear her better if she did.

Taken aback by the closeness, Cheryl politely asked, "Is there anything you need, Pamela?"

Pamela wasn't her normal reserved demeanor when meeting with a client. Instead, she seemed overly excited. Some would describe it as hyperactive. Cheryl wasn't accustomed to this behavior and didn't want to deal with any quirky activity, especially today. She had plans with her boyfriend and was eager for the work day to end so she could drive to Sedona for a lovely weekend filled with snowy mountains and refreshing air. All she wanted was peace and quiet. Cheryl subtly breathed deeply to ascertain if the smell of alcohol exuded from Pamela. When none did, she was relieved.

With a radiant smile, unbecoming of the moment, Pamela replied, "I'm just here to speak with Daniel."

Cheryl's eyebrows furled and her upper lip raised as the corners of her mouth downturned. She was obviously confused by Pamela's inquiry.

"He's still in Puerto Rico...at the celebrations," she responded, hoping the unwelcome guest would immediately leave and the weird encounter would be over.

As Cheryl ignored Pamela and pretended to work on some indistinct project, she heard footsteps.

"Cheryl, can I get a certified copy...," John said as he approached the reception area. Seeing Pamela in the corner of his eye, John abruptly turned towards her. "...Hi, Pam. How are you doing? I thought you were in Puerto Rico with Daniel."

Cheryl's ears perked up at the revelation. It was a piece of gossip she wasn't aware of. She continued fake working as the two talked, ensuring her eyes were diverted to avoid revealing her true intent.

"Oh, I was. I had to come back for some personal business," Pamela remarked. Her voice unconsciously broke as her words tapered off.

"It must be lovely this time of year," John said, hoping to distract her and draw out some salacious details he knew Cheryl would later discuss with other members of the firm.

John motioned to Cheryl to let Pamela inside the office away from the reception area. Cheryl reluctantly complied. Pamela was appreciative of his gesture and walked through the inner door but not before smiling at Cheryl. Cheryl reciprocated with a forced smile.

Gesturing with his right arm to direct Pamela to the nearest conference room, John added, "I wish I was in Puerto Rico. Maybe next time. I hear there will be a celebration at their Maui hotel next year. I'm going to convince Daniel to let me go to that one."

"I didn't know about Maui," Pamela revealed. *"Daniel must be holding out on me,"* she thought.

"Oh, yes. I hear it was Regal Wisteria's first hotel outside of Japan. Their clientele love the Hawaiian islands and visit often since it's so close compared to the States or Europe, I suppose."

"I can imagine," Pamela replied, trying not to reveal any personal knowledge she had about Regal Wisteria or Gerald Ravan.

Just then Carl and Robin approached the conference room eager to speak with Pamela.

"You got back from Puerto Rico. How exciting!! You must have had a great time," Robin enthusiastically inquired.

Robin sat down to soak in everything Pamela would say about the trip. In contrast, Carl quietly sat down next to John. His mind was still on other things but definitely not work. Robin dragged him along to get him out of his office and the sullen mood he had all day.

"Yes, it was beautiful. The food was scrumptious. They roasted an entire pig for the guests and had all types of local foods. I can't remember how to pronounce the names but there were a lot of fried items and fresh *ceviche* with octopus. Now that was delicious." The attorneys could almost see Pamela salivating while describing the delicacies she ate. "The music was awesome."

She shimmied instinctively when her mind recalled the celebratory atmosphere.

Pamela told the attorneys about the *bomba* dancers they watched under the moonlight and how one night they did a little salsa dancing.

"Daniel doesn't have any rhythm. I'm surprised he tried salsa dancing," Cheryl said when she drew near to the conference room. Her inquisitiveness got the best of her.

"No, he doesn't," Pamela giggled in response as she looked in Cheryl's direction. "He did the best he could and didn't mind when I was dancing with other people."

"Well, you guys aren't dating so why would he mind," Cheryl insisted, somewhat overly protective of her boss.

"Of course, not. I was just saying how much of a gentleman he is. That's all. I didn't mean anything by it."

Cheryl huffed at the meager explanation but relented. She walked back to her desk with disgust that she let her curiosity get the best of her.

"Did you do anything else?" Robin prodded once Cheryl was out of earshot.

"We were supposed to go horseback riding on the nearby beach. The hotel even chartered a boat so guests could go deep-sea fishing later in the week. I know I wanted to do that," Pamela beamed.

Even Carl was impressed at her comment. He tried harder not to reveal his mood or what he was thinking.

"I hear the deep-sea fishing is great there - marlin, mahi mahi, billfish, tuna," John interrupted. "I know I'd do that too."

"No one cares whether you like fishing," Robin declared. "It's about Daniel and Pamela. Not you. Let her finish."

John was surprised at Robin's attitude. She had never spoken to him in this manner before especially not in front of anyone. He was the senior associate in the firm and had more seniority than Robin. *She should respect that*, he thought while mentally noting he needed to speak with her once the visitor was gone. For the moment, he let it go.

Sensing the tension, Pamela said, "Enough about me already. Daniel told me you're in trial with Marissa. How's the trial going?"

John was pleased with the question and eager to discuss the trial.

"It's a great experience. Whether we're convincing the jury to see the accident the way we want them to is a different story. I'm not sure we're there yet. I think we're convincing some jurors but it may not be enough."

"You'll get there. I'm certain of it. I'm just sorry I wasn't able to help out on this case," Pamela expressed.

"I appreciate it. This is a straightforward case. Maybe we can use your help on the next one."

Before Pamela could respond, the group in the conference room could hear a voice coming from the reception area. John was disappointed at the distraction.

"My name is Corina Walker. I'm here to see Daniel Mendoza."

Cheryl looked up and wondered why.

## 20 CORINA

### Phoenix, Arizona
### The Same Day

When Corina woke up earlier that day, she was pleasantly surprised she slept in longer than expected for a Friday morning. Luckily for her, it was her day off. Her work schedule required her to work nine-hour shifts every day of the week. The perk for working long hours was a day off every other week. For obvious reasons, she selected Fridays as her day off. Having this schedule meant Corina could enjoy three-day weekends twice a month which allowed her to take mini-vacations to San Diego, Hawaii, Cabo, or Cancun because the flights there were quick and inexpensive. Traveling to further destinations like the east coast, the Caribbean, or other foreign countries required Corina to use her vacation time. Working at her job for decades also came with perks. With five weeks of vacation a year, she frequently traveled abroad often and enjoyed new adventures in distant lands.

Oftentimes, it meant traveling without her family

and friends who didn't have the luxury of numerous vacation days nor the commitment to spend their hard-earned money on luxurious things like travel. Corina was accustomed to the excuses and, for the most part, enjoyed traveling alone to accomplish her personal goal of visiting all fifty states and all seven continents. But she wanted more.

When she first met Daniel, they both shared their love of travel. Corina believed she had found a travel partner as well as a potential lover. Daniel, however, traveled as part of his job and less frequently on vacation. As the named partner of a boutique defense firm, it was difficult for Daniel to make himself available for personal vacations. Vacationing five times a year for a week or more each time was certainly out of the question. Work was a jealous mistress who summoned Daniel even when he went on vacation.

During the first trip when Daniel wasn't able to accompany Corina, she wanted to involve him in her experience by FaceTiming him, sending him pictures of her adventures, and enticing him with plans for their own secret rendezvous. Despite this, Corina felt Daniel was distracted whenever they talked or texted. A part of her wondered if he was envious of her ability to take time off from work and enjoy life while Daniel was too preoccupied by it.

When Daniel occasionally mentioned he should retire from the practice of law, Corina, eight years his junior, encouraged him. She too wanted to retire early at age fifty-five when she was fully vested in her company's retirement plan and could fund her travels without working. She imagined the two of them traveling the world together. She dreamt of seeing Victoria Falls, the Egyptian pyramids, and even the natural hot springs of Turkey. The plans to far-off lands were still five years away. In the meantime, she had plans to see the Florida Everglades, Mardi Gras in New Orleans, and the Freedom Trail in Boston, among others.

In the previous year, she attended the firm's Christmas party with Daniel. She had a great time and enjoyed his company. Daniel was excited when Corina mentioned she booked a trip to New York City for New Years and invited him to attend. He'd planned on accompanying her and even booked a flight, but an unexpected lawsuit was transferred to his firm last minute. He withdrew from the trip to tend to business.

Corina was disappointed. She planned a carriage ride in Central Park, a trip to the Statue of Liberty, and also wanted to take the Staten Island ferry for the spectacular views of the New York harbor. She felt unexpectedly lonely without Daniel when she accomplished those adventures on her own even though traveling alone was nothing new for her. Upon her return to Arizona, Corina decided it was in her best interest to move on and let the repeated disappointments escape from her heart.

She slowly started pulling away from him. She ended the evening dinners together on her Fridays off from work. She stopped returning his calls or his text messages wishing her a good night. When he sent her a link to a romantic song he wanted her to listen to, she simply ignored it.

For whatever reason Daniel didn't take the hint and back off. Perhaps he was enamored by her. She really didn't know or fully understand his persistence. Sometimes, she responded to his texts asking about her day or when he let her know he was thinking of her. She wondered if that encouraged him.

*It was simply banter. Nothing serious,* she reasoned.

When he asked her to accompany him to the celebrations at the Regal Isabela in Puerto Rico, she was shocked. Although they texted each other, they hadn't been on a date in nearly a year. She didn't want to deflate his ego but was flattered he still wanted to pursue her even if they weren't the perfect pair. She politely declined and struggled with telling him why. The look in his eyes revealed disappointment. It also touched her heart.

After Corina got dressed that morning, she ran a few errands and contemplated the other things she needed to do that weekend. Believing Daniel already returned from Puerto Rico, she decided to bring him some lunch. The night before she made her signature dish of chicken enchiladas with kale. The green leafy addition to the dish gave it a unique flavor and texture. Daniel incessantly teased her about the special ingredient whenever she discussed making the dish. Despite the mocking, she reassured him kale added the necessary vegetables to her meals and encouraged her to have a balanced and healthy diet.

Daniel often suggested Corina invite him over for dinner to try the dish. She never did. But on that day, she decided to bring him a plate as a gesture that she appreciated his invitation to the Caribbean and as a heartfelt apology for not attending.

As she approached the glass enclosure surrounding the receptionist's desk at the Mendoza law firm, she carried a plate of enchiladas in an insulated food carrier.

She announced, "My name is Corina Walker. I'm here to see Daniel Mendoza."

Cheryl looked up and replied, "I'm sorry. He's not here right now. He's in Puerto Rico."

"Oh my. I thought he was coming back."

"No, no. The celebrations are a few more days," Cheryl explained.

"But he texted me yesterday he was taking a flight back. Did his plans change?"

Corina was embarrassed but wanted to get to the bottom of it. Standing her up again would be the final straw. Not that they were a couple or had made an informal commitment to each other. But she expected Daniel to keep his word he would see her or at the very least let her know that things had changed.

"To be honest, I'm not sure why he would have texted you that. I can speak with his legal assistant to confirm whether his plans changed," Cheryl offered.

"Please do,"

"I'll be right back."

Ignoring the discussions in the conference room with Pamela and the other attorneys, Cheryl headed to Lydia's cubicle down the hallway closer to Daniel's office. She could see his office was dark and un-occupied.

"Hey, Lydia. I have someone here for Daniel. She says Daniel texted her saying he would be back today. Do you know anything about that?"

Lydia was puzzled by the request but checked her emails and her calendar for any indication Daniel let her know he was coming back early.

"I don't see anything saying he was headed back early. He normally asks me to change his flight reservations. I never did. Are you sure she understood correctly?"

Remembering the look on Corina's face, Cheryl replied, "The young lady sincerely believes Daniel was supposed to be in Arizona today."

"It's unlike Daniel to change his plans and not let me know."

Lydia contemplated calling the hotel in Puerto Rico to confirm whether Daniel was still a guest. But she didn't want to disturb Daniel during his vacation. It was his first vacation in a long time and one he really needed.

"I think you should let her know she's mistaken," Lydia suggested.

"Okay. I will."

Cheryl headed back to the reception area when Pamela exited the conference room as she said goodbye to the other attorneys. Quickly walking passed her, Cheryl sat down at the reception desk and said, "Ms. Walker, Daniel is still in Puerto Rico. He wasn't supposed to come back early."

Before Corina reacted to the news, Pamela overhead the conversation on her way out of the office and interrupted.

"I'm sorry, Cheryl. But Daniel told me he was coming back early because of some personal issues I had to deal with."

"Oh, really," Cheryl said in disbelief.

Even Corina was surprised at the revelation.

"Now, I'm really confused," Corina added. "If he's supposed to be back, where is he? Does anyone know?"

## 21 DINNER

### Phoenix, Arizona
### The Same Night

The waiter approached the table just as Carl struggled to push the chair closer to Samantha so she could sit down. Both back wooden legs scratched the marble floor as he pushed making a loud screeching sound resulting in several of the other dinner guests quickly turning their heads, wondering what was going on. Carl was embarrassed. Samantha not so much. She was just happy to be at a fancy restaurant in Scottsdale overlooking the valley.

The waiter originally intended on assisting Carl with his overt, chivalrous act but instead decided it was proper to let the guest take care of his dinner date. He also did not want to upstage the floundering guest or sully the mood.

"Thank you, babe."

Samantha's voice was sweet with a hint of glowing love and affection, unlike how she spoke with Carl nearly a year ago after moving back from Florida and leaving a failed budding relationship behind.

Then, she was stern and demanding towards Carl, wanting to see their daughter, Senovia, and wanting to be a part of her life, for the good and bad. At the time, she had no idea her and Carl would break down the walls and begin to learn to trust each other again despite their recent divorce and his sordid affairs which ruined their marriage.

Without their daughter's love, they couldn't have overcome their various obstacles. Senovia was giddy and innocent. She saw the world with new and refreshing eyes the way young kids do, which helped them to see it that way as well. Senovia was also forgiving and understanding when her father explained to her how mommy was away for work for so long when really it was for adult reasons she was too young to understand. Seeing her mother once more, only brought the joy Senovia needed in her life that her father and her grandmother could not bring without her mother present. There was something special about a mother's bond with her daughter which Senovia longed for and needed.

At first, Samantha would take Senovia so they could spend time alone together. There were the play times at the trampoline park, Disney movies during an early morning matinee, eating chicken tenders at a fast-food restaurant Senovia loved, or greedily chowing down chocolate ice cream for fun, especially during the hot Arizona summer days. But as the newness of being with her mom again wore off, Senovia began asking why her mom wasn't there for dinner or why she didn't sleep overnight. Her mother stayed somewhere else instead of the family home. Senovia yearned for her mother to tuck her in at night, read her a bedtime story, help her with her homework, and just be there for her like mothers are.

Carl agreed to let Samantha move in, especially after Carl's mother explained that forgiveness breeds contentment and that both former husband and wife needed to forgive each other to move on and to allow Senovia to grow. It wasn't until one Saturday morning when Senovia was walking hand in hand with her father and then grabbed her mother's hand did the three of them unite together again. Senovia was in the middle with her little hands squeezing her parents' hands on each side of her. She was content they were all together again.

At that moment, Carl knew he had lost all animosity and so did Samantha. There was a budding love, a weird romance of sorts from of old like when the two first met. How did it return? He could not explain it. Neither could Samantha. He wondered whether it was the true reason why Samantha returned to Arizona. She could have fought for full custody of Senovia and lived with her daughter in her surrogate state of Florida. But she chose not to. She chose to come back. In some ways, it meant more to Carl than he first realized.

To accommodate the new arrangement, his mother started babysitting Senovia like she did that night so the two of them could have time together alone and rekindle what was lost. They were simple dates at first focused on discussing Senovia rather than truly getting to know each other again. Eventually came the discussions of each other siblings and parents, work, and friends. And then there were gatherings at a local pizza joint downtown near the Heritage Square where they could eat and then walk

DANIEL MALDONADO

around the vintage location and reminisce about past times together.

The future was never discussed. Only just the moment. Tonight, however, was different. Carl purposed to breach the subject of his future with Samantha. Now that he was comfortable working at the Mendoza law firm and filled a niche that gave him a sense of security, he could focus more on what he really wanted in life besides raising his daughter.

The dream he let go of so long after graduating from law school returned. The dream of a family. Of one true love. Of sacrifice beyond sacrifice. Of happiness beyond measure. Was it really something he could obtain after having failed at it so miserably? He knew Samantha had no right to forgive him for his overwhelming pride and infidelity. She shouldn't even under Carl's own reasoning. Why did she? He could not fully understand.

All he knew, as he sat there in a French restaurant at the Regal Phoenix Resort and Spa with the sparkling lights of the valley echoing into the main dining area and stars twinkling in the distance was that he wanted her in his life again and hoped she loved him too.

"*Monsieur. Mademoiselle.* It's a wonderful evening. Isn't it?" the waiter finally asked once Carl and Samantha were situated.

They both agreed.

"Is tonight a special occasion?" the waiter inquired like he did with every couple who patronized the restaurant.

The question made Carl nervous.

"No. Not really. We're just enjoying the lovely view and the atmosphere."

Carl knew his response didn't make any sense, especially after the weird look Samantha gave him from across the table.

"The view is stunning," Samantha agreed as her eyes greedily consumed it.

She was impressed with Carl's choice of restaurant and encouraged that he was willing to spend the time to plan a romantic evening together despite his busy work schedule.

"This is definitely the place for you," the waiter added. "We have it all here. I can bring you some drinks. If you are ready, I can also order some appetizers for you. Take your time. We are in no hurry."

The waiter was about to walk away when Samantha said, "I'd like a fruity drink. Do you have any recommendations?"

"Sure. I recommend a Kir Royale. You'd love it."

"I've never heard of it. What is it?'

"It's a very popular cocktail the French started drinking after the last great war. It's named after a priest, a hero of the French resistance. It's made with a blackcurrant liqueur and Champagne. Very delicious."

"Sounds interesting. Almost like a French mimosa," Samantha replied with a beaming smile.

"Not quite," the waiter said not wanting to display any offense at the comparison.

"Well, I'd like to try it. And you, Carl?"

After quickly assessing the situation, Carl said, "I'll take one too."

"Good," the waiter responded. "I'll be back with your drinks."

Finally alone again, Carl hesitated before breaching the subject he wanted to speak with

Samantha about and why he had taken her to one of the most romantic restaurants in Phoenix. Having a professional connection with the hotel owners didn't hurt. Carl knew the restaurant would go above and beyond as a result and make his date feel special. So far, it was working.

"Samantha," Carl whispered as he awkwardly and lovingly stared deep into her eyes once she turned her head towards him.

"What? Why are you acting this way?" she asked after recognizing his childlike demeanor. Her facial expression suddenly changed from giddiness to worry. She didn't understand why. "Is something wrong at work?"

"No. No. It's nothing like that. I'm happy at work. I'm happy at home too," he slyly admitted.

His flattering comment brought her smile back.

"I'm happy as well. I can't believe the time has passed so quickly. Who'd have thought I would be living in the same house as my ex...you." She corrected herself.

"Yeah, I know. I..."

The night his mother moved out of Carl's home flashed before his eyes causing him to stutter and lose focus on what he was going to tell Samantha. He'd always imagined his mother moving out would be a difficult night filled with drama. He thought his mother would be embittered especially because Samantha was back in her son's life and the reason for her displacement from his home. To his surprise, it wasn't like that. His mother was civil and cordial and even eager to move out. Perhaps, she felt she'd accomplished her goal.

With a renewed spirit, Carl reached across the

table to hold Samantha's hand. He wanted to announce how she meant the world to him, how he deeply loved her and needed her in his life, how he wanted to be a family again, and how this time he would treat her like the queen she was and not take her love for granted like he did before. For a brief moment, he struggled with his own shame for having hurt her so and almost let go of her hand out of despair. She could see it reflecting in his eyes, but he buried it deep inside him again and mustered the strength and fortitude to convey his feelings for her.

"Samantha, I know I'm not the perfect man, far from it. But having you in my life makes me strive to be a good man, a man who can love you the way you deserve. It would do me a great honor if you would marry me again."

He pulled out a three-carat, Harry Winston emerald-cut engagement ring and was about to get on bended knee when Samantha stopped him.

———

The older male captor held Daniel's iPhone in his hand and scanned for various text messages to gather information about his unsuspecting captive. He read about the trial in Phoenix and the many group texts exchanged between Daniel and the other members of the firm. He also saw the text message to Corina letting her know he was on his way back to Phoenix.

Realizing his captive was an attorney and worried the firm and possibly authorities would be looking for Daniel if they considered him missing, the older male sent a group text: "I'm still in Puerto Rico having fun. Don't worry about me."

Sweat beaded down his forehead.

Carl's iPhone vibrated upon receipt of the text message as he was about to get down on one knee to propose to Samantha. The other firm member's phones also received the group text.

## 22 COPAS

### San Juan, Puerto Rico
### The Same Night

Johnny walked into the office of his fellow *copa*, Luis. On either side of Johnny were two tall, bulky men who were apparently his bodyguards. They both had sidearms at the ready even though this was a meeting with a fellow family member. Johnny was just being cautious. Given the latest developments, Johnny wasn't sure if a rival mafia or even a disgruntled member of the family would turn on them. For all he knew, Luis may be a turncoat out of fear of their boss, *Chango*.

He knew Luis wouldn't betray him out of a sense of loyalty to *Chango*. Too often, Luis complained about how they did all the work and *Chango* took all the credit. Both *copas* organized business deals with other countries and presented them to *Chango*. They ensured the relationship with any new partners was on the up and up. They vented every possible contingency which could get *La Familia* in trouble with the authorities, not just the local ones, but also the feds or

143

international authorities. Both Luis and Johnny traveled abroad and risked their lives with dangerous criminals to make these new ventures happen while *Chango* stayed comfortably in the lap of luxury in his mansion in San Juan.

They reasoned that taking all the risk meant they should have gotten a bigger slice of the pie, but they didn't. Their cut of the profits of the international ventures was no higher than any other enterprise the mafia was into even if they had little to no involvement in that enterprise. It didn't make sense not to reward them for their hard work and the expansion of the family business abroad. The repeated slights left a bitter taste in their mouths.

As *copas*, Luis and Johnny executed *Chango's* orders without question. If *Chango* gave a kill order, the *copas* had one of their men carry it out and guaranteed the individual would be executed with undeniable proof and no way to trace the murder back to the family. Although *Chango* was the boss, Luis and Johnny ran the day-to-day activities of the family and commanded the soldiers as well as the *castas*, the made men of the family. The *copas* were extremely loyal to *Chango*. But they had doubts he was just as loyal to them.

Having known *Chango* since they were little children, Johnny and Luis expected to be bosses one day. Once *Chango's* wife got pregnant and had their son, doubts crept in. *Chango* was secretly grooming his son to take over. The other members of the family explained to the *copas* it was normal for *Chango* to want to pass the family business to his son. It's what all *El Grans* did. Johnny and Luis, however, felt they started the family with *Chango* and only coronated him as the *El Gran* out of respect not because he had any claim to the title.

After the other family members realized *Chango's* son was reckless and uncontrollable, it only furthered the *copas'* argument he wasn't qualified to lead the family and they should. In fact, it was Johnny's idea to send *Chango's* son to Arizona to escape the family's wrath after he stole the mafia money, including his own. Johnny also suggested *Chango's* son could take advantage of Johnny's business connections in Arizona, which included his forte, prostitution, and running guns and drugs to add another source of revenue for the family. *Chango* was appreciative of Johnny's proposal. It allowed his son to stay safe and save face.

*Chango's* son was expected to use the increased profits to pay back the debt owed to the family members. When the business wasn't profitable and more money was missing and only a paltry sum of the debt was repaid, the *copas* feared the worse. *Chango's* son had merely taken his shenanigans to the States and hadn't truly reformed like he'd promised. *Chango*, however, wouldn't listen to them when they suggested his son betrayed the family a second time. He insisted they were trying to defame his son and wouldn't give him the opportunity to redeem himself. When *Chango's* son was conveniently missing, it outraged the *copas* even more. They suspected foul play and some machination secretly orchestrated by *Chango*.

When Gerald Ravan reported *Chango's* son was staying at his hotel, the Regal Isabela, their suspicions were confirmed. Johnny arranged for his capture with two of his more obscure soldiers who *Chango* wasn't aware of. The two soldiers had no loyalty to *Chango*. Their sole loyalty was to Johnny. He wanted it that way. But he now needed to loop Luis into the whole affair if it stood any chance of obtaining his long-term goal.

"Welcome. Sit down," Luis said as he gestured to the seat across his desk. "Can I get you a drink?"

Johnny obliged and sat down. His stare was ominous, but he didn't want to make Luis feel uncomfortable. He only wanted to suss him out.

"A cold Medalla will hit the spot," Johnny answered as he watched one of Luis' men exit the room to obtain his preferred local beer.

"So what is it that my brother needs so late in the evening?"

Although not biological brothers, the two *copas* were more than just brothers in arms. They had grown up like brothers living next to each other and sacrificed so much together in the name of the family. In some ways, they were more than brothers. Once after a near-fatal encounter, Johnny had to give Luis his blood to save his life. That truth was never brought up between the men. It was an unspoken reality that Luis literally owed his life to Johnny. Johnny never asked for a favor until now.

"I have a proposition for you."

"A proposition? Which one? I hope it's not that *loco* idea you keep mentioning with the Venezuelans. It's never going to happen. They're too...out there."

"No, it's not that. It's more serious."

"I'm all ears," Luis remarked as he stood up eager to hear it.

"I wanted you to be the first to know I have *Chango's* son."

Luis's jaw dropped.

"You're serious. I thought he was dead."

146

"We were led to believe that but he's not. I have him and I'm willing to work with you so we can make a deal with *Chango*."

"What kind of deal?"

"I think it's time *Chango* steps aside and let us run the family. Don't you? After this debacle, can anyone in the family trust him?" Johnny saw the receptiveness in Luis's eyes. With a calmer voice, he continued, "I can take the east side of his territory and you, the west side."

Luis understood Johnny's proposal meant Luis would get the more lucrative territory. He wasn't sure if the split was a sign of Johnny's weak hand or if it was a means to lure him into a risky endeavor. *Chango* would not willingly leave his position despite his failing health and even if the other members of the family were disappointed in his recent behavior towards his son.

"That's a generous offer. But why?"

"Well, my expertise has always been prostitution. It's what I love. It's what I'm good at. Entertainment. Guns and drugs are not what I want to focus on. You've always been the brains in that area. So there's no need for me to be greedy."

Luis nodded. The proposal made sense after all.

"So what do you want me to do?"

"I need you to work your magic, Luis. You're closer to *Chango's* family than I am. He'll listen to you and won't become a hothead with you like he will with me if I broach the proposal. You know what I mean. He's been like that with me since we were in preschool. You've seen it yourself many times."

"He's gonna want to know where his son is."

"I'm not willing to give away my only ace at this

time. I'll tell you, the both of you, once we have a formal agreement in place."

"He's not gonna like that but I'll try to work with it for now. *Chango* will want some assurances his son is alive and treated well if you know what I mean."

"He's alive alright but with a few missing parts, nothing significant."

Luis gritted his teeth and refrained from making a disapproving comment. Instead, he stood up and reached out to shake Johnny's hand.

"I'll do the best I can under the circumstances. Within the hour, you'll hear from me in our usual way."

Johnny was pleased with himself and walked out of Luis's office with his bodyguards. Once Johnny was in the hallway walking towards the front door and out of earshot, a shadowy figure revealed itself.

"Mrs. Quintana, I had no idea this was what the meeting was going to be about. I promise you and *Chango* on the grave of my mother, God bless her soul, that I was not involved in any of this."

She stood silent for a moment in deep contemplation before responding. After a deep sigh, she said, "I know you weren't. But this may be a good thing."

## 23 WIDOW

Phoenix, Arizona
Two Days Later

"Mrs. Hernandez...Selinda, can you tell the jury what happened when you arrived at the crash scene," Danica Bridgers asked and then turned her body towards the jury so she could watch their reaction.

"Like I said, I got there as fast as I could. I don't remember who told me he was in an accident, but I knew it couldn't have been my husband. Carlos...his body was lifeless. When I first saw him, I thought he was dead. Blood was everywhere. Streaming out of his head. His head was squashed like someone hit him with a hammer or something. I tried to get closer to hold him, to tell him that I loved him, but they...the paramedics wouldn't let me. They asked me to stay back because they were trying to save him...I couldn't. He was...is my husband. I ran to him, but the police officer restrained me. I tried to get loose. I was flaying my arms and pushing my body away, but the officer was too strong. I know now there was nothing I could have done for him, not in those last moments."

Selinda's eyes teared up.

Danica walked from the lectern at the well of the courtroom back to the plaintiffs' counsel's table to grab a box of tissues to give to Selinda. All eyes were on Danica as she displayed a level of compassion for her client.

"Your honor, may I approach the witness," Danica asked.

"Yes, you may," Judge Furman instructed.

"Here," Danica said once she reached the witness stand.

"Thank you," Selinda replied as she grabbed the tissue box and wiped the tears from her eyes, cheek, and even the stray tears that managed to reach her neck.

"Do you need to take a break?" Judge Furman asked. "I know it's early in the day, but we can accommodate it if you'd like."

The judge's voice was calming, not like the stern, assertive voice she used when talking to counsel or other witnesses.

"I just need a second to compose myself, your honor. I'll be fine."

"Take your time," the judge added.

"Thank you."

Pulling another tissue from the box, Mrs. Hernandez wiped her tears again and this time blew her nose. She took a deep breath and looked up at her attorney who was back at the lectern.

"I'm ready," she announced as her voice broke once more.

"Thank you, Selinda," Danica said. "When did you learn your husband passed away?"

"I was on my way to the hospital. I let my older son drive because it was just too much for me at the time. I didn't know what happened or why. When I got to the hospital, the emergency room nurse told me he passed away."

She sobbed again and grabbed another tissue.

Not wanting to overwhelm her client with the details, Danica questioned her about a different topic.

"Can you tell the jury about how your life and the life of your children have changed since Carlos passed away?"

"Carlos was my world. We were childhood sweethearts. We met when we were really young. Three or four years old. I can't remember exactly. Some family members claimed our parents betrothed each other when we were infants. It was an interesting love story, but I don't know if it was true or not. I just know I loved him with all my heart, and he loved me tenderly like no one else could."

"What sorts of things did you do together?" Danica asked.

"Everything. We would go to sports games together. He loved baseball games. We had season tickets to the Diamondbacks, and we would take the kids, clients, or family when they were in town. We would hike Camelback mountain. He loved it. It invigorated him like he was on top of the world. We literally were. Our marriage improved once we moved to Phoenix and started our business."

Knowing the judge didn't like such open-ended questions allowing a witness to speak forever, Danica politely interrupted her client at this point because it was an appropriate segue.

"Selinda, can you tell the jury about your company?"

"Yes, yes," she brightened up at the question. "We weren't just lovers. We were also business partners. I was the company's accountant, but Carlos was the brains of the business. He ran everything and the profits soared. He was good at bringing in customers, wining and dining them, and convincing them to buy our products."

"What kind of business is C and S?"

"It was an import business. We imported things from all over the world. Whatever our clients needed or wanted. Carlos knew how to make it happen and it did."

She was bubbling with pride at the thought of her husband.

"Why do you say, 'was' in referring to the company?"

"Well, it's not doing well anymore. I'm a good accountant but I'm not the rainmaker Carlos is. We lost a lot of clients after he passed away. Some gave us a chance for a while but even they abandoned us. I was just so depressed and now alone with the kids, I couldn't keep up. I had difficulty going into the office because it just reminded me of Carlos."

"Did you hire someone to replace Carlos?"

"I did. We tried several people in his position, but no one had Carlo's expertise or his ability to schmooze clients. He got that from his father."

It was the first time Selinda smiled on the stand since she was first introduced to the jury as a witness earlier that morning.

"And how has the loss of their father affected your children?"

"They're devastated. Both of them are in counseling," she admitted.

"Why is that?"

"They miss their father so much. They loved him more than life itself. He was so involved in raising the kids, not like some fathers. He would help them with their homework, go to all of their activities, school plays, recitals, and stuff like that. He attended every PTA meeting. Now that's all gone. I did those things with the kids too before he passed but now that there is only one parent and the business is struggling, I don't have time to do all the things I used to. And I'm not a man. I can't replace the father figure in their lives no matter how much I try."

"Thank you, Selinda. Your honor, I have no further questions."

"Mr. Davis, your witness," the judge declared.

John looked at Marissa before picking up his binder and heading toward the lectern to ask questions. Marissa seemed to be rejuvenated after spending the weekend with her family. He was happy to take the lead in deposing Mrs. Hernandez because it gave him the chance to shine and to also show Marissa he was a man of his word.

"Mrs. Hernandez, my condolences for the death of your husband," John said.

"Thank you, sir."

"I'm going to bring up plaintiff's Exhibit 52. Do you see that on your monitor?" John asked after clicking a button on his remote mouse to bring up the requested exhibit.

"Yes, I do."

"Thank you."

As with all exhibits shown to a witness that were already admitted into evidence by the judge, John could publish the exhibit to the jury. The exhibit was displayed on the monitors in front of the judge and counsel as well as the large monitors facing the jury and the gallery.

"Mrs. Hernandez, can you tell me what is plaintiff's Exhibit 52?"

"It looks like the police report."

"Have you seen the police report before?" John asked.

"I'm sure I have a long time ago. I just don't remember to be honest."

"Well, Officer Hickman testified already in this case. Do you remember Officer Hickman? He testified he was the officer who prepared the police report. You were in attendance when he testified, correct?"

"Yes, I was," she admitted.

"And you remember Officer Hickman testified when questioned by your attorney, I believe it was Ms. Bridgers, about how the police report is based upon notes the officer takes on the scene and the report is finalized at the police department once he gets back there, correct?"

"Yes, that's what he testified to."

"Do you remember Officer Hickman testifying he's been a police officer for over twenty years, and he takes meticulous notes?"

"Oh yes, I remember he testified to that."

"Did you have any reason to believe Officer Hickman was being dishonest when he testified he takes meticulous notes and his report is reliable?"

"No, I have no reason to doubt that. He was a very polite and professional police officer."

Selinda smiled at the thought of the officer testifying. As her attorneys explained, the officer was a favorable witness who made a great impression on the jury.

"Thank you," John said before asking his next question. "I'm going to show you page eight of plaintiff's Exhibit 52, which is the police report. Do you see how Officer Hickman summarizes the different times in his report where significant things happen?"

"Oh yes, I see that."

"He notes the time he arrived on the scene, doesn't he?"

"Yes, I see that."

"He notes he is the first officer on the scene, doesn't he?"

"Yes. Yes, he was."

"He notes when other officers arrive on the scene, correct?"

"Yes. I didn't realize there were so many officers who came."

"Do you have any reason to believe Officer Hickman's entries as to when he arrived and when other officers arrived were incorrect?"

"No, I don't. He's definitely correct. He's very meticulous," Selinda said as she gave an awkward smile to the jury.

She was confused why she was questioned about the arrival of the various police officers.

"Do you see where he noted the time you arrived on the scene?"

She squinted at the monitor to search for the entry.

155

"It's entry number ten if you don't mind me helping you out with that," John said.

"Thank you. I see it now. Yes, it's entry number ten like you said."

"And what time did Officer Hickman indicate you arrived on the scene?"

"He entered 1:28 p.m."

"Do you have any reason to doubt Officer Hickman was inaccurate in recording when you arrived on the scene?"

"No. No, I don't."

"And that's consistent with your earlier testimony that you were with your son doing something and around 1 p.m. you were informed your husband was in an accident. Do you remember testifying to that effect?"

"Yes, I do. It's true. I received the call around 1 p.m. It must have been after 1 p.m. because what we were doing ended at 1 p.m. and it had already finished by the time I received the call."

"And how long did you say it took you to get to where the accident was on Scottsdale Road near 68th Street?"

"It took about twenty to twenty-five minutes. We weren't too far from the intersection but because of the traffic it took longer than expected," she explained.

"So you would agree with Officer Hickman's report when he indicated you arrived on scene at 1:28 p.m.?"

"Give or take a few minutes. It took me some time to park and then walk to where my husband was."

"I understand. Turning back to page eight of the police report, what time does Officer Hickman report your husband left in the ambulance to the hospital?"

She looked at her monitor again for the answer.

"He wrote 1:10 p.m."

"Isn't that at least eighteen minutes before you arrived on the scene?"

"Yes, it is."

"So your early testimony on how you saw your husband at the accident scene was incorrect. He was gone well before you arrived, correct?"

"I may have been mistaken but I did see the blood spatter from his head injury on the asphalt when I was there. I clearly remember that. It's a memory I'll never forget for the rest of my life."

"You testified earlier that you arrived at the hospital with your son and was informed your husband passed away. Isn't that correct?"

"Yes. I was told that."

"But isn't it true you never saw your husband at the hospital or even at the funeral home because he was cremated before you arrived?"

"Yes, I never saw him."

"And you didn't arrive at the hospital in the ambulance transporting your husband from the accident scene, correct?"

"I didn't."

"It was Dr. Weimar who rode in the ambulance with your husband, correct?"

"I don't know."

"Well, you were in the courtroom when Dr. Weimar testified he did. Do you remember that testimony?"

"Yes, I do."

"Any reason to dispute Dr. Weimar's testimony

that he rode in the ambulance with your husband to the hospital?"

"No, I don't have any reason to doubt he's telling the truth."

"So, Dr. Weimar arrived on the scene before you did even though you were close to that intersection, correct?"

"I supposed so," she admitted.

"When you testified you saw your husband's head at the accident scene looking like it was smashed with a hammer, it wasn't true, correct?"

"I'm confused. I must have seen his autopsy photos and I'm getting the two mixed up."

"Is it your testimony, Mrs. Hernandez, you were able to see the autopsy photos defense counsel were never provided and have never seen? Is that what you are telling the jury?"

"I don't know. I'm so confused. I just know his head was smashed like with a hammer. I must have been told that by someone. The police officer. The paramedics. Dr. Weimar. I just don't remember."

Selinda became more agitated and fidgety on the witness stand.

"Can we take a break, your honor?" Danica asked.

"I think this is a good time to take a break," Judge Furman replied.

"All rise," the bailiff immediately announced.

# 24 OUT OF ORDER

### Phoenix, Arizona
### The Same Day

"Mrs. Hernandez, you are now dismissed," Judge Furman said after her counsel, Danica Bridgers, announced she had no more questions on her redirect of her client.

Walking out of the witness stand, Selinda then sat down at the plaintiffs' counsel's table. She intended on walking straight out of the courtroom because she needed a break after being emotionally drained from testifying. However, she knew her testimony and the cross-examination were something she needed to endure to see this through. It was also for her children who needed closure in their own way. They looked proudly at their mom and gave her a hug when she sat down.

"Counsel, you can call your next witness," the judge announced.

When Marissa stood up, the judge was confused because it was still the plaintiffs' case-in-chief and not the time for the defense counsel to call their witnesses.

"Your honor," Marissa said. "The parties have a procedural issue for the court to address. May we approach the bench?"

The judge nodded and beckoned them with her hands. Both Doug Clarkson and Marissa walked toward the judge. She turned on the white noise generator so the jury and the rest of the courtroom could not hear their discussion.

"Please proceed," the judge commanded after noticing the court reporter was ready to transcribe the bench conference.

"The parties have agreed to call the defendants' traffic engineering expert, Dr. Andrew Kominski, out of order. There is a scheduling conflict Mr. Clarkson is willing to accommodate. Dr. Kominski also has a trial in Florida where he's scheduled to testify on the same day we intended on calling him as a witness in this trial, your honor. We apologize for the oversight but had no idea of the double-booking until last night," Marissa explained.

"Counsel, do you agree?" the judge questioned Doug Clarkson to ascertain if he actually consented on behalf of the Hernandezes.

"Yes, we agree. John and Marissa have always accommodated us, your honor, and we're happy to return the favor," he responded hoping to score points with the judge for his personal satisfaction.

"Because counsel are in agreement, you may proceed," the judge declared.

After letting the jury know Dr. Kominski was testifying out of order and after the bailiff administered the oath to the witness, Marissa proceeded to ask him questions.

"Good afternoon, Dr. Kominski. Can you explain to the jury your educational background?" she asked.

"I've earned a Doctor of Philosophy in civil engineering from Rice University. I am a registered professional civil engineer in Arizona, a certified professional traffic operation engineer, and an accredited traffic accident reconstructionist."

The jury was impressed by his credentials but wondered if he was just another paid expert. Given his experience, some jurors were open-minded and willing to listen to what he was going to say.

"What is traffic engineering?"

Turning to the jury, Dr. Kominski said, "Traffic engineering is a branch of civil engineering. The discipline uses engineering techniques to achieve various goals, for example, the safe and efficient movement of people and goods on roadways. As a traffic engineer, I research the safe and efficient flow of traffic which can include road geometry, sidewalks and crosswalks, and traffic signs and lights. It can also include researching road surface markings."

"Although you are also an accident reconstructionist, what is your role today?"

"I'm only here to testify as a traffic engineer, but I believe my understanding of accident reconstruction helps me to understand all components of a case before rendering an opinion."

"And you were retained by my office as an expert for the Weavers, correct?"

"Yes, I was."

"What was the scope of your retention as a traffic engineer?"

"I was asked to use my education, training, and experience and apply the analytical techniques and principles of transportation engineering and statistics to evaluate the factors that contributed to the subject accident."

"How did you arrive at your opinions?"

"I reviewed materials provided by your office. I did a site inspection. After reviewing my site inspection, I performed an analysis and formed my opinions."

"Did you review any engineering plans for the site?"

"Yes, I did. I obtained them from the city. I also understand that the plaintiffs' expert had a copy of the plans. When I reviewed his file, they were in there as well. So it wasn't something I needed to do but it worked out in the end."

The witness seemed pleased with himself although the jury not so much.

"You mentioned going to the site. What did you do at the site?" Marissa asked hoping to regain the jury's attention.

"I took photos. I used a drone to take videos of the site and I also took measurements."

An aerial photograph of the accident site was displayed on all of the monitors in the courtroom.

"Doctor, could you please confirm the photograph on the monitor shows the area where you observed the beginning of the lane shift?"

"Yes, it is."

Dr. Kominski used the digital pen associated with

his monitor on the witness stand to circle that part of the photograph where the lane shift was so the jury could see what he was referring to.

He continued, "Traveling westbound on Scottsdale Road the roadway shifts approximately five feet for a distance of approximately one hundred and fifty feet. The shift is not unusual in the transportation field and can be encountered at other roadways within the greater Phoenix metropolitan area."

"Did you locate the gouge mark that was made by Mr. Hernandez's vehicle?"

"Yes, I did."

He encircled the gouge mark on the photograph and drew an arrow towards it making it easier to detect.

"After reviewing all the materials provided including the engineering plans and after doing a site inspection, can you tell the jury your opinions?"

"Yes. Assuming Mr. Weaver was traveling in the middle of his lane of travel, even if he had not steered and instead continued straight, his vehicle would not have entered the middle lane even with the design shift. There would have been at least fourteen inches between the shuttle van and the middle lane where Mr. Hernandez's Lexus was traveling in."

"Thank you, doctor. Can you explain to the jury what your opinion means?"

"Absolutely. It means Mr. Weaver didn't drift into Mr. Hernandez's lane of travel. It also means Mr. Hernandez didn't inadvertently drift into the far left lane. Given the location of the gouge mark, the only way this accident could have occurred is if Mr. Hernandez intentionally entered into Mr. Weaver's lane."

"Are you certain of that?"

"Yes, I am. My opinions are provided to a reasonable degree of engineering certainty."

## 25 RENEWAL

Phoenix, Arizona
Later That Early Evening

As Marissa walked outside the Mendoza law firm towards the elevator bay, Carl rushed out after her.

"Hey, Marissa. Wait up," he said as he lugged his briefcase over his shoulder. He grabbed it tighter so he could walk faster to catch up to her.

Marissa was determined to get away, away from the office and the memory of that day. Carl wondered why. Before the elevator doors closed, Carl put his right hand in between them so the doors would automatically open as part of the safety feature.

Seeing Marissa facing toward him, unfazed and deep in concentration, Carl asked, "Didn't you hear me? What's wrong Marissa?"

Once the elevator doors slammed closed, it was as if Marissa snapped out of a hypnotic trance. Her stony smile upset Carl.

"Are you mad at me?" he inquired, unsure of the rationale behind her perplexing demeanor.

"No, no."

Her first words broke her eerie silence. She was certainly transfixed by something. Carl wanted to get to the bottom of it.

"Then what is it? I've been calling you since you left your office. I have..."

"It's not you, Carl," she reluctantly admitted.

He backed off once he heard her voice break. Obviously, something more serious was affecting her and he decided not to take it personally anymore.

"It's just that...John...I...," Marissa uncharacteristically stammered.

She took a deep breath as the elevator doors opened on the first floor of the building. She quickly exited and walked towards the front door almost as if she wanted to escape from the interrogation. The rotunda was darker than normal because the sun set earlier in the day at that time of year. Carl followed after her. This time without saying a word. Realizing no one was around or more importantly not caring if anyone was around, Marissa suddenly stopped and faced Carl.

"I'm so mad. I can't believe him. He was so aggressive...too aggressive. I don't know if we can recover."

Carl listened attentively, not wanting to interrupt her, which would have only discouraged Marissa from sharing what was on her mind. It was unlike her to hold back. They'd been friends for years and there had never been secrets between them. He wondered if John had taken his infatuation with Marissa too far.

Once he realized she wasn't going to say anything more, he asked, "What do you mean by recover?"

She shook her head in frustration.

"The jury was so mad at him...at us now. I saw their stares at John...at me. Some jurors were crossing their arms tightly in disgust. Others squinted their eyes just wanting it to stop. I wanted it to stop myself," she admitted. "But I couldn't do anything."

"Wow, what did he do?"

"He was asking the wife about what she saw at the accident scene. Her husband's dead. The poor lady is broken and suffering from the loss of her husband and John was just focused on whether she saw his lifeless body or not."

"Oh no."

The words just unconsciously escaped Carl's mouth. He regretted them after realizing it. He didn't want to make things worse for Marissa.

"You're telling me," she said after hearing them. "The jury doesn't care about those things. They just saw John as being spiteful. Now they're against us. It's all my fault. All my fault."

"It's not your fault, Marissa," Carl said reassuringly. "You did nothing wrong."

"I shouldn't have spent the weekend with my family. I should have questioned the wife myself. At least, the jury wouldn't have felt like a man was attacking a woman on the stand. I would have been more professional, and I wouldn't have asked all of those stupid questions that just upset the wife and the jury."

"I don't know what to say. Have you talked to John about it? Has he explained why he focused so much on those questions?"

Seeing the look in her eyes, Carl understood she was too riled up to have spoken to John sooner.

"Well, you need to go home, relax, eat, and when

you're feeling better, give John a call. I'm sure he'll listen to reason. He'll explain it to you if you let him."

Marissa took another deep breath and nodded as Carl shared his thoughts on the situation. She appreciated his willingness to calm her down and bring her off the ledge.

"I will," she affirmed, still trying to convince herself it was the right thing to do.

"If he's wrong, God knows he may be, he'll listen to you and the two of you can come up with a way to fix it. I'm sure you will."

A smile finally graced Marissa's face.

"So what did you want?" she asked after finally realizing there was a reason Carl wanted to talk to her after all which had nothing to do with her trial apparently.

Feeling awkward someone might come down the elevator, see them in the rotunda, and overhear a personal conversation, Carl motioned towards the front door of the office building. He walked further into the Rotunda. Marissa got the hint and followed him.

Once they were out the double doors and walking towards the parking garage, Carl said, "I know this is going to sound crazy, but I just needed your advice."

Marissa became more interested.

"I finally did it."

Marissa's eyebrows furled in confusion. Upon seeing her facial expression, Carl realized he wasn't being clear enough.

"I asked Samantha to marry me again."

"You're joking." After seeing the disappointment on Carl's face, she added, "You're really serious. I can't believe it to be honest with you. It's unexpected."

"I know. But things between Samantha and I have gotten a lot better. Better than I expected. I realize I truly love her. I really do."

He hoped his profession of love towards his ex-wife would convince Marissa he was sincere.

"But is she ready to accept your love? It's been a hard road. The two of you both made mistakes but, to be honest, Carl, you really are the one to blame. You made a huge mistake with all those...those affairs."

Marissa tried desperately to hide her disgust and disappointment with Carl at that moment. But over the years of their friendship, when they discussed his marriage and the divorce, Marissa repeatedly made it clear how she felt about his actions. Tonight, she didn't need to remind him.

"Yeah, I know that. I've owned up to my mistakes and have taken responsibility for them," he admitted.

"But it's not easy for a woman to forgive one infidelity."

Her voice peaked when saying "one" to emphasize there was more than one in this instance.

"Is she truly healed from all the pain and hurt from the marriage...from the divorce? To be honest with you, Carl, if I was in her position, I wouldn't be. It would take years to forgive you and trust you again. I don't know if any woman would."

Carl hung on to every word Marissa said. Although he knew she'd never been married, Carl also knew Marissa suffered through relationships where there was infidelity. She was speaking from first-hand experience.

"I would have given her more time," she added.

"I know, now," he admitted as he processed Marissa's advice. "I was just so excited to express my love for her I didn't think about it. I should have spoken to you or my mom before I asked her to marry me again."

His voice tapered off at the realization.

Not wanting to focus on the negative, Marissa asked, "What did Samantha say when you proposed?"

Perhaps she was wrong, and Carl had good news to convey but she doubted it.

"She stopped me from proposing which took me off guard. I was going to insist but I could see it in her eyes. She told me she didn't know whether she could ever marry anyone let alone marry me again. She didn't say 'no.' She said she wanted to think about it. But I know if she wanted to marry me, she would have let me propose."

Carl wanted to let Marissa know how he planned the proposal, picked a romantic restaurant, and a lovely engagement ring. Given Marissa's previous comments, he knew it wasn't appropriate or relevant to their discussion.

"I'm not surprised she reacted that way. But don't be too discouraged. You guys are still living together and trying to work it out. Who knows? Maybe they'll be a wedding in the future."

After Carl gave Marissa a sober smile, he told her goodbye and drove off in his car.

# 26 REALIZATION

An Undisclosed Location in Puerto Rico
The Same Night

Daniel awoke in extreme pain. Every part of his body was bruised and sore. Even his neck was sore from leaning on its side while awkwardly slumped on the chair restraining him. He had no idea how long he was unconscious. Righting his head, he was still unable to see his surroundings because he was still blindfolded. He had difficulty breathing and wasn't sure if the captors cracked his ribs from their repeated beatings. Certain his lungs hadn't collapsed from a puncture, Daniel was relieved he had only bruised ribs. He struggled to twist his body so he could sit up straight in the chair. The movement was grueling and caused excruciating pain.

Despite the unending distress to his body, he wanted to know what happened since the last encounter with the captors. He couldn't hear them in the other room but wasn't sure if the ringing in his ears was the reason or if they had left them unattended again.

*Did the guy tell them where the money was? Maybe they're looking for the money in the right place now?* he thought.

Daniel had his doubts given the other captive's resiliency and unwillingness to cooperate. He listened for the other captive in the room and could hear a faint noise. It almost sounded like moaning. Uncertain if the captive was beaten senseless like he was while unconscious, Daniel wondered if the captive was awake.

*Can he hear me?*

Daniel wasn't sure if it was a hopeless endeavor to communicate with the other captive given his previous unsuccessful attempts to partner with him.

Before he could say anything, he heard a chair moving from across the room. Because no one had entered the room, Daniel concluded the other captive was still alive and conscious at the very least. Whether the captive was badly beaten or able to assist Daniel, he did not know.

Then Daniel heard the captive whispering. He listened very closely to figure out what was said. From what Daniel could discern, it sounded like the captive was talking to himself, encouraging himself to be strong, and reassuring himself his father's men would rescue him.

*Who is he? Who is his father? Will they rescue me too or will I...,* Daniel thought before stopping himself.

The picture of a shallow grave filled his head. He worked diligently to rid himself of negative thoughts. He needed to survive and not let his fears get the best of him.

*Focus. I need to focus. If I know who he is, maybe*

*it will make sense and I can figure out how to get out of here.*

Never seeing the man's face made it difficult for Daniel to know for certain who was the other captive. Daniel concentrated hard on what little information he knew. The only thing Daniel remembered from the beatings besides the pain was the captive yelling, "I don't know that *puto*!!"

He smiled at the captive's derogatory description of him and his defiance. Once his temporary amusement subsided, Daniel realized the captive's voice seemed familiar. He must have heard it before, but he couldn't picture when or where.

*Was he an employee at the Regal Isabela?* Daniel wondered.

It didn't make sense that the captive was an employee.

*What would a hotel employee be doing staying in a casita?* he asked himself.

He remembered Gerald Ravan telling him years ago employees were not allowed to patronize any Regal Wisteria hotels even after they left the employ of the company.

*Surely, Gerald would have enforced company policy, especially during a celebration when he was present. It can't be an employee. He has to be a guest. Was he there for the celebrations or just on vacation?*

Searching his mind's eye, Daniel wondered if he'd met the captive at one of the celebrations he and Pamela attended. He pictured walking into the hotel lobby but could not remember hearing someone with a similar voice. He pictured the female *bomba* dancers entertaining everyone near the resort's outdoor restaurant. So many couples were at the event enjoying it. All the men were mesmerized by the swaying of their bodies and their flamboyant, traditional dresses. Daniel remembered staring at the men as they reacted in a way not to upset their partners.

*The captive could have been mingling with the other couples and dancing with the crowd. The casita looked like only a single man lived there,* he remembered.

He scanned his memory of the events for any single men in attendance. None came to mind. He was disappointed with himself.

*Maybe I heard his voice when I previously stayed in Puerto Rico,* Daniel mused in desperation wanting somehow to remember who he was.

Straining his brain only made his head hurt even more. Daniel wished his medical needs were attended to, but he knew his captors would never bring anyone to his location who could place them in jeopardy and report it to the police. He had to bear the pain for now but didn't know for how long.

*What are they waiting for? They must not have found the money.*

He had no idea whose money they were looking for and how much. It seemed irrelevant to the situation but took his mind off the pain.

And then It dawned on him.

*Once they find the money, both me and the other guy will be dead.*

The stark reality of his pending death haunted him. His despair increased as he became desperate for a way out. He resisted struggling to get himself free because it was useless and only wasting his valuable energy. He tried to calm himself but to no avail. More thoughts muddled his mind.

*Is Pam looking for me? She doesn't even know I'm missing.*

Realizing Pam had left the island and was tending to her father, Daniel knew she couldn't have been looking for him. He became even more despondent.

*Is Gerald Ravan looking for me? His men can find me. They are well-trained for this kind of thing.*

Daniel hoped Gerald was searching for him. After all, he was Gerald's guest.

*Surely, he knows I'm no longer at the resort. I've been gone for some time now. He must have figured out I've missed a lot of events.*

The thought gave him comfort even if it was only for a moment.

Suddenly without any forewarning, the door burst open. Daniel could hear the rushing sound of two pairs of feet coming from the other side of the room.

"Where are you taking me?"

No response or explanation was given.

The door quickly shut as violently as it was opened.

Daniel was now alone. Or was he?

## 27 AIRLINE

### Scottsdale, Arizona
### The Same Night

Pamela quietly watched her father as he rested in the hospital bed. He was still ill despite having been in the hospital for several days. She admired his gray hair which was frazzled from lying in bed practically all day every day. He showered on occasion but didn't focus on grooming himself as much as he used to when at home. She brushed his hair every time she visited him, but he cared less if he looked like the handsome man of his youth or what Pamela was accustomed to seeing when they lived together. Besides her daily visits, her sister visited once, which pleased her father. Most of the time, her father was alone in the hospital and had no reason to look his best. Her heart ached for him, but she stood strong for her father.

Knowing there was nothing she could do for him, she exited his hospital room and walked to the terrace at the back of the hospital. It was where she spoke with Dr. Thamm months ago when her father was last hospitalized. She desired a secluded place to focus on work for a moment while her father was resting. The terrace was the only place she could think of to get away from it all. She checked her email and text messages and then called the office.

"Virginia," she said when the phone was finally answered.

"Hey, boss. How are things going?" the investigator said while preoccupied with preparing paperwork for a case she'd been working on.

"I'm okay. I just wanted to check on things."

"There's no need to worry. We're handling business like we said we would. I know you've been back for a few days, but we didn't expect you to come back until tonight. So, we're not doing anything differently than what we originally expected. Just relax and spend time with your dad."

Virginia hoped she could persuade Pamela to forget about work, but she knew Pamela couldn't. It was in her blood. Pamela was raised to be a perfectionist. Her martial arts studies and her military background only reinforced it.

"I know. I..."

"Nothing's going on right now. We've finished the Bishop assignment. I'm actually filling out the final report right now."

"Good," Pamela said with a sense of relief.

Once the conversation ended, Pamela checked her phone again for any messages from Daniel. He told her he'd visit her father in the hospital once he got back in town. It had been several days since he agreed to fly back early to Phoenix. Pamela thought his involvement with the celebrations at the Regal Isabela and his interactions with Gerald Ravan may have delayed him from flying back to Phoenix. She wasn't as concerned because she was used to Daniel's busy schedule. His schedule wasn't nearly as hectic or disruptive as her own.

But like Virginia reminded her, the originally planned trip ended today. Daniel should have flown back by now. Not hearing from him was unexpected especially given his promise. Daniel was not one to break a promise, definitely not carelessly. She wanted to confirm he would be visiting her father soon, so she dialed Daniel's cell phone.

"You've reached the desk of Daniel Mendoza. I'm not in right now...."

The call went straight to voicemail.

*He's probably with Corina,* Pamela thought.

She smiled wishing him the best of times with a new woman and regretting Corina hadn't traveled to Puerto Rico with Daniel as he originally desired. However, a nagging thought gnawed at her. She hoped nothing happened to him. At first, she dismissed her concerns as intrusive thoughts, but it continued to haunt her.

*I'd rather be safe than sorry*, she convinced herself.

She dialed Virginia again.

"Are you going to stop worrying about work already?" Virginia lectured surprised her boss called back so quickly.

"I'm sorry but I need you to do something for me."

When Virginia noticed the concern in Pamela's voice, she eased up and said, "Sure. What is it?"

"Can you find out if Daniel Mendoza made his flight back to Phoenix? I think he was scheduled on Delta today."

Virginia accessed the airline company with her

special software program to ascertain Pamela's request.

"It doesn't look like he made the flight," Virginia explained after scanning the day's flights on her computer screen.

Pamela's heart sank. Her fears seemed more real, but she continued to hold out hope.

"Is there any way to check if he switched to a different airline or left on a different day?"

Clicking into another special federal program giving her access to flight schedules and passenger lists throughout the country, Virginia checked flights leaving the three international airports in Puerto Rico for the past few days.

"He didn't leave on any other flights," she told Pamela. "If you want, I can check the video feeds for the airports to see if he even arrived and when."

"No," Pamela responded. "He may still be at the hotel and decided to extend his trip. Can you call the Regal Isabela and find out if Daniel's still there?"

"Hold on."

Virginia called the resort's front desk and explained her request to a helpful manager. She then switched back to her call with Pamela.

"Daniel never checked out of the resort. They put me on hold. They're having someone check the casita to see if he's still there."

"Okay."

Pamela's heart raced at the thought of the tossed casita adjacent to the one where she and Daniel stayed on their trip. She imagined something similar happening to Daniel because of their investigation into the abducted resort guest. She dismissed her concerns as fanciful thinking sullied by her many years of being a private investigator who mainly saw the bad side of humanity.

Pamela heard the phone click over. As she waited for Virginia to speak with the hotel employee, she unconsciously started pacing the hospital terrace. Fortunately, she was alone, and no one was distracted by her unsettledness.

"His luggage is still in the room," Virginia said once she returned to the call. "They have no idea where he is."

"This is not good," Pamela declared. "It's not like Daniel to just drop off the face of the earth for no good reason."

Noticing Pamela was worried about Daniel's well-being, Virginia suggested, "George is in Orlando for business and some time off with his wife. It's only a short flight to San Juan from there. Do you want me to have him fly to the island and look into it?"

"I'd hate to interrupt his vacation," Pamela bemoaned.

"It's nothing. George won't mind. He likes Daniel and will want to make sure he's okay."

Pamela relented to the idea.

"Thanks, Virginia."

"Don't worry about it, Pam. Just focus on your father. We'll get to the bottom of this."

## 28 HOSPITAL

Scottsdale, Arizona
At The Same Time

When Gerald Ravan entered the hospital room for Gavin Williams, he was overjoyed to see his old friend. Gavin was starting to wake up. His eyes slowly opened revealing deep pain and sorrow but also a glimmer of confusion. Gerald sat on the edge of the hospital bed while he awaited a fully conscious patient.

Drawing a cigarette pack from his coat pocket, Gerald extended it towards the now-awake Gavin and asked, "Want one?"

Gavin groggily shook his head and said, "I quit a long time ago."

"True. I should have remembered that," Gerald replied with a slight smirk.

Once Gerald brought a cigarette to his mouth and pulled out a lighter, Gavin declared, "You can't smoke in here. It's a hospital."

The recovering patient squirmed in his bed apparently from a blast of pain due to overexerting himself.

Displaying a dumbfounded look, Gavin said, "I forgot. You Americans are so strict with everything. Europeans are more liberal in that way. We can smoke anywhere. No problem."

He smiled and returned the cigarette pack to its original location.

"You're looking good my friend. It's good to see you again," Gerald remarked after the ordeal over the cigarette seemed over.

Gavin smiled.

"It's good to see you too. I hope the flight from Tokyo wasn't too bad."

Gerald explained he had just arrived from Puerto Rico after participating in the tenth anniversary celebrations for the resort.

"I wish you could have come," Gerald said.

"I know. It would have been nice. I'm glad Pam went. She said she had fun." He looked around the hospital room for his daughter but didn't see her. "Where is she?"

"I saw her dart outside before I came in the room. I'm sure she'll be back soon," Gerald replied.

The two buddies reminisced about the good ole days together and how Gavin was in the special forces and transitioned to working with the Regal Wisteria once he retired from the military. Gerald first met Gavin when he competed in Aikido tournaments in Tokyo years ago. Gerald attended because Regal Wisteria sponsored the tournaments. Watching a young American male compete with grace and skill using a modern, Japanese martial art was a rare opportunity. Gerald was enamored by him and their budding relationship, both personal and business, started that day. They also reminisced about how Gerald eventually watched Pamela compete in the Aikido tournaments when Gavin first coached her as a child.

"She was a badass," Gerald gleamed. "Remember the time she threw that Swedish guy? What's his name? He was soooo huge."

Gavin beamed as the memory of his young daughter defeating a guy twice her size filled him with joy.

"Lars...Lars Johannson. I remember him. He was six feet five inches. He looked like a giant and was as strong as an ox."

Gavin tried in vain to lift both arms to demonstrate the Swedish competitor's height, but his body wouldn't cooperate. He was still in pain.

Not wanting to highlight any of Gavin's limitations, Gerald pretended not to notice and kept talking.

"Yes, that's him. Good ole, Lars. He was a big talker but when it came to Pam, he fell short every time. The look on his face during the award ceremony was priceless," he added.

"Yeah, I was proud my girl took first place and that bully only made it to second place."

"She's a lot like you, Gavin. It's no wonder she followed in your footsteps and became special forces as well."

Gerald looked like he was a proud father himself even though Pamela only worked for him. The two understood the unique relationship Gerald had with Pamela but rarely spoke about it. Today was no different.

"I am so glad she did. I can see how happy and

dedicated it has made her," Gavin admitted. He unexpectedly lowered his head in shame despite the jovial conversation. After a long, uncomfortable pause, he continued, "The only regret I have in my old age is Cameron not going into the military. He was just as good an athlete as Pamela if not better. He even practiced Aikido with me and loved it. He never wanted to compete or follow the rules. He was stubborn and liked doing his own thing. I just don't know why he was a rebel in that way."

The seriousness in Gavin's eyes revealed his pain, this time not from his illness but the pain a father feels when a child is lost and never returns to the fold.

"I haven't seen him in years. Decades. I've heard from Milagros that he's in town, but he hasn't visited me yet."

Gavin's voice broke. It was the first time Gerald had seen him this way.

"He won't tell anyone what he's been doing all this time. I don't know why. He's still bitter towards me for pushing him into Aikido and wanting him to go to the military. I was just trying to turn him into a disciplined man who could face every challenge this dark world demanded. Was I wrong for that? Did I push him too hard? I just don't know, Gerry."

Gerald was lost for words. Seeing his longtime friend in such agony and knowing his physical condition was deteriorating over the past year made Gerald reconsider everything. He had a secret he held close after all these years despite their deep connection. Now, he realized he needed to reveal the secret even if it meant losing his friendship.

"Cameron's been working for me all this time, but he never wanted me to tell you. I needed to honor his request. I battled with it every day. I wanted to tell you so many times because you seemed so disappointed in him. I wanted you to know what he was doing and how successful he was so you could be proud of him the way you were so proud of Pam and the way I am so proud of him. I need to tell you now. You deserve to know. I pulled him off an assignment and asked him to visit you this week. He needs to make things right with you. No more silly childhood resentment. I don't know why he hasn't visited you yet. Cameron's stubborn just like his father. But you also need to forgive him, Gavin, for his choices. This time for real. Not just giving lip service to forgiving him. He's heard what you've said about him all these years.

"When I told Cameron about what you've been dealing with, he had a heart-to-heart with himself like he needed to. He's been avoiding reconciling with you all this time no matter how many times I've spoken to him about it over the years. He finally realized his part in all this. He wants to make amends and knows there may not be a lot of time left. That's why he's here today. I don't know how long you have to live. I'm hoping it's plenty more years. We're doing the best we can to make it so you can beat this thing. But as I've told you before, I can't make any guarantees. All I can say is that we'll do everything we can to make you comfortable and deal with the pain you're going through. I promise you, Gavin."

Gerald's words stung deeply. He was shocked by the betrayal and resented it. But at the same time, Gerald gave Gavin hope like he never had in the past years since he'd been dealing with his illness. He missed his boy and he wanted to be a family again even if it was only for just a moment.

The door unexpectedly opened. Both Gavin and Gerald turned toward the door. It was Cameron. Gerald got up from the bed.

"I will leave you two alone."

Gerald walked towards the door and squeezed Cameron's shoulder before exiting the hospital room. Cameron took a step closer toward his father.

## 29 TEAM UP

Scottsdale, Arizona
Moments Later

When Gerald exited the hospital room, he almost bumped into Pamela who was returning from the terrace. He stepped back just in time to avoid a collision.

"Hi, Gerry. I didn't know you were coming to visit dad," she said once she realized who he was. "You should have let me know."

Gerald hugged her and explained, "It was a surprise for both you and Gavin. I was just in the hospital room talking to him. I'm happy to finally see him again. I want you to know Cameron's in with him now. It looks like they want some privacy."

Gerald slyly looked towards the hospital room door to ensure it was closed. He was initially worried Pamela would enter the room as soon as she returned and would interrupt the father-son conversation. Once he told her about the unexpected visit from her brother and she appeared reluctant to enter the room and engage him.

*It's a good thing*, Gerald thought.

"I'm surprised he's here after all this time. I've been trying to get a hold of him. He won't take my calls. Milagros spoke with him but she's just as secretive as he is. Do you know why he's here?"

Gerald's face went blank. He didn't want to give it away but at the same time, he already told Gavin. It was only a matter of time before Pamela would find out. He decided to tell her as well. Sadness clouded her facial features when she heard his explanation.

"Why wouldn't you tell me after all this time? He's my brother. I had no idea he was working for you too. How could you?" Pamela fumed.

She backed up when Gerald approached to hug her. Relenting, she eventually embraced him and sobbed on his shoulder. They held each other for a while until she felt enough emotional release to talk about it again.

"I understand it's not ideal and you may never trust me again. But this is what Cameron wanted. He wanted anonymity because he felt whatever he did or was doing the family was going to judge him for it because he wasn't doing what the family wanted. I know it doesn't mean much but Cameron kept tabs on you. He'd come into my office when he was not on assignment. We'd catch up and afterward he would ask me about you, ask to see any photos of you, whether you won a tournament, how your private investigator business was doing. He wanted to know it all.

"I didn't hesitate to tell him everything but, to be honest, I'd prefer he speak to you guys directly instead of me being the middle man. When I'd ask him to reach out to you and your dad, he would brush me off and sometimes get upset, really upset, at my suggestion. I knew pushing it would make things worse not just for me but also for you."

Pamela listened attentively, pleased her older brother expressed some concern about her even if he never reached out personally to talk to her or their father.

"Give it some time," Gerald requested. "I know you want to talk to him. He's talking to your dad about it, all of it. I'm sure it won't be easy for both of them. But when they're done and it's time, he'll want to talk to you as well."

Gerald started walking toward the terrace where Pamela had come from. She instinctively followed out of concern their voices were penetrating her father's hospital room. The last thing Pamela wanted was for her brother to hear her arguing about him and possibly ruining the moment with their father or worst yet making it even more difficult for her to reconcile with him.

When they were on the terrace, Gerald looked into her eyes and asked, "Before we had a conversation about Cameron and all this stuff, you seemed preoccupied when we bumped into each other in the hall. What was on your mind?'

"It's Daniel," Pamela admitted.

"What about him?"

Pamela didn't know how to explain it, but she knew Gerald would listen to her and understand no matter how weird it sounded. He was always that way with her. It's why she looked at him as a second father figure.

"He's missing. We...I don't know where he is.

He's not in Phoenix and he definitely never left
Puerto Rico. We checked."

"It's unlike him to disappear for no reason. Is he
with that new woman you mentioned to me before? It
seemed like their relationship was on the mend."

"We don't know. I've asked Virginia to discretely
look into it. He may be at her place or, you know,
somewhere special. The last thing I want to do is ruin
a romantic time. It would be embarrassing. Besides,
Daniel deserves some time alone. But to be honest,
Gerry, I think there's more to it. I can't explain it. I'm
worried about his safety."

"You're not one to make a snap decision. It's unlike you to rush into anything. If you feel there's something more, I trust your judgment."

Gerald knew Pamela had never steered him
wrong. Her instincts were unparalleled. But there
was something different in how Pamela expressed her
concerns about Daniel's whereabouts. At that moment, he realized Daniel meant more to Pamela than
what she'd led him to believe.

"I understand what you mean. I sent George to
the island so he can figure out what happened but, to
be honest, I want to go back to Puerto Rico and look
into it myself now that dad is doing a lot better."

Pamela also wanted to avoid the conundrum between Cameron and their father. They could work it
out on their own. She would face her brother later
once her mind was at ease and Daniel was located.

"If you're serious about going back to the island,
you can use my private jet. It will give me an excuse
to spend more time with your father."

"Thank you."

Watching Pamela brighten at the offer, Gerald decided to take it a step further.

"I can have my security team at the Regal Isabela meet you and George if it turns out there's something more serious going on. They are equipped for anything."

Having seen them in action herself many times before, Pamela knew it was an offer she couldn't pass up if she found herself in a precarious position. Her martial arts and gun shooting skills were top-notch, but she had no idea what was in store should things take a turn for the worse and her fears come to fruition. She remembered the horrifying scene at the neighboring casita. She struggled to keep the thoughts of Daniel being tortured from ruminating in her head.

*No, that's not happening,* she convinced herself. *I have to stay positive for Daniel's sake.*

"I really think it may be nothing. I may be overreacting but if it comes to that I'll definitely take you up on your offer," Pamela responded.

# 30 NEGOTIATIONS

## An Undisclosed Location in San Juan, Puerto Rico
## Two A.M. The Next Day

*C*hango, the head of *La Familia*, walked into a large room in a building pre-arranged for an early morning secret meeting between him and his two *copas*. Escorted by his bodyguards and his closest advisor, he sat at the far end of the table. He was clearly disturbed and uncomfortably sat tapping his fingers on the table while gazing at the door for his *copas* to enter. Sweat slowly dripped down his forehead. One of his bodyguards effortlessly wiped the sweat off with a handkerchief. *Chango* did not flinch because he was used to attentiveness from his employees. The bodyguard stepped back into formation behind *Chango* and beside his compatriot after fulfilling an unspoken duty.

Entering next was Luis. He arranged the meeting as requested by his fellow *copa*, Johnny. He too was accompanied by his bodyguards.

Luis walked to the other side of the room to greet *Chango*.

"It's good to see you, my old friend," he said. "My apologies for having to wake you up so early to deal with this...this unfortunate situation."

*Chango* refused to rise and greet his childhood friend with their customary greeting of an embrace and kissing each other on the cheek. Although Luis could have taken it as an insult, he brushed it off knowing *Chango* wasn't in the mood. After all, prior to the meeting, Luis was the one who broke the news that *Chango's* son had been captured by Johnny. Luis suspected *Chango* thought he was involved as well. He adamantly denied it but wasn't sure if *Chango* believed him.

Further, near the center of the table, Luis sat down to take his role as the go-between. He seemed confident and almost arrogant in enjoying taking center stage in the conflict. It was almost as if Luis believed he was born to be a mediator of sorts. The two sat in silence as they waited for Johnny to arrive so the negotiations could begin.

After thirty minutes passed, one of *Chango's* bodyguards leaned over and whispered into *Chango's* ear. *Chango* sat up with a blank stare upon receiving the news. Moments later, Johnny entered. He walked in with his typical swagger and flare the other two were accustomed to. Johnny did whatever he could to hide a smirk on his face. He wasn't successful. *Chango* wasn't pleased with his arrogance. Neither was Luis as he believed it may hamper things and undermine his efforts.

Once Johnny and his bodyguards were settled, Luis announced, "*Chango*...Johnny. We are here tonight to deal with a family dispute. We are all friends, and we should be able to resolve this like family. Don't you agree?"

He looked at both men for affirmation.

*Chango* nodded with a slight disdain.

"I agreed to come here in good faith based upon your word, Luis. Nothing more," he said while staring across the table at Johnny.

"Well, that's a start. Johnny?" Luis asked hoping his fellow *copa* would restrain himself.

"Luis, I appreciate you setting up this meeting. But *Chango* has to admit, he doesn't have...how you say...the strongest hand here tonight. If we all agree upon that, I think this night will be productive and we can...well...we can put it all behind us."

"Coño," *Chango* whispered under his breath, but his words traveled as far as where Luis sat but not nearly as far as where Johnny was seated across the room.

Johnny could see *Chango* mouthing the curse word even if he couldn't hear it. He could also see *Chango's* eyes bulging. It brought him a sense of joy. He reveled in knowing it was only a matter of time before his long-sought-after goal would be achieved. He would no longer be subjected to the childhood whims of his nemesis and could take his rightful place in the family.

"I provided *Chango* with your terms, Johnny. He is considering them. We both know *Chango* has wanted to play a smaller role in the family. Stepping aside is a totally different thing. He's not happy over this whole thing with his son and efforts to try to force his hand. *Chango*?" Luis said.

"I admit my son hasn't been behaving these past few years. It's my fault. I overindulged him in ways a father does. You both are fathers and know what I mean. But this business of torturing my son to find out where he hid the money? It's outrageous and uncalled for. I guaranteed he would repay all the money he stole with a hefty interest rate. I personally put up my villa in Ponce as collateral for my guarantee. So I don't know why Johnny needed to do all this. He agreed to the terms. I didn't force him. All I want is my son back and for this to be over so we can go back to the way things were."

*Chango's* voice became angry at the last request.

"We haven't seen a dime in all this time," Johnny declared. His nostrils were flaring.

"I've asked you to be patient. This endeavor on the mainland isn't an instant...get-rich-quick scheme. All sides need to be patient," *Chango* explained. "Including you, Johnny."

"I've waited long enough. I know from my connections in the States nothing is being done like we were promised. Whether your son is behind the delay or stealing again, I don't know. I just know I'm not getting my money. None of us are and something needs to be done about it."

"Johnny, please. No insults," Luis admonished. "We are old pals, and we need to respect each other and our families. Making unfounded accusations isn't helping anything."

"Thank you," *Chango* agreed. "I don't know why you're being this way, Johnny. So disrespectful. What have I done for you to mistreat me or my family? I leave you alone to run your business the way you see fit. It's a lucrative business. I've not interfered in any way. When you needed money to expand the business, I gave you the money with no strings attached because you are like a brother to me. You are a brother to me, both you and Luis."

Johnny jumped out of his seat out of frustration and the insinuation he had been treated like a brother this whole time.

"I didn't need your money," he declared. "I..."

Johnny heard gunshots outside the building in the far distance. The sound caught him by surprise.

———

The cooler breeze from the Atlantic Ocean comforted Johnny's men from the tropical heat. Johnny brought two vehicles to the location of the meeting. One was the vehicle he came in and the other vehicle was filled with loyal soldiers to ensure his safety in addition to his bodyguards.

A third vehicle was hiding a few blocks away. Inside the third vehicle, was *Chango's* son guarded by three men. They were awaiting instructions to bring him to the location if the negotiations were successful. The men were bored waiting for the call. The two men seated in the front of the vehicle were munching on Puerto Rican snacks. While the third was seated in the back with a gun pointed at their captive.

Smelling the delicious food, the man in the back seat said, "It's not fair. You guys need to share."

"You didn't share those *alcapurrias* you ate this morning," the driver said while greedily smacking on his food. He looked at the man beside him with a devilish smile.

"Yeah, now you want our stuff. No way man," the guy said as he continued munching on food.

Looking in the rearview mirror for his reaction,

the driver saw his fellow soldier in the back of the vehicle suddenly slump over after a bullet pierced the back window causing the glass to spray wildly inside. Another bullet barely missed the driver and hit the windshield.

"What the... Take off!!" the front passenger exclaimed as an array of bullets showered the vehicle.

———

Once Luis recognized there was a shootout nearby, he stood up as well worried there would be an attack on the building and his life would be in danger. His bodyguards grabbed their weapons and faced the door, the only entrance to the room. Luis looked over to *Chango* who was unfazed by the commotion and unconcerned for his safety.

"You did this. Didn't you?" Luis protested. "Why?"

"Just relax. It'll all be over in a few minutes," *Chango* declared.

Turning to *Chango*, Johnny ranted, "You tried to cheat me out of my due. Don't think I'll forget this. You may never see your son again. Never!!"

Johnny stormed out of the room with his bodyguards. They were armed and ready to confront any obstacles.

# 31 CONFESSION

## Phoenix, Arizona
## The Same Early Morning

As Marissa sauntered closer to the kitchen in a bathrobe, she was still sleepy and tried to keep her eyes open. The weight of her eyelids made her blink uncontrollably. She tried rubbing her eyes with her hands to wake up but even then she was so tired she didn't really want to wake up. What she really wanted to do was walk to her mother's kitchen on autopilot, grab something quick to eat or drink, and return to her inviting bed effortlessly as if she was sleepwalking.

She was not sleepwalking. Her mind was filled with thoughts of the trial, and it was making it hard to relax and go to sleep. It was only out of mental exhaustion that her body complied with her previous command to lie down. Now, it was not enough to keep her in bed. She needed to break the cycle of her thoughts so she could keep them under her control and subdue her fears.

When she finally passed through the doorway

leading to the kitchen, she resisted flicking on the light switch out of concern any sudden bright light would shock her into full consciousness. That was the last thing she wanted at the moment. After a few more steps, she could see the flicker of light in the room which gave her pause.

"*Mija*, what are you doing up so early? You should be asleep. You have a trial tomorrow," her mother chided. "Go back to bed."

Marissa tried to tell her body to comply, but it resisted. Perhaps, it was the smell of Mexican sweet bread filling the room mixed with the sweet aroma of arabica coffee beans. When it filled her nostrils, she was suddenly awake as if it was the middle of the day rather than the middle of the night. What further drew Marissa's attention was her mother biting into a homemade *concha* which she had baked during the day while Marissa was in court. The sweets were apparently for the visiting guests, but her mother appeared to be eating the last one.

Once Marissa noticed the tasty treat, she scurried over next to her mother and said, "It smells so good. I'm sure *tía* loved them. It was nice of you to make her favorite dessert."

Realizing all of the treats were eaten before Marissa came home, her mother broke the remaining sweet bread in half and handed her daughter the biggest piece. She greedily took it and took a big bite.

"Can I...?" she said with a full mouth.

Before Marissa could finish her question, her mother smiled and passed the large mug of coffee across the table so she could gulp down the refreshment.

"Thank you, *mami*," she said almost as if she had returned to a childlike state.

Marissa's mother stood up and was about to head back to bed herself when Marissa touched her forearm and asked, "Can we talk for a minute?"

"Sure, *mija*. What do you need?"

"I...I don't need anything. I just wanted to..."

Marissa struggled with revealing her secret out of concern it would not only disappoint her mother but also her father and the rest of the family. Not to mention, she vowed to her aunt, Carmen, and her uncle, Manuel, she would not reveal it to anyone, not even to her mother. The promise was for the sake of Gabriela and, of course, to keep the personal health issues her aunt and uncle faced a secret. To them, it was somewhat embarrassing despite the many times Marissa tried to convince them otherwise.

There was something about the reality of the trial which gnawed at her and made Marissa realize life was precious and loved ones could be taken away at any moment. She needed to make things right before she too would be in the same position as Mrs. Hernandez - missing a loved one and never being able to say goodbye before they left this world. Marissa didn't want to live with the same regrets.

"Mom. I have something to tell you. Something I should have told you a long time ago but couldn't. It was wrong for me to keep it from you, but I promised. Keeping the secret...my secret...was too much for me," she admitted.

Marissa wanted to bury her face in her arms and hide from her mother and the rest of the world.

"It's okay, *mija*. Whatever it is, we're here for you - me and *papi*."

Marissa nodded her head and wiped a tear almost escaping down her cheek.

"I know. I know. I...I have a confession to make."

Marissa's mother gave her a puzzled look but kept silent. She didn't want to interrupt her daughter for fear it would cause her not to reveal it.

"I know this sounds strange and you may not believe me, but as God is my witness, I'm telling you the truth. Gabriela...Gabriela is my daughter."

"No, no, no, *mija*. I know you feel like she's your daughter because you've spent so much time with her while you lived with your aunt in Chihuahua. But she's your cousin. Gabriela's your cousin," her mother tried in vain to explain with an innocent smile.

"I know you think she's my cousin. But I actually got pregnant. I hid it from you and *papi*."

Marissa held back the tears. She didn't want her emotions to overwhelm her during this critical moment. She wanted to be strong the way she always had been even if it was during her most vulnerable point.

"But I never saw you pregnant," her mother commented. "You never had a baby bump. Nothing."

Marissa acknowledged her mother's confusion by gently nodding her head.

"Because I...if you remember, I left for Chihuahua very early in my pregnancy before I was showing. I told *Tía* Carmen about my pregnancy. She convinced me to go to Mexico and stay with her so I can take time away from work and decide what I wanted to do."

"Why not stay here and talk to me and your father about it? We would have been there for you. I don't understand."

Her mother stood up as an anxious reaction to the situation and an unconscious way to escape from the reality of their conversation. She was about to pace the kitchen but this time when Marissa touched her forearm it caused her mother to bow her head and weep.

"I was ashamed because I wasn't married, and I never wanted to be a single mom. I didn't think you would approve," Marissa admitted.

Mother and daughter embraced. At first, the embrace was gentle, but it tightened as the realization of what Marissa told her mother fully came to her understanding.

"I...I have a granddaughter," her mother declared proudly but with restraint so as not to wake her guests, including Gabriela.

Hearing the proclamation, Marissa slumped in her mother's arms.

"It's not that simple, mom. *Tia* carmen and *Tio* Manuel adopted Gabriela. I signed the paperwork. She's their daughter now, not my daughter."

"Don't be silly. They'll give her back to you."

"I...I don't know if I want her back."

"What do you mean? She's your daughter. Of course, you want her back."

"With my job, my career, it's not that simple. I don't know if I want Gabriela to be a part of my life. It's too complicated."

"*Mija*, I know it seems overwhelming. No one is ever prepared to have a child. They struggle with whether they can take care of it. It's not like there's a manual for raising kids. I certainly didn't have a manual. I learned like everyone else. But your father and I can be there for you. We can babysit when you have to work late or like today be in trial. I don't want you to miss out. Life is so much more fulfilling when you have someone who unconditionally loves you. It gives life more meaning."

Marissa listened attentively to her mother's advice even though she struggled with it and struggled with seeing herself as a single mom.

"But Carmen will be so disappointed in me if I...I just can't. It's not right for me to betray them in this way. They've taken good care of her. It's not right for me to take Gabriela away from them. They love her so much."

"They will continue to love her just in a different way. Just like you will love her in a different way once you are her mom."

Marissa's eyes gleamed although they also displayed her confusion and self-doubt.

Seeing her daughter this way, her mother volunteered, "I can speak with them if you'd like."

"I...I haven't decided yet," Marissa admitted.

"It's okay, *mija*. There's no rush."

Marissa's mother moved Marissa's bangs from her eyes, kissed her tears away, and gently kissed her cheeks. The two continued hugging.

## 32 DRIVER

Phoenix, Arizona
Later That Same Day

"Mr. Weaver, you were running a little late back to the resort, correct?" Doug Clarkson asked while standing in front of the plaintiffs' counsel table.

His client, Selinda Hernandez, observed as the driver of the shuttle bus was on the witness stand. Although she had attended every day of the trial and saw Mr. Weaver every day with defense counsel, she wanted to watch as the man who killed her husband would finally be held responsible for hurting him and her family. It's what she had waited for all this time.

"I...I was only a few minutes late. It wasn't a big deal. At that time of day there were very few guests needing a shuttle bus. I don't...if I remember correctly, dispatch told me no one was waiting for a ride. So, no, from my point of view, I wasn't late."

"Mr. Weaver, according to you, you weren't late, but you were speeding at the time of the crash, weren't you?" Mr. Clarkson asked with a confounded expression.

He turned to the jury and shrugged his shoulders.

"I don't believe I was. I was going around the speed limit," he nervously responded.

"If an expert were to testify, you were going over the speed limit and were speeding, you aren't able to dispute that, correct?"

"It's been a while since the accident. I can't remember my exact speed at the time. I wasn't looking at the speedometer. I would have been traveling at the speed limit and no more than a mile or two above the speed limit, if at all. It's my habit to travel the speed limit and no faster."

"Weren't you speeding when you crossed into my client's lane and rammed his car?"

"I didn't ram his car. He came into my lane and hit me," Mr. Weaver insisted.

The jury stared at him listening attentively to every word. They didn't seem taken aback by Mr. Clarkson's aggressive questioning. By the time Mr. Weaver was on the stand, they had gotten used to his style. It was more entertaining compared to the defense counsel's methodology of questioning.

"We'll let the jury decide that," Doug said as he switched topics. "You were driving a shuttle bus, correct?"

"Yes, I was."

"And it's owned by the Regal Phoenix Resort and Spa, correct?"

"Yes."

"You were a resort employee at the time of the crash, correct?"

"Yes, I was. I'm still employed by the resort."

"Everything you did that day including getting into the crash with Mr. Hernandez was done in your capacity as an employee of the resort, correct?"

"That's correct."

"The shuttle bus is a huge vehicle compared to my client's Lexus, correct?"

Mr. Clarkson stretched out his arms simulating how long the shuttle bus was and when mentioning the Lexus, he brought them closer together.

"It is about the size of a small school bus."

"Doesn't the shuttle bus have blind spots where you aren't able to see vehicles in either lane next to you?"

"The shuttle bus has dual side mirrors with wide-angle glass on each side of the vehicle. It allows me to see everything to the left and right of the bus. If I move my head while looking in the mirrors there is absolutely no blind spot. None at all."

Mr. Weaver was confident in his answer. He wasn't sure if he was too confident and whether it was something that would come back to bite him.

"That assumes you're paying attention, doesn't it?"

"I pay attention when I drive. It's what the resort is paying me to do. In the last twenty years of driving for the resort, I've never been in an accident. I've never even gotten a traffic ticket."

Mr. Weaver remembered Marissa coaching him to volunteer this information at the pertinent time to educate the jury about his driving history. He held back a smile knowing she would be proud of him for bringing up these facts at this moment.

"So you didn't fiddle with the radio knobs or any of the controls?"

"No, I did not."

"Were you on the phone at the time of the accident?"

"We aren't allowed phones. I leave mine in my locker."

"Were there any passengers in the vehicle?"

"Just one," he answered.

"And who was that passenger?"

"My wife, Rose."

"Where was your wife seated?"

"She was seated in the nearest seat in the aisle across from the driver's seat."

"She was seated there because you could see her while driving, correct?"

"Yes. She often comes with me while I'm driving the shuttle bus."

"You were talking to your wife while driving the shuttle bus back to the resort."

"No, I wasn't."

"Isn't it true Mr. Weaver you were distracted talking to your wife as the crash occurred and you rammed the bus into my client's vehicle?"

"No, that isn't true. That didn't happen."

———

"You did a great job on cross-examination," Marissa told Martin Weaver during the break. "We just have your redirect and you'll be finished testifying."

"Thanks. This is exhausting, worse than my deposition," he said while wiping sweat from his brow.

"He's a lot more aggressive this time," John added. "We think plaintiffs' counsel is concerned he's losing the jury and he's trying to make it up during your cross-examination."

"Great. He's using me as a punching bag," Martin fumed. "I'm just glad it's over. There's just one thing I want to know. Mr. Clarkson was questioning me so far away at the counsel's table. Why wasn't he leaning up against the witness box questioning me face to face?"

Marissa and John looked at each other and smirked.

"You've watched too much television. That's totally fake," Marissa said.

"Yeah, attorneys can't do that," John explained. "They can question you at the lectern or at the counsel's table, but they can't get right in your face or ask questions in front of the jury."

"Really? I didn't know that. I'm so surprised," Martin admitted.

"It's why I don't watch legal dramas," Marissa said. "I get upset when I watch them because I know they're so fake and not realistic at all."

"I'm the same way," John said. "I guess TV shows do that for dramatic effect probably to keep both actors in the same shot or add some added tension and drama."

"There's enough tension and stress in a real trial," Martin declared.

John put his hand on Martin's shoulder to comfort and encourage him.

"We need to get back into the courtroom. Looks like the break is over," Marissa said while turning towards the door.

"Martin, before the break, do you remember Mr. Clarkson asking if you were distracted by talking to Rose when the accident occurred?" Marissa asked.

"Yes, I remember that question," Martin responded.

"Can you tell the jury if you were talking to your wife during the ride back to the resort?"

"No, we weren't talking to each other at all for the whole trip."

"Why is that?"

"Rose has Alzheimer's..."

"Objection," Mr. Clarkson announced as he quickly jumped out of the seat. "Your honor, may we have a bench conference to discuss this?" he asked.

"Counsel may approach the bench," the judge commanded.

Doug Clarkson and Danica Bridgers walked to the bench along with Marissa and John. Both Martin and the jury watched as the parade of lawyers approached. However, they couldn't hear what the attorneys were going to say because the judge turned on the white noise generator.

"Mr. Clarkson," the judge said once all four attorneys were situated.

"Thank you, your honor. We don't believe Mrs. Weaver's health issues are relevant. In fact, it's unduly prejudicial and solely designed to arouse sympathy in the jury. We request that your honor preclude Mr. Weaver or any other witnesses from testifying she has Alzheimer's. This case is about which vehicle entered the other's lane of travel and who caused the crash. Mrs. Weaver's Alzheimer's doesn't make any material fact any more or less probable. Even if the Court is willing to accept the information as relevant, it is certainly outweighed by the danger that it unfairly prejudices the jury."

"Your honor, if I may," Marissa said once she realized Doug was finished with his argument. "Mrs. Weaver's health condition is totally relevant. Plaintiff's counsel opened the door when he cross-examined Mr. Weaver and insinuated he was distracted talking to his wife. Given the extent of her Alzheimer's condition at the time, Mrs. Weaver had limited speech functions. She wasn't talking to her husband and wasn't distracting him like plaintiff's counsel is insinuating because of her specific health condition. If we aren't allowed to explain to the jury why she couldn't speak with her husband, then the jury will have false information and will make the assumption they were talking to each other and may incorrectly conclude that Mr. Weaver was distracted. That's extremely prejudicial to the Weavers, your honor."

Before Mr. Clarkson could respond to Marissa's point, the judge interjected, "Counsel you opened the door by asking the question if Mr. Weaver was distracted. Her health condition is relevant to the issue of distraction, and I will allow it. If you'd like, I can remind the jury that they are to decide this case based on the facts and not any sympathy for any party, including the plaintiffs or the defendants. Is that acceptable?"

"I'm fine with that, your honor," Marissa said.

Mr. Clarkson also reluctantly agreed after realizing he'd lost the argument.

"Good," the judge said and then reminded the jury about their role in deciding the case.

"Martin, can you finish what you were going to

say before the bench conference with the judge?" Marissa asked.

"Of course. Rose has Alzheimer's. She had it for years and has limited speech capabilities. She likes going on the rides with me because it brings her pleasure, but we don't talk during those trips."

"Were you distracted in any way by your wife when driving back to the resort?"

"No, not at all. She loves the rides and is so enamored by the views she is too busy and lets me do my job. She's very proud of me."

Martin smiled as he looked at the jury. His wife wasn't present during the trial because of her health issues. Unable to smile at his wife made Martin sad. He tried to be strong for his absent wife at that moment and kept up his smile.

"Martin, were you able to speak with Mr. Hernandez after the accident?" Marissa continued.

"No, I wasn't. By the time I exited the shuttle bus with my wife, got her to a safe place on the sidewalk, and walked to the Lexus, he was surrounded by paramedics."

"Was Dr. Weimar with Mr. Hernandez when you approached?"

"I didn't know who he was at the time. But having met him during the lawsuit, I now know he was with the group of people with Mr. Hernandez when I got to his car. They were treating him, and Dr. Weimar was getting into the ambulance as I approached."

"Did you speak with Mrs. Hernandez at the scene of the accident?"

"Yes, I did. It was several minutes later. I don't know exactly how much later. We...Rose and I were standing around waiting for the police to do their job and she walked up to us. She was very pleasant, smiling, and asked how we were doing. I told her we were fine and had no injuries except for the shock from the impact."

"Anything else Mrs. Hernandez talked to you about?"

"Well, she said she was driving home. I thought that was strange since her husband was injured and was taken to the hospital. I would have thought she would drive to the hospital instead."

"Are you sure she told you she was driving home?"

"I'm certain she said that. She even drove in a different direction from where the ambulance was headed. It was strange. Very strange."

## 33 VIDEO

### Isabela, Puerto Rico
### The Same Day

When Pamela arrived at the Regal Isabela resort she was tired and not really looking forward to it. The long flight took its toll on her. She was stressed from having to leave her father again. This time, however, he wasn't alone. At least her older brother, Cameron, was spending the weekend at her house to take care of their father. Even her sister, Milagros, agreed to drop by on occasion to check on their father. All of her family working together to care for her father brought Pamela some relief. Just not enough to keep her from worrying altogether.

The additional stress and worry wreaking havoc on Pamela's mental health was caused by the unknown whereabouts of Daniel Mendoza. She still had not heard from him or learned what happened to him since she left Puerto Rico earlier the previous week. Her senior investigator, George, already traveled to Puerto Rico from Florida and laid the groundwork for her arrival. He was waiting for her in the lobby.

"How was your flight?" George asked as he grabbed her luggage and gave it to the hotel employee to place on the golf cart to take to the casita.

The accommodations were comped for Pamela by Gerald Ravan himself.

"Thank you, George. I'm a little exhausted. I tried to sleep on the plane. The flight was packed with no room to stretch out. I just couldn't take the company jet back. It wasn't right. Not when Gerry was still in Arizona visiting my father," she explained.

George agreed.

Realizing the seriousness of her mission, Pamela composed herself, focused on why she was there, and asked, "What did you find out? Is Daniel still in the hotel?"

"I checked with everyone and even checked the casita you guys stayed in. He never left the resort. Not willingly, it looks like."

George walked to the golf cart expecting Pamela to follow. She dreaded having to see the casita again but knew she had to eventually face the reality Daniel was missing. She reluctantly climbed into the golf cart and was driven to casita number seven. She opened the unlocked door to the casita and scanned the suite. No one was inside.

"It looks eerie," Pamela said. "So quiet. I can't believe I was just here. It seems so long ago."

She searched the casita as George watched. He didn't want to interrupt her because he knew she needed to concentrate to be on top of her game. The casita was nearly impeccable. It was in stark contrast to the neighboring casita she previously examined with Daniel where everything was strewn everywhere. That casita was a total mess. Seeing this casita the same way it was when she stayed there gave Pamela some hope.

Walking into the bathroom, Pamela remembered soaking in the oversized, rectangular tub and the fresh rose petals floating on the water. Soft jazz played in the background. Daniel shyly fed her some grapes with his eyes partially closed. He didn't want to do it, but she insisted he leave the terrace where he was enjoying the view and give her food while she bathed. She was hungry after all and knew he would comply after putting up a fuss. She shook the memory from her mind and focused on what was important at that moment.

She walked to the bathroom sink. She picked up a toothbrush and razor blade lying on the countertop and examined them.

"These are Daniel's," she said as she showed them to George. "I remember his brand."

She omitted letting George know she also saw these identical hygiene products in Daniel's master bathroom many times before.

*He won't understand,* she convinced herself although she suspected both George and Virginia were aware of her unusual obsession with Daniel due to her work requirements.

"I don't think he left willingly," George reiterated. "The entire casita looks exactly how it would be if Daniel was still staying here."

He knew his boss wanted to see it for herself even if he'd previously described the scene to her when they were in the lobby. Although Pamela completely trusted her investigators, this particular assignment was too personal for her to let them handle it on their own. She needed to be involved in every step of the process even if it annoyed them. George understood and accommodated her in every way he could without taking offense to her decisions.

Once she finished searching the entire casita, Pamela stood in the middle of it, lowered her head, and rested her chin on her closed fist. She then shut her eyes and concentrated intensely. She could faintly smell Daniel's cologne, his body sweat, and the salty air sweeping in from the coast. Her mind pictured the closet she recently examined. All of Daniel's dress clothes he packed for the trip were neatly hanging on the rack. Not one was missing. Even all of his shoes were in the closet. Something seemed out of place, but she couldn't remember exactly what. Then it dawned on her.

"His beach sandals. They're gone," Pamela exclaimed.

She rushed into the bedroom area of the casita, searched under the bed, and opened up the dresser drawers.

"One of his swim trunks is also missing," she added with a smile. "He must have gone to the beach."

The thought gave her relief but was immediately followed with concern. Her smile instantly became a frown. George noticed it.

"I know what you're thinking," George said. "The waters are a little hazardous this time of year. Crashing waves are normal making the rocky coastline even more dangerous. You don't really think..."

"No. Daniel's a great swimmer. However, he prefers to just relax and enjoy the ocean view. I doubt he would have gone into the ocean especially if it was high tide or there were crashing waves."

Although Pamela hadn't gone to the beach herself when she stayed at the resort, she vaguely knew where it was. She remembered seeing a resort map during her previous stay. She found a resort book on the desk and flipped to the page with the resort map. Looking at the map, she saw how the infamous maintenance road where the mysterious guest was taken away in an Escalade was also near the pathway leading to the beach.

"I think if something happened to Daniel, they would have left through this maintenance road," she said while pointing to the road on the map so George could quickly locate it.

Pamela remembered the security guard who gave her access to the video feed for the maintenance road when she was looking into the missing captive guest. She called Gerald Ravan so he could expedite access to the video feed to determine if something also happened to Daniel.

"Thanks, Gerry. I appreciate it," she said before hanging up the call. "He's having one of the guards bring us any relevant video," Pamela told George as she walked onto the terrace. "Can you feel the breeze?"

The warm, Caribbean air swept through her long blonde hair almost causing it to float away from her neck. She was relieved if only for a moment. Before long, a knock at the door disturbed her peace.

"Thank you, sir," George said after receiving a Manilla envelope from the resort employee.

He closed the door and headed towards Pamela. She seemed oblivious to his presence. He wanted to let her enjoy the moment a little longer but knew time was of the essence. Nudging her with the Manilla envelope, Pamela finally awoke from her self-induced trance.

"Sorry, George."

She grabbed the package and opened it. Inside was a USB drive which she assumed had a digital copy of the video feed. Also inside was an eight-by-ten photograph of a black Escalade on the maintenance road. The photo was clearly captured from a video feed. This time the Escalade's license plate was visible.

## 34 HIGHWAY 18

### San Juan, Puerto Rico
### The Same Day

"H*ermano*, it's good to see you again," George said after tightly hugging his long-time friend, Alberto. "I'm impressed. You still look good."

George eyed Alberto up and down as if he was checking out a lovely woman in a classy bar on a Friday night. Alberto was used to this irksome treatment. For whatever reason, George's expressions of brotherly affection no longer disturbed him. Once he realized years ago George was sincere and only intended to make Alberto feel young again despite the passage of rough years, he no longer objected to George's antics.

"You're looking good too if I may say so myself," the older Puerto Rican male expressed with a beaming smile. "I haven't seen you in a while now. What brings you to my island?"

Before George could respond, Alberto's eyes spotted Virginia standing next to George.

"And the lovely lady, who is she?" Alberto seductively inquired as he stepped forward, reached for her hand, and gently pecked the back of it; squeezing a little to emphasize his admiration.

"Why thank you," Virginia gleamed, unsure why his prowess took her off guard.

She was not easily impressed with pickup lines after having heard so many silver-tongued devils flatter her as part of the job. There was something about his handsome looks and Latin charm which mystified her. To the casual observer, Alberto's piercing hazel eyes were the obvious culprit. Many women were captivated by them and unwittingly succumbed to his desires.

George watched the pageantry as if it was a sort of mating ritual he was very accustomed to.

"Alright, alright. We know you're a charmer," George said as he separated the two. "But seriously, we're here on official business."

Alberto stepped back, flicked his black, wavy hair, and turned to George.

"My apologies. Please, let me know what you need. I am at your service."

"No worries, Al. I just need a favor. You owe me from the time we were in Havana."

"I do!! Oh yes, I do. Did he ever tell you about Havana?" Alberto asked Virginia who unexpectedly blushed. "We were in-country on a very secret covert operation. I mean only the top brass knew...."

"Now, you know you're not supposed to talk about any of that with anyone," George said as he glared at Alberto only half-seriously. George loved recanting stories from their youth in the military but only to service men and women, not civilians. He never told civilians what branch he served in or whether he was in the special forces like Pamela. He kept that and how he met Pamela a secret even to his fellow private investigator, Virginia.

"Well, I can regale you some other time if you'd like?" Alberto teased Virginia hoping she would bite at the invitation.

George gently nudged her. Virginia simply smiled instead of answering. Alberto took the hint.

"We're just here to find some information about a vehicle. That's all. A black Escalade," George said while showing Alberto his cell phone containing a photo of the captured video feed.

"I see," Alberto responded while he entered the license plate number into the police computer system to identify the vehicle's owner. "Looks, like a mister Johnny Lozado owns the vehicle."

"Johnny Lozado? That name sounds familiar," George said.

Seeing Alberto's puzzled look, George mouthed something to him so Virginia couldn't hear.

"Let me double-check if it's the Johnny Lozado you are thinking of."

Alberto punched a few more keys on his computer and then said, "Yes. It's definitely him. His photo came up on my computer screen. And I know that face. I will never forget it."

"Well, the boss isn't going to like that," George remarked.

Wanting to ensure they were being thorough and not sleeping on the job, Virginia asked, "Can you check if the Escalade had a GPS tracker installed?"

She smiled to soften her request. He definitely took the bait.

"Sure, let me see." After a few more clicks on his

keyboard, Alberto said, "Looks like this model has a factory GPS installed but the purchaser requested the dealership remove it as a condition of the sale. I'm sorry I couldn't help you with that."

"What about CCTV? Are you able to track the vehicle once it left the Regal Isabela? Maybe you can find out where it is now," she subtly suggested.

"I'm not an expert on that. I dabble on occasion when needed of course, but not too often," Alberto said with a charming smile. This time he sat closer to his computer and intently gazed at the screen while feverishly pushing buttons and clicking the mouse. "There, I found the Escalade at the hotel."

George and Virginia stepped closer to the screen.

"That's great!!" George exclaimed and slapped Alberto on the shoulder.

"Looks like the Escalade headed east on PR-2. That's the highway headed towards San Juan."

"Yeah, we took that highway when we drove here today," George acknowledged.

"Can you zoom in so we can see the passengers?" Virginia asked.

The video became a close-up of the black Escalade speedily traveling the freeway. The trio watched looking for any clues of anyone inside.

"All of the back windows are tinted. We can see into the front windows and the windshield," Alberto said.

"Dammit," George said. "We can see the driver, a young Hispanic male, but no one else. Pam's not going to be happy we can't verify if Daniel's in the Escalade."

"I don't think it'll deter her. She'll want us to track it down and see for ourselves...," Virginia explained.

She almost disclosed who they were looking for but stopped herself before saying it.

"Let me check if the Escalade exited the highway before getting to San Juan. I'm going to check if the Escalade reached the interchange." Alberto switched his view of the CCTV cameras to the one recording the highway interchange. "Yes, it did."

He pointed to the screen where the Escalade merged into PR-22.

"So far, it looks like they're heading to San Juan," Virginia interjected.

"You're correct. Now, let me see if they made it here."

Alberto switched to local CCTV cameras looking for the Escalade. The screen rapidly displayed various views of the capital city.

"There it is," George pointed to a camera feed with the Escalade still driving on a four-lane freeway. "Where is that?"

Alberto looked at the video and replied, "That's Highway 18. They're heading south."

"Can you find out where they went from San Juan?" Virginia asked.

"I can try."

After clicking a few more buttons and trying other alternatives, Alberto eventually admitted defeat.

"I'm sorry my friends but all of the CCTV cameras south of this point on Highway 18 were down for maintenance. They were being upgraded and tested at the time. I can't tell if the Escalade exited the highway or continued south."

"What about any footage on any highways further

223

south of Highway 18?" George asked hoping they would get lucky with a stab in the dark.

"Unfortunately, that part of the island is the mountainous region with very little traffic. There are no cameras in that area," Alberto replied.

"You did your best, my friend. We appreciate all of your help," George stated.

"Your praise means a lot to me, but you know what I want for all my efforts, I want..."

"Of course, I will have the finest bourbon sent to you once I'm back in the States. You earned it."

Alberto smiled and licked his lips in anticipation of receiving the libation.

"That will definitely do," he added.

Once the two friends gave each other a farewell embrace, Alberto gazed into Virginia's eyes with seductive affection. She sneakily placed her business card in his pant pocket. George was none the wiser. Then the two investigators took off in their rental car and headed toward Highway 18.

## 35 CLOSING ARGUMENT

### Phoenix, Arizona
### The Same Day

"All right. Please be seated. The record will show the presence of the jury, the parties, and counsel. Good afternoon, ladies and gentlemen. At this time, the attorneys will give their closing arguments. Mr. Clarkson?" the judge announced.

Doug walked to the middle of the jury box and began his closing arguments.

"Ladies and gentlemen of the jury, my team would like to thank you for the two-week-long consideration and attention in this case. Also, I'd like to thank our co-counsel for their professionalism and the Court and staff for allowing us to try our case and for putting up with us. I think it's a very humbling experience to have someone put their life in your hands and rely on your skill and your talent to achieve justice for them. And that is what Selinda and her children have allowed me to do. And it's humbling, and it's frightening because you don't want to let them down.

"You want to make sure that everything comes out

the right way because they don't get a chance in five years or in ten years to come back. This is their only chance for justice right now. Today. And throughout the course of the trial, I may have done something that you all didn't like, or asked a question that you guys didn't like, or made an argument that you didn't like. Or I may not have let opposing counsel speak and objected to their question. But don't take that out on Selinda or the kids. Any kind of shortcoming I have as an attorney, don't take it out on my clients.

"Verdict is Latin for seek the truth. And that is what I said in my opening statement, that you guys are the seekers of truth. You are the finders of fact. And I indicated that our case needs to be viewed through a common-sense lens, and that common-sense lens will show that Mr. Weaver was at fault for this crash."

Doug looked at the jury as they watched him attentively. One or two jurors had their jury notebooks open and were ready to take notes when Mr. Clarkson said something substantive and critical to the case. He took a step closer to the jury box and continued.

"And throughout the entirety of the testimony these past two weeks, the answer has been a resounding yes, consistently. The judge has given you some jury instructions. And before I get into what we discussed these past weeks, I want to talk about one jury instruction, the preponderance of the evidence – more true than not. It may sound confusing, but it's really simple on a basic level. We all have seen Lady Justice with the blindfold and the scales that are even. All my clients have to do to fulfill our burden is to ever so slightly change those scales. A grain of salt or a feather will allow us to meet our burden, but we have done more than that these past weeks. We have shown that Mr. Weaver was at fault, clearly.

"Our version of events makes sense because it's true. Michael McDowell's account of events matches the physical evidence because it's true. The defense has tried to manufacture what happened, but Mr. Weaver and Mr. Kominski's accounts are diametrically opposed to the physical evidence. They have no foundation. And like a house with a bad foundation, it's going to collapse. The plaintiffs' case is true. The plaintiffs' case makes sense from a common-sense perspective.

"You've heard from Michael McDowell, plaintiff's expert reconstructionist, a former detective of the city of Phoenix, seven-and-a-half years investigating vehicular crimes. He testified that Mr. Weaver was traveling faster and was coming up from Mr. Hernandez's rear; it is undisputed that Mr. Weaver was over the speed limit. Mr. McDowell testified that Mr. Weaver drifted into Mr. Hernandez's lane, pulling him forward. And then because of the speed differential, the Lexus did a clockwise spin causing Mr. Hernandez to be ejected from his vehicle."

A photo of the accident scene was displayed on all monitors for the jury to see.

"You've seen numerous photos of Mr. Hernandez's Lexus and the location of the accident. The defense's own accident reconstructionist testified that a lazy drift takes two or three seconds. It wouldn't have taken place according to the defense. In his theory, it only takes place with an intentional move, an intentional move to get from one lane to the next but there is absolutely no evidence of that.

227

None. Mr. Sineda, plaintiff's traffic engineer's opinion is also clear. There is an offset. If the striping moves, the lane is moving. You saw a picture from Mr. Sineda, who was with the City of Phoenix Traffic Department for twenty—plus years. He took the picture showing the lane in which Mr. Weaver was traveling and you could clearly see the offset.

"We're dealing with a car collision; we're not dealing with a plane collision. We see what we see on the road. We've all driven. We see from that perspective daily how a road moves, how a road changes. And for all of you that may be photographers or have interests in any kind of photographs or any kind of pictures, it's clear that the picture on the monitor right now that's the most realistic picture, not from above. We're driving; we're not flying."

The photo of the accident scene was removed from the monitors. In its place was a montage of photos showing the Hernandez family: an individual photo of Carlos and then of Selinda, wedding photos, photos of the couple in a hospital room with their newborn baby, photos of Carlos playing with the kids, Carlos grilling food on a BBQ and the kids laughing and being silly, vacation photos, and a photo of his headstone at the cemetery with the inscription - "Loving Father, Husband, Son, and Sibling." Doug Clarkson waited for the jury to absorb all of the photos before continuing.

"Now what happened to Carlos really isn't in much dispute. You heard Dr. Weimar testify that he was ejected from the Lexus. As a result, his head hit the ground causing a fatal head injury. Those were Dr. Weimar's words. This tragic accident is perma-

228

nent. Carlos is not coming back. Sadly, his wife and kids will never see him again. Never.

"And sometimes at the end of trials, juries say, well, I wish you would've told me what you wanted to ask for. I don't like that you asked me to just come up with a number. So I think what I'm going to do now is show you what I think would be a just settlement for Selinda based on what the Hernandez family has gone through, and what they will go through. If you look at your jury instructions, you will see that if you find for Selinda Hernandez, usually the items that you must provide for what has happened to them. We're going to take it out of order. Number three, reasonable expenses of necessary medical care treatment and services rendered. We need you to award the $166,000 for the ambulance and the hospital bills. They made a valiant effort to save Carlos.

"Item number two is for pain and suffering. Selinda talked in great detail about the pain she suffers as a result of the loss of her husband and the pain the children suffer. Selinda talked in detail about how she can't sleep like she once did. We all know what sleep deprivation does to us. It affects us mentally, physically, and causes a variety of issues. But most of all the suffering of losing your spouse, your provider, and the father of your children is immeasurable.

Doug turned to his clients with a look of compassion. Selinda and both children faced him and then the jury. He then continued his closing argument.

"Now the jury instruction also allows you to award what Carlos would have earned and could have provided for his children and his wife had he stayed alive and never was involved in this fatal crash. The instructions indicate Carlo's additional life expectancy is forty-five years. There is the loss of enjoyment of life, that is, participation in life's activities, we talked about the things that Selinda can no longer do with her husband or what the children can no longer do with their father. We've assigned one hundred thousand dollars a year for that loss over the course of forty-five years which in total is four point five million dollars. What we're asking this jury to do is return a verdict in the amount of six million dollars to make Selinda and the children whole. Now six million dollars is a number that I think is just. You may not. It's your prerogative to go lower or higher; the jury decides. This is not a runaway verdict. This is a number that is commensurate with what Selinda and the children have undergone and what they will undergo in the future.

"I've had the distinct honor of representing Selinda these past few years. And I have the unbelievable ability to represent victims of horrible, horrible tragedies as part of my work and see some of the worst things imaginable. People that are broken, people that pass away, people that lose so much, and those are tragedies. But what sticks out about Selinda is the way she perseveres, her toughness. No matter how many times she gets knocked down, she gets back up. She continues to fight and to take care of her children. She is one that will never relent. She is dogged, dogged in her pursuit of justice.

"When I was a history major at Arizona State University and I remember, my sophomore year I was taking a class about the American Revolution. And there was a quote from Benjamin Franklin that kind of put me on the path to law school. He said justice will not be served unless those who are unaffected are as outraged as those who are. I hope we've affected you during these weeks in Selinda's pursuit of justice. I hope we've shown you the way. Thank you.

Doug Clarkson sat down next to Selinda. Judge Furman looked at the clock and noticed it was nearing five p.m. Turning to the jury, she said, "Looks like we are out of time. We are going to adjourn until tomorrow morning."

"All rise," the bailiff announced.

## 36  CELL PHONE

San Juan, Puerto Rico
The Same Day

As the white rental car accelerated onto Highway 18, George and Virginia wondered where Daniel Mendoza could have been taken and why Johnny Lozado would have kidnapped him from the Regal Isabela resort. They were at a loss having no idea what transpired once Pamela left Puerto Rico early to be by her father's side. All they knew was he was missing and had not made contact with Pamela, the firm, or even any of his family members or friends, including Corina, a woman Daniel recently pursued. He would have contacted Corina at the very least if he was safe especially because she had finally reached out to him wanting to spend more time together. It didn't make sense to them, but should it have?

George and Virginia really only knew Daniel as part of their working relationship with Pamela. They surreptitiously surveilled him at times even though he was their client. Why? They didn't exactly know. All they knew was that Pamela asked them to do it and so they complied. During those times, they found nothing strange or dubious about Daniel. He was a dedicated attorney with no family life and very few friends, most of whom lived out of state. Other than work and sometimes attending live theater often by himself, Daniel hadn't exhibited any unscrupulous behavior. Even his relationship with Gerald Ravan was strictly professional. How or why he was involved with the Puerto Rican mafia was a mystery.

"Johnny? Johnny Lozado is a pimp if you will. He's a member of *La Familia*, one of the largest Puerto Rican mafias on the island. They're huge with their greedy tendrils into everything - drugs, gambling, prostitution, guns, booze. And it's not just on the island. *La Familia* traffics their goods from Central and South America to the States or to other Caribbean islands. Being part of the United States and a huge coastline makes Puerto Rico an ideal segue for *La Familia* to conduct its international business," George explained after Virginia inquired about the owner of the Escalade and who he was.

George knew it was only a matter of time before Virginia asked him how he knew this notorious family and whether he was involved himself somehow. He wanted to avoid the conversation as much as possible given his desire to keep his background hidden and of course, his secretive nature. After conveying a rudimentary knowledge of *La Familia*, George decided the tactic to avoid further discussion was to switch topics.

"I saw you eyeing Alberto back there. Don't deny it," he said.

"I'm not going to deny it. He is a handsome man,

but that's all. I was just enjoying the view." Virginia grinned.

"Good. I've known Alberto for a long time. We... we've spent a lot of free time together and he is a heartbreaker if you know what I mean. I'm not going to call him a womanizer. He's on the brink of that. But he's my friend. I've seen him break a lot of hearts over the years and the last thing I want him to do is break..."

"I'm a big girl, George. I don't need your protection. Everyone is entitled to have fun every once in a while, even me. What I choose to do and with whom is my business...my business. Not yours."

"Okay. I'll back off. I did my duty and I warned you. You won't be able to deny that," he said before realizing it came across as she would inevitably experience a heartache like the rest of the playthings Alberto dabbled with. "I'm not saying you're going to fall for his charms," he added to lessen the blow. "I'm just saying..."

"You don't want to tell me 'I told you so' in the future. I know you, George. I appreciate your concerns and I heard you."

Seeing the seriousness of her expression, George decided to let it go. After all, they were on a mission even if it seemed a hopeless one at this point.

Virginia grabbed her cell phone and dialed Pamela's number. She looked at her phone, but it continued displaying "dialing."

"The reception is bad here," she said. "Real bad."

"Which phone carrier do you have?" George asked.

"I have AT&T."

"There you go. I don't know if you noticed all

those *Claro* signs we passed since we left the Regal Isabela. But that's the main phone company on the island. You can still use other carriers, but they just have spotty service. Use my phone. It's Verizon. They work in conjunction with *Claro*."

Handing his phone to her, Virginia then called Pamela.

"Hi, Virginia. Any news?" Pamela's voice was stern yet still worrisome.

"We've tracked down who owns the Escalade. Some guy named Johnny Lozado," she responded.

She heard Pamela gasp. Not wanting to alarm them further, Pamela didn't address her knowledge of the owner.

"Did you guys track the vehicle?"

"We can't. It doesn't have GPS. We're just heading in the direction of the vehicle's last known position but, to be honest, this is going to be extremely difficult. We'll never find the Escalade by just driving around aimlessly," Virginia admitted unsure it was the right thing to say in light of her boss's concerns for Daniel's well-being.

"Let me see what I can do," Pamela said before ending the call.

"She's going to call us back, I suppose," Virginia told George.

"Good," George replied.

He let off the gas so he wasn't traveling farther than necessary if Pamela had other directions they should be headed.

"So were you really in Havana?" Virginia asked unexpectedly.

She wanted to pass the time while they waited. George thought he dodged the topic.

"It was a long time ago. Way before I met you and way before I met Pam."

"So when you were young, like me?"

"Yeah, those were the good ole days. No worries. Excitement. Fun."

"But it couldn't have been fun if you were there on...what did Alberto say...a covert operation. Sounds serious."

"He was exaggerating," George said hoping to throw her off track. He knew she was a seasoned investigator with dogged determination, a lot like Pamela. He had a hand in training her and knew she wouldn't give up easily. "You know I'm not all work. I love to have fun. At that age, I couldn't turn down a dare, even a dangerous one. I've grown out of it. Somewhat."

George smirked. Virginia wasn't sure if it was due to his recent comment or memories of his past adventures. She wondered if they were gallant, sordid, or both. She suspected they were both.

George's phone rang and Virginia answered.

"I contacted one of my connections," Pamela said. "We think we know where Daniel's at. We tracked his cellphone number to some city about thirty miles south of San Juan. I'll send you the coordinates."

Virginia was relieved they finally had another lead.

"Good. We're on our way," Virginia said while she signaled to George the good news.

"I'm on my way. I'll be there too," Pamela insisted.

"I've got the coordinates," Virginia announced. "Keep going south."

"Yes, ma'am," George said.

———

When the rental car finally arrived at the coordinates, George parked a little distance away so they would walk up to the site without drawing attention to themselves. The neighborhood was upscale with primarily locals living there as indicated by the aroma of Puerto Rican food filling the air along with Latin music blaring from practically every home. Exiting the vehicle, they wandered as if they were lost tourists pretending to enjoy the views. Noticing they weren't being followed or stared at by the neighbors, they walked closer.

"I don't see the Escalade," Virginia said as they approached.

"It may be in a carport or in a garage and not parked on the street," he suggested while scanning the homes for the wanted Escalade.

She wondered which of the homes had Daniel inside. The neighborhood didn't seem like a bastion of crime, but perhaps it was a lair for criminals to escape the big city and enjoy the town as a weekend getaway. Looking at George's phone, Virginia realized the coordinates were not for the inside of a home but actually on the side of the road. She quickened her pace. George did as well.

Bending over, she picked up a cell phone with a significantly cracked screen. When she touched the home button, a dim photo of Daniel standing in a sentry box at Fort El Morro appeared.

237

## 37  THE CITY OF FOG

Cayey, Puerto Rico
The Same Day

When Virginia picked up the shattered cell phone, she showed it to George. He too noticed the faint picture of Daniel Mendoza on the screen and then entered the passcode to unlock the phone. Checking the call history, George noticed there had been no calls made for the past few days. A couple of missed calls were received from Corina Walker and a few from Cheryl, the receptionist at the law firm. Even Marissa and John called once or twice.

"How did you know the passcode?" Virginia asked.

"Don't you remember the assignment Pam gave me during the royalty case? I had to check his cell phone to see if Daniel was receiving threatening calls or text messages about the Shirvani murder or any other of the murders because Pam was concerned about his safety. She knew he wouldn't tell her about it. She'd seen Daniel enter his passcode a couple of times and gave it to me to check on occasion when he...he wasn't looking."

George's devious smile was telling. Virginia glared at him with suspicion while wondering if he took liberties with his "assignment."

"I only did what she told me to do. I didn't do anything else. I promise. I'm no pervert."

"You better not have. Pam wouldn't like that."

"What do you think? There were photos of Daniel and some woman being...you know...intimate?"

"We've been in this business forever. We've both seen things we've never suspected even from the nicest of people."

"I'm there with you on that but I wasn't tasked with finding out dirt about Daniel. At least..."

George decided it was better to leave the topic alone before he put his foot further in his mouth and couldn't get it out. He knew Virginia would never let it go even as the conversation stood. Anything more would only make her future interrogations on the topic worse.

"Forget it for now. We need to focus on finding him instead of any gossip," Virginia said as she turned away from George to the street.

Looking at the neighboring homes, Virginia saw a few people muddling about. One particular elderly woman was staring at them apparently because they stood out. Virginia smiled but the woman's face remained stoic.

"She clearly doesn't like us being here," Virginia said to George.

"It's okay. She's probably a part of the informal neighborhood watch. It's typical of the island. People here are friendly once they get to know you. Let's go say 'Hi' and see if she knows anything that can help us."

Virginia reluctantly agreed.

"*Buenos días, señora*," George said as he approached the woman.

She was pleased he spoke Spanish. She conversed with him in her native tongue. Virginia listened as the two engaged in a lively discussion as if they had been friends for decades. She smiled and wildly gesticulated at times until she pointed in a particular direction to indicate something to George.

"*Gracias*," he said and then hugged her.

"*De nada*," the woman rejoined after patting him on the back before entering her house.

Staring at him for answers, George finally explained, "She's invited us for dinner later. I told her we are busy but might make it. *Bistec y arroz con habichuelas*. Sounds delicious. You'd like it..."

"Not that. About the case. What did she say about the case?"

"Oh, she was very helpful. She watches this neighborhood like a hawk and sees everything. She remembers seeing the black Escalade a few days ago. Someone tossed the cell phone out the window. She saw a man wearing a black hood in the back seat before the window rolled up. Lucky for us, she knows that Escalade. She's seen it many times in the past and told me where it went. It's not too far from here."

"Great. I'll let Pam know."

Virginia texted Pamela what the two learned and where they were headed.

The rental car headed south on Highway PR-52 and snaked through the mountains and lovely scenery until the pair of investigators reached the higher elevation with another neighborhood of affluent locals. Knowing the approximate location of the Escalade, this time they parked in a driveway at a home the elderly woman told George would be temporarily vacant because the residents were visiting relatives in the States.

Still inside the rental car, Virginia took out her binoculars and scoped out the house where the Escalade was parked. The two-story residence seemed tranquil. Palm trees and elm trees laced the rear of the house and along its sides. A mountain range could be seen in the distance. A large balcony above the two-car garage had two exterior doors.

"Looks like the bigger door leads to the master bedroom," Virginia whispered to George as if someone was listening besides him. "The smaller door may lead to another bedroom. What do you think?"

She handed George the binoculars, who then spied the house himself.

"Could be. It could also just be a second door for a very large master bedroom. I've seen similar designs before. A secondary bedroom isn't going to be right next to the master bedroom. They're usually on the opposite side of the house. If Daniel's in this house, my bet is he's kept in a bedroom in the back away from the street."

He handed her back the binoculars.

"Then we can't confirm he's inside from the street. We'll have to get closer," Virginia explained.

"That's risky. It won't be an easy task without tipping off the kidnappers."

"I'm up for it."

"Are you kidding me? We can't make any more moves without the boss giving us the green light."

"I'm sure she will. Call her," Virginia responded while still gazing through the binoculars at the house.

He complied with the request.

"Yeah, we're here," George said into his cell phone. "No, we haven't seen anyone. Just the Escalade. The woman said there were two individuals in the front seats. She's seen them before but doesn't know their names. No one does." He stopped talking and listened. "Okay."

After ending the call, George told Virginia, "She's going to be here in about ten minutes and will check it out herself."

"Okay."

Virginia was secretly relieved.

"Do we still have any snacks?" George asked. "I'm starving."

"Check the glove compartment," Virginia replied.

Opening it, George found a candy bar, a package of cheese cracker sandwiches, and a bag of plantain chips. He gave Virginia a snarky look.

"It's all I could find in the vending machine at the rental place. Don't blame me?"

"It'll do for now."

He ate a couple of chips but dreamed of the Puerto Rican meal the elderly woman promised. It brought some joy to his otherwise frustrating day.

*I'll have to thank her for all of her help. It was invaluable*, he reminded himself.

Putting another chip in his mouth, George was about to start chewing again when he saw something that caught his attention.

"Hey..."

The chip fell out of his mouth before he could finish. He pointed in a direction to alert Virginia of his concerns.

Using the binoculars, Virginia spotted a person crouching close to the property they were staking out.

"It's Pamela," she announced.

———

The weather was cooler than she expected but Pamela wasn't distracted by it or the higher elevation. She was focused on one thing and one thing only: verifying whether Daniel was inside the residence. She hoped he was safe and alive but that was a secondary concern at the moment.

Hiding behind one of the large trees in the neighbor's yard, Pamela checked the front door and the adjacent windows to determine if anyone was inside. From what she could see, the front rooms were devoid of any individuals. She sneaked to the next tree closer to the house. Nothing seemed out of the ordinary until she saw one of the side windows was covered with what appeared to be aluminum foil. The rest of the windows on that side of the house weren't covered up.

*This is strange for a rich neighborhood*, Pamela thought as she scanned the area for the kidnapers.

The place seemed empty, so she quickly crouch-walked to the covered window. Noticing the aluminum foil on the bottom left of the window was peeled upward, Pamela moved her body to look through the gap inside. She saw a near-empty room. Facing her with a blindfold on was Daniel Mendoza. His head was down, and the rest of his body wasn't moving. She wasn't sure if he was unconscious. Turning her head to see the rest of the room, she saw a young, Puerto Rican male enter the room and walk to a second chair with a male restrained to it. Pamela could only see the back of the person's head.

## 38  INTERRUPTION

Cayey, Puerto Rico
Moments Later

"Y ou want some chips?" George asked Virginia as he crunched on a couple himself.

She looked at the near-empty bag and then back at George.

"No. It's the last thing on my mind."

"They're not bad for local chips."

As he plopped another one into his mouth, the rear passenger door opened and quickly shut. George looked in the rear-view mirror and saw Pamela seated in the back. She was calm and collected like she normally is when faced with adverse assignments. But this was different. It involved one of her clients and a close one at that. George and Virginia were surprised she was still serene despite her personal stake in the outcome. Not to mention the distractions she'd been dealing with the past week with her father in the hospital. They had always admired her for her fortitude but today their admiration reached a higher level.

Pleased she was taking a hands-on approach, George asked, "Boss, what's the sitrep?"

The two investigators turned around to face their boss. They were apprehensive to hear the news.

"He's in there. I saw him tied up with another guy. It may be the guest at the resort we witnessed being abducted. It may be someone else. I really don't know. But I definitely saw Daniel."

"Good," Virginia said with a sense of relief their hard work paid off and the mystery was finally solved.

"Where is he?" George anxiously asked.

"He's in a room in the back of the house. I'm not sure if he's unconscious or not or even if he's alive. He didn't move when one of the kidnappers entered the room to check on the other guy."

Pamela's voice never trembled while speaking even though both George and Virginia knew she was concerned about his safety. Even they were. Virginia reached over and touched Pamela's knee. She appreciated the gesture.

"How many tangos are in the house?" George inquired, wanting to distract her from any disturbing thoughts about Daniel's well-being.

"At least two. Possibly three. I circled around the back of the house and looked inside all of the windows. Looks like there's a young male and an older one watching over them. But it was bizarre. They were unsettled like something recently happened," Pamela responded.

"You don't think they will...," Virginia pondered.

"They would have done it by now if that was their intent," Pamela sternly remarked. "Daniel's face was bruised. I think he's been tortured like the guest who was tortured at the resort. I think they want something from them. I just don't know what it could be."

Pamela pushed out the memory of casita number eight from her mind so she could concentrate on the present. The last thing she wanted to visualize was Daniel being mortally wounded. She contemplated telling them about the multiple deep holes she saw dug in the backyard. She wasn't sure if it was relevant to rescuing Daniel and the other male. She also didn't want to distract them with needless information. She wanted them focused on one thing - rescuing Daniel.

"Well, we outnumber them," George concluded. "I think we should go for it. What do you say, boss?"

He looked at her hoping she would give the green light to extract Daniel. For the first time, he saw hesitation in Pamela's eyes. Even Virginia noticed it. Pamela was deep in thought.

After mulling it over briefly, Pamela asked, "Your friend, Alberto. Do you think he can get us the plans for this house? I don't want to go in there blind."

"He has connections. I'm sure he will do what he can for us. He still owes me."

When Pamela nodded giving her approval, George dialed his friend and made the request. He explained to Alberto the true reasons why they were in Puerto Rico and needed the information about the black Escalade. George then apologized for omitting it when they were in person together in San Juan. Realizing George was sincere, and this was a personal request, Alberto was eager to provide what was needed.

"Now, you'll owe me," he declared to George who wasn't happy to be in that position.

"If you say so," George coyly replied.

Alberto picked up a pad and pen and asked George for the information needed to obtain the relevant document. "The name of the City?"

"Cayey...9692," he told Alberto when he inquired about the house's street number.

"I'll call you back."

"*Gracias, hermano.*"

George gave Pamela the thumbs up. He was also pleased his connections were useful to their mission.

Within five minutes, George's cell phone buzzed. He received a text message with the blueprints for the house. In turn, he forwarded the text to Virginia and Pamela.

"I told you he could do it," George grinned.

Pulling up the blueprints, Pamela said, "It looks like the kidnappers are watching television in the family room." She pointed to it on her phone as she explained the plan. "Daniel's in this room. I will enter from here and I need you guys to take out the kidnappers."

"This is a good entry point," George said as he pointed to a patio door on the opposite side of the house closest to the family room.

"Agreed," Pamela said.

"We can do this!!" George excitedly exclaimed while opening his windbreaker and flipping open the leather flap to his shoulder holster. He then quickly removed his gun. "I'm ready. I'm always ready."

His devious smile returned after disengaging the safety.

Pamela also pulled out her concealed gun and looked at Virginia.

"I didn't bring mine. Sorry. I had no idea it would lead to anything like this," she confessed.

"Here." George handed her his second gun holstered on his left side. "I know you can handle yourself with all those practice sessions. Just point and shoot like we trained."

Virginia awkwardly nodded despite desperately wanting to hide her misgivings. She mustered the strength to proceed.

As George was about to open the car door, another black Escalade approached the home, drove up the driveway, and parked in front of the garage. Two men exited the vehicle and knocked on the front door. The younger captor opened the door and let them in.

## Cayey, Puerto Rico
## Later That Night

With the moonlight shining on her back, Virginia positioned her body so she could kick down the side patio door. Before she could strike the door, George tapped her shoulder, walked in front of her, and twisted the door knob.

"This is Puerto Rico. People trust their neighbors." He then grinned before slowly opening the door and entered.

Pointing his gun to his left and then his right, once he confirmed the entry point was clear, George walked further into the home. Virginia followed aiming her gun as well. The two headed to the family room where Pamela had verified the occupants were hunkering down while guarding the captives. During the previous hours, Pamela confirmed a second time the captors were primarily in the family room after the two additional men arrived on the premises.

Light, sounds, and voices emanating from the family room confirmed Pamela's intel was still reliable. As they neared the family room entryway, George looked around the corner seeing two men sitting on a couch watching television. They were laughing and drinking beer oblivious to the ensuing circumstance.

"This fool is funny," one male said to the other and then swigged some more beer. He burped loudly and lazily wiped his mouth with his sleeve.

"He is," the other male agreed while burping louder as a sign of his superior prowess compared to his companion.

George turned his head toward Virginia to get her attention. He then faced the two men and made a circle with his index finger and thumb while pointing his other fingers, extended, at the two men. Virginia acknowledged his signal by nodding. With his hand above his head, George pointed to the left side of the family room and motioned Virginia to cover that area. He indicated he'd cover the right side. Stealthily entering the left side of the room, Virginia continued further when her hip inadvertently touched a lamp on a nightstand causing it to tip over. The noise startled the two men who quickly turned around to face the rear of the room.

Seeing Virginia and George aggressively pointing guns at them, the two men panicked and jumped to their feet. One male jumped over the couch, lunging at Virginia. She shot twice putting him down. Fearful he would suffer the same fate, the other male raised both his hands allowing George to restrain him.

At the same time, Pamela entered the house through the rear door and scurried toward the room she knew Daniel and the other gentlemen were restrained in. She faced no opposition which pleased her and worried her at the same time. Opening the door to the room, Pamela rushed toward Daniel who panicked because he was unable to see who entered due to his blindfold. Wondering if another beating was forthcoming, Daniel braced himself for the impact.

Sensing his anxiety, Pamela whispered, "It's me."

Recognizing her voice, Daniel sighed in relief. His body loosened.

"Pamela," he quivered.

She hushed him worried the other occupants would hear.

"Yes, it's me."

She removed his blindfold. Untying his restraints, Pamela then assisted Daniel in standing. His muscles were mildly atrophied in addition to his body being bruised. He stumbled getting up. Pamela kept him from falling.

A bullet whizzed by Pamela's head. A second bullet almost grazed her shoulder. Pamela turned towards the door and saw the younger captor nervously aiming a gun at her. He was obviously an inexperienced shooter. Realizing hitting his targets was more complicated than he expected, he looked for the older captor who was busy removing the other captive from the room. The younger one followed the older one out.

As Pamela looked on in the confusion, she wondered whether George and Virginia successfully restrained the two men in the family room or if they would soon enter the room to prevent her from rescuing Daniel. She preemptively aimed her gun at the door. When no one entered, she resumed taking care of Daniel.

"Were you hit?" she asked Daniel.

He feverishly checked his body for any bullets. Pamela checked as well.

"No, I wasn't."

She was pleased with his response, grabbed and held him tight, and unexpectedly kissed him on the lips. Confused by her overt display of affection, he originally was taken aback. However, he could not resist her at that moment and started kissing her back. He immediately stopped after remembering he still liked Corina and still wanted something between them.

Daniel backed up and looked at Pamela. He didn't know why she expressed herself in that way at this moment amidst the danger and uncertainty. It was totally unlike her.

"What are you...," Daniel asked.

Pamela brushed the comment off with her own confused look, shrugged her shoulders, and implied she had no idea what he was talking about. She then continued helping him walk outside the room by holding him with her left arm across his back. Her right hand held her gun tightly. Daniel limped forward using all of his strength to exit the room. It was the moment he'd been waiting for all through the darkness of the past days. He wasn't sure how many days passed. All he knew was he wanted, no he needed, his freedom.

When they exited the door to the backyard, Daniel smiled. The cool Caribbean night was refreshing. He felt alive again. He was pleased Pamela came to rescue him although at times he doubted she even knew what happened and would come to his rescue. As he happily continued hobbling through the backyard with Pamela's assistance, a man charged at them.

"Stop," the man commanded.

He was dressed in fashionable clothing unlike the men guarding the captives. Pamela noticed he was aiming a gun at them. She froze. So did Daniel.

"I'm just here for my friend," she said after surmising the man was a local resident and unlikely affiliated with the mafia holding Daniel and the other captive.

"I don't know who you are, but you're not welcome here," he said as he took a few more steps closer to them.

"Sir, please step aside. I don't want to hurt you," Pamela replied.

The man gave her a strange, territorial look.

"You're in no position to tell me what to do," he said before noticing she also had a gun in her hand now aimed at him.

She looked menacingly at the local hoping he'd still back down. Out of the shadows, another individual walked towards them from behind the local man.

*Just what I needed. More tangos*, Pamela thought.

Daniel became increasingly worried.

The second male aimed his weapon at the man in front of him rather than Pamela.

"Drop the gun," he told the well-dressed man.

"Cameron?!!" Pamela said as her voice echoed in the night.

## 40  ILLNESS

Phoenix, Arizona
The Next Morning

After the bailiff announced the jurors were entering the courtroom, the entire gallery rose including the attorneys and their clients to show respect to the jury. Once the jurors were seated, the judge instructed everyone else to sit down. She then welcomed the jurors and also the parties.

Facing the jury, Judge Furman said, "I want to thank you for your patience. Yesterday, we were unable to finish closing arguments. Today, the defendants have their closing arguments and then Mr. Clarkson can make a rebuttal."

The jurors nodded as they were eager to hear what the defendants had to say.

"Ms. Robles?"

Marissa stood up and walked to the lectern in the middle of the courtroom.

"Thank you, your honor. May it please the Court? Ladies and gentlemen of the jury, we've sat through all the evidence and the testimony these past two weeks. You know what the simple issue is in this case, and that's who caused the accident. They claim that Martin drifted into Mr. Hernandez's lane. We claim that Mr. Hernandez entered into Martin's lane, causing the accident, and that his unfortunate death is his fault. You're going to be able to review all of the evidence again with all of the exhibits, and it's up to you to decide what happened."

Noticing the first exhibit hadn't appeared on the monitors, Marissa walked to the defense counsel's table and conferred with John Davis to resolve any of the technical issues. An aerial view of the accident location suddenly appeared on the monitors. She then returned to the lectern.

"Sorry, it's a little -- it's a little slow. We should have set it up sooner," Marissa said with a nervous smile she hoped the jury didn't notice. "One of the things plaintiffs' Counsel said repeatedly while he was cross-examining witnesses is, you have to be attentive; you have to know your surroundings. They seem to imply that Martin wasn't attentive, but that's not true. We proved that he was attentive. What did he testify to? He testified that as he was going westbound on Camelback Road, he saw Mr. Hernandez's Lexus making his right turn from 68th Street. He was aware the Lexus turned into the middle lane. Unfortunately, Mr. Hernandez wasn't able to testify if he was aware of the shuttle bus Martin was driving. But we do have the motorcyclist who was riding behind the Lexus. You remember his testimony. What did he testify to? As the motorcyclist is traveling west on Camelback Road, he noticed Mr. Hernandez didn't look into his side-view mirrors and didn't turn his head to look at the lane to his left. Mr. Hernandez is not aware of his surroundings. The motorcyclist said the entire time Mr. Hernandez was looking straight. He was looking straight."

Marissa held out both her arms to emphasize the direction Mr. Hernandez was looking.

"Martin's very familiar with these roads since he's been working at the Regal Phoenix Resort and Spa for over twenty years and has to use this particular road to get to the resort. He's been very consistent during his original recorded statement given to the adjuster several years ago, his deposition testimony taken by Mr. Clarkson before trial, and even his trial testimony earlier this week that he was always in the left lane. He stayed in the left lane, and Mr. Hernandez hit him. Remember what the motorcyclist testified to. After the accident, the motorcyclist came up to the Weavers and asked them how they were doing. The motorcyclist testified that Martin told him the same thing shortly after the accident: the Lexus hit him. Martin hasn't been inconsistent. So it's not the truth to say he was inattentive. He was attentive. On the other hand, Mr. Hernandez never knew the shuttle bus was in the left lane.

"I want to show you Exhibit 95. Remember this exhibit? This is the photo of Camelback Road, but Exhibit 95 is the one that I had the plaintiffs' accident reconstructionist, Mike McDowell, draw on. And remember he made these drawings as to how the street was? And he kept on saying, well, this picture is compressed, compressed. He said that three times, compressed. He also said, this picture makes it look like the lateral offset was right there -- and he testified the offset was further up about sixty feet from the intersection. This photograph isn't the truth; this isn't the truth."

Pointing to the monitors showing the distorted Exhibit 95, Marissa shook her head in disapproval. The jurors looked on in silence not giving away whether they agreed with her argument.

"What was the truth? Dr. Kominsky, the defendants' traffic engineering expert, showed you the 360-degree model he made of the accident scene. The model showed the offset wasn't as pronounced as this exhibit makes it out to be. You saw the model with your own eyes. That was the truth, not this."

"Can you switch?," Marissa told John who displayed another exhibit on the monitors.

The monitors showed an excerpt of the jury instructions.

"The judge instructed you as to the burden of proof in this case. Plaintiffs must prove Martin Weaver was at fault for the accident, Mr. Hernandez was fatally injured, and their damages. We've proven over the past two weeks Mr. Hernandez was at fault, and his unfortunate death was a result of his own negligence. It's sad that he passed away and my client has expressed his condolences, but the Weavers were not responsible for that. Mr. Hernandez entered into our lane. And we're confident that when you review all of the evidence and what you've heard, what you've seen, you'll come to that same conclusion."

Another exhibit appeared on the monitors.

"This is Exhibit 83, remember? The defendants' accident reconstructionist, Hank Richardson, said he took this photo with his drone. He located where the gouge mark was which is where the red arrow is pointing to."

Marissa pointed to the area of the photo where the arrow was so the jurors could clearly see the gouge mark.

"Based upon the speeds the vehicles were traveling, he calculated where the actual impact would be. It was south of the gouge because we know the impact isn't at the gouge because the gouge occurred after the Lexus spun. And he calculated the original impact was twenty-nine feet south of the gouge. And at that point, the lateral offset is only six inches, not five feet; that's the number that you heard from Mr. Sineda, the plaintiffs' traffic engineer. Plaintiffs' experts claim that Martin drifted into the middle lane because there was a five-foot offset he didn't notice and he failed to follow the actual lane because he was distracted.

"The truth is there was no drifting, no drifting. Martin's shuttle bus didn't drift into the middle lane. How do we know that? You heard all four experts who testified. Mr. Sineda and Mr. McDowell both testified there was no physical evidence that Martin was drifting. No physical evidence. There was no testimony from Martin that he was drifting, none at all. And there's no testimony that he was inattentive. That was just speculation; speculation isn't the truth.

"The worst part about it is they didn't even bother to calculate where the impact occurred. I think, even Mr. McDowell— he pawned it off. He said that wasn't my job. Was that a search for the truth? He was an accident reconstructionist just like Hank. If Hank could figure it out, couldn't he? And, in fact, he agreed to Hank's calculations. We showed you Mr. McDowell's deposition testimony. He said, yeah, the impact occurred twenty-nine feet south of the gouge. And I asked him, well, you agree with Hank, don't you? And he said, yes. And then I showed him Hank's report which indicated the offset was only six inches at that point. And then I asked him, well, did you measure the offset at the impact there? He said he went to the impact area, but he didn't measure the offset. That wasn't a search for the truth. But he did admit the offset was only six inches, six inches."

This time, Marissa mimicked the six inches by placing her hands apart at the approximate distance and showing them to the jurors to demonstrate how small it was.

"Well, we know what the truth is, Dr. Kominsky told us. Remember, I'm not going to pull it out, but it's Exhibit 109 where he did the drawing yesterday. If Martin's in the middle of the left lane at the transition, there is plenty of room at that point, remember? And Dr. Kominski testified if you let go of the steering wheel, and you just allow the shuttle bus to move forward; you don't do anything; the vehicle will go straight for sixty feet, which is where that gouge mark is. Where will the shuttle bus be? One foot left of the dashed line between the two lanes which is in Martin's own lane. That's the truth, and it's undisputed. So Martin certainly didn't drift into Mr. Hernandez's lane."

Marissa turned to John and said, "Can you go back to the previous exhibit? Go to the next one."

"This one?" John asked as he switched exhibits.

"Yes, that one," Marissa replied after smiling at John with approval. "The other thing Dr. Kominsky testified to is, when he monitored the traffic patterns at that location, eighty-nine percent of drivers drifted inside or shifted lanes into Martin's lane. Only eleven percent drifted or shifted into Mr. Hernandez's lane.

What did Mr. Sineda say? He said five percent, which is even less. There's no evidence of any drifting. It's just not the truth that Martin drifted into Mr. Hernandez's lane; they're just speculating. The truth is he was in his own lane when the accident occurred."

Marissa took a sip of water to calm her nerves and then continued with her closing argument.

"The other thing they are arguing is that Martin was distracted and drifted into the middle lane because he was talking to his wife, Rose. We know this isn't true. Rose was not able to testify because of her Alzheimer's disease but Martin testified she was content watching the road and looking at the scenery. She wasn't talking to him and distracting him because her Alzheimer's makes speaking extremely difficult. There's simply no evidence that somehow Rose caused Martin to not see the Lexus in the middle lane."

Another exhibit showing a different jury instruction appeared on the monitors. Marissa walked to the large monitor facing the jury so she could explain this particular jury instruction.

"You were instructed about the negligence per se aspect of this case. And it says, a person shall drive a vehicle as nearly as practical entirely within a single lane and shall not move that vehicle from that lane until the driver has first ascertained that the movement can be made with safety."

The jurors followed along as Marissa read the instruction from the monitor.

"And then it says, if you find from the evidence that a person has violated this law, that person is negligent. The jury instruction doesn't say Martin is negligent because you will have the opportunity to find that person is Mr. Hernandez. Mr. Hernandez was negligent; he violated that statute. He entered into Martin's lane without first ascertaining whether the movement could be made safely; he didn't even know the shuttle bus was there.

"We've proven that Mr. Hernandez was negligent per se because all of the evidence, even their experts' own testimony, leads to one and only one conclusion: Mr. Hernandez entered Martin's lane. Also, there's not going to be any jury instruction that says, just because you're speeding, you're automatically at fault...."

As Marissa continued with her closing argument, one of the jurors reached out to the bailiff. Marissa could see them speaking in the corner of her eye. She tried not to allow their discussion to distract her from the closing argument. Before long, the judge interrupted Marissa.

"Counsel, can you stop? It seems something is going on in the jury box. Bailiff?"

"Your honor, I apologize but I think we have an emergency," the bailiff said.

The bailiff grabbed the juror's arm and led the juror out of the courtroom as everyone watched. Returning to the courtroom a few minutes later, the bailiff walked to the bench and whispered to the judge.

Addressing counsel, the judge said, "Juror number six is very ill and has been taken to the emergency room. We will need to recess and determine if the juror can return or if we need to continue without juror number six and use an alternate."

# 41 DECISION

### Cayey, Puerto Rico
### That Same Morning

Several of Gerald's security detail escorted two of the four mafia men into vehicles to transport them away from the house to the police department in San Juan. The wounded man was critically injured but felt better as he was temporarily treated. He would be transported to a local hospital in a separate vehicle. George and Virginia looked on as they realized only one Escalade was parked in the driveway. Two of the mafia men apparently escaped in the other Escalade with the captive before Cameron and the security team arrived.

The two private investigators were somewhat disappointed but relieved when they saw Pamela assisting Daniel and exiting the front door. They rushed to help them.

"We're okay," Pamela insisted as she helped Daniel sit down on the front lawn.

He was in a weakened state but tried to keep an upbeat attitude as displayed by a silly grin he couldn't control. It faded into a grimace once the pain returned after the adrenaline rush subsided.

Right behind them was Cameron. He was alone having let the neighbor go after speaking with the man and ascertaining the neighbor wasn't a part of the kidnapping but thought Pamela and the others were engaged in a home invasion. His story checked out after Cameron alerted his security detail, and they confirmed his credentials with their police connections. Cameron first whispered something into the ear of one of his men and then walked toward Daniel and Pamela on the front lawn.

"Hey, sis. Can we talk?" he asked after stowing his weapon.

She looked at Daniel who nodded and said, "I'll be fine."

Walking further down the driveway toward the street, the siblings seemed comfortable with each other as if their relationship hadn't been estranged the past few years.

"I talked to Dad," Cameron said. "We worked it out. Well, there are some kinks but we're working things out and...and I want to work things out with you as well. But before we can talk about the past, I need to know what's going on here. All of it."

Surprised he was coincidentally in a small town in the middle of the Caribbean, Pamela asked, "What are you doing here? How did you find me?"

"Well, Gerry was worried about you and Daniel. After Dad and I were finished, he asked me to provide backup and sent me on the company jet after you. Once my team and I were here, it was easy to track you. Even Stevie Wonder could have seen your bread crumbs from a mile away."

Pamela was secretly grateful she hadn't taken Gerald up on his offer to take the jet back to Puerto Rico.

*If I had, Cameron wouldn't have been here*, she thought.

"I appreciate his concerns, but I didn't need any backup," Pamela told her brother.

"It looked like you did to me. That neighbor had the drop on you."

"It's nothing I couldn't handle. I've gotten out of worse before."

"I know. Gerry's told me a lot about you. I'm very proud of how your career and your work with Gerry has gone."

Cameron gave her the look of approval he always did as an older brother which warmed her heart. But she immediately put up a wall not wanting to let him in just yet.

"Don't do that," she said.

"Do what?"

"Do what you always do. Pretend like there isn't anything wrong between us when there is and then move on to do your own thing. Dad may have forgiven you very easily. But he knows he may not have a lot of time. It isn't going to be that easy with me, Cameron. I've given you many chances before and you've broken my trust every time."

He could see the hurt in her eyes while hearing it in her voice. It's what he expected. So he just listened.

"I'm just here for my client. Me and my team rescued him. He's safe now and we just want to go home."

"What about the other captive?" Cameron asked.

Pamela hadn't realized he was gone. She assumed either Virginia and George stopped them when they fled, or the security team had them. Looking around the yard, she couldn't see the older and younger captors or the captive. She was disappointed in herself yet resolved in her convictions. Speaking with her brother always made her that way.

"I'm not sure I should still be involved. If we hadn't gotten involved in the first place, Daniel would never have been kidnapped. Just let the local police handle it. I've got to get back to Phoenix to be with Dad and to take Daniel home."

Cameron hadn't realized his sister would feel guilty about everything. It was unlike her to respond this way. Gerald warned him there was something different about Pamela's relationship with Daniel, but he didn't really believe it. He assumed there couldn't be anything romantic between the two because of the significant age difference. After all, Daniel didn't seem to be Pamela's type.

*Maybe as an older male, Pamela considers him more like a father figure the way she does with Gerry,* Cameron reasoned.

But the look on her face dispossessed him of that belief. There was something more. He couldn't put his finger on it and knew it wasn't his place to ask, at least not at this moment.

"It's up to you. If that's what you decide, I can have the local police look into the kidnapping."

Cameron walked away from Pamela and spoke with his men. She watched him before heading back to Daniel who was being tended to by George and Virginia.

"You're right. They only look bruised and not

fractured," George agreed as Daniel lowered his shirt once George was finished inspecting his torso.

Daniel was pleased despite the agonizing pain.

"We should get you to a hospital," Virginia suggested. "That way they can take a look at you."

"I'm fine. Just a little bruised and battered. But I can take it. I don't need a doctor."

Daniel tried to exude strength despite having a black eye with numerous cuts and bruises and dried blood flowing down his face which contradicted his assertion. The knot on his head was the size of a walnut giving him an awkward appearance.

"You're not fine," Pamela said as she approached. "You look like hell. These guys won't tell you, but you know me, I will. Let us take you to a doctor. It doesn't have to be at a hospital, but we can arrange a private doctor to treat you. There's no shame in that."

Daniel nodded and tried to stand up, nearly losing his balance because his legs were used to being restrained. George and Pamela helped him stand. When he was finally steady enough to walk, he looked for the other captive but didn't find it.

"Where is the other guy?" Daniel asked. "I want to talk to him."

Daniel continued frantically looking for him and almost stumbled.

"He's not here. They took him," Pamela explained.

"Where?"

"We don't know. It just happened too fast," George said.

"We have to find him," Daniel insisted.

"Why? He's long gone, and we have you. That's why we came here. Not for him," Pamela said.

She didn't want to explain that the captive wasn't her client and she had no professional obligation to him. Although she was originally intrigued by what happened when she was vacationing with Daniel at the resort, the intervening issues had dampened her interest and enthusiasm. Realizing he needed to convince Pamela it was a good idea, Daniel explained how the captive's voice seemed familiar to him and how the two captors tortured both of them to pressure him to reveal the whereabouts of hidden money.

"I have to think it was more than just money they're after," Daniel suggested. "You saw those holes in the backyard. Maybe jewelry or some heirloom. I just don't know but the way they were insistent on finding it makes me think there was something more, something personal."

"These guys are part of the Puerto Rican mafia," Pamela finally revealed. "It's big time. We inadvertently got in the middle of it but now it's time for the police to take over and handle it."

Daniel couldn't hide his disappointment.

"I get that. I do. But this guy, they're going to kill him. I just know it. We're here. I think they're close. They aren't running away because what they need is here. Somewhere in this house or on the property. By the time, the authorities come, if they aren't personally involved with the mafia, it may be too late."

Pamela sighed. She knew he wasn't going to let it go. A part of her didn't want to let it go either. It wasn't who she was.

"If you really want to, we can go after him."

"Hot dog," George said as he did a little ditty. "I'm ready."

He smiled eager to get back into the game and

looked at Virginia for her reaction. Virginia wasn't as pleased having already shot one of them. It was the first time she'd shot at anyone and the feeling of taking someone's life still haunted her. Having never been in the military like George and Pamela, she wasn't looking for another fight, but she knew it was ultimately what she signed up for when she came to Puerto Rico. She was never asked to come but came on her own for Daniel's sake and because she knew it would mean a lot to Pamela.

*I can't leave them now*, she pondered and then holstered the gun George previously gave her.

## 42 THREATS

An Undisclosed Place in Puerto Rico
That Same Morning

"Coño, who were those people?" the younger captor asked the older one. "We barely escaped." He was breathing hard and clearly out of his depth. "I didn't sign up for this."

The older man stared at him in disbelief, shaking his head to physically display his inner feelings.

"Yes, you did. We both did. What did you expect after agreeing to kidnap the boss's son? *Coquito* and *empanadillas*? We're getting what we deserve for backstabbing *El Gran*."

Pacing the area like a stressed animal, the older male became more and more furious as he thought about their predicament and their pending doom at the hands of the head of their family.

*I only agreed to the coup so I can make it big. Now this!* he thought.

"Wait a minute. The lady I shot at, she was a blondie. She didn't look *Boricua*. Not at all," the younger one suggested.

Looking up, the older male stared at him originally thinking he was on to something but quickly dismissed it.

"You don't think *Boricua women* dye their hair? You're kidding yourself. You're worse than I thought," he responded while stomping his right foot out of frustration.

"No, listen to me. I know *Boricua* women dye their hair. I'm not stupid. But this woman didn't have the typical facial features. She didn't look Hispanic at all. Besides, she went for the other guy, not him."

He looked at the captive who was still restrained inside the Escalade. The older male gave a puzzled looked when the younger one kept talking.

"If she was hired by *El Gran* to get his son back, she could have easily rescued him first. Why did she run to the farthest part of the room to rescue the other guy? It doesn't make sense. Why would *El Gran* care about the other guy? Or even know he was there or who he was? We don't know who he is."

The older male stopped pacing and placed his hands on his hips.

"You're making more sense now. Who knows who she is? Maybe she works for the feds?" he suggested. "That's the last thing we need. Johnny better end this takeover quickly. It's lasting a lot longer than we were originally told. I...."

Before he knew it, the younger male rushed towards the Escalade. He was excited and panicked at the same time.

Opening the rear passenger door, the younger male yelled at his captive, "You think you're smart making us run around looking for your treasure trove like we're some pirates. But we know better now.

Look at you trying to pretend like you're strong, but we know your game. We know you're weak and worried. You thought you were getting saved. Huh? But you didn't. They didn't even come close to saving you. They don't want you. They wanted the other guy.

"Your daddy wants nothing to do with you now. He probably thinks you were killed in the shootout earlier. He didn't even send any of his men to save you. You're pathetic."

The younger male spat at his face in defiance. The captive became angry, but his restraints prevented him from lashing out. He looked away and ignored his captor. He didn't want to give the others the pleasure of seeing him upset or fazed by their maltreatment.

The older male pushed aside the younger so he could be next to their captive.

Looking like he was possessed, the older male grabbed the gun from his compatriot and declared, "My partner is correct. You're not getting away from us. This can go one of two ways. Either you tell us where the money is and maybe we'll let you live, or you don't and you leave in a body bag. It's up to you. Frankly, if I was you I would choose the former and live for another day. It's just money. You can always make more of it or your daddy can just give you more of it. But you only have one life. Just one."

The captive realized his honor was something they hadn't thought of as an option. If he had none, he would have easily rolled over and given them what they wanted a long time ago. But he didn't give his captors much credit.

*They'll never know what it means to have honor.*

*They're foot soldiers, low men on the totem pole and are easily misled over money. They reek of desperation.*

He remained silent despite their desperate plea for him to disclose the whereabouts of his bounty from stealing from the other family members.

"Suit yourself."

The older man shot the captive's right kneecap. He writhed in pain as blood gushed out. He couldn't grab his knee or move given his restraints. Shutting the door, the older male told the younger one to follow him. Pulling out his cell phone, he dialed Johnny.

"Tell me some good news," Johnny requested.

"I know you said not to hurt him, but he must have been injured in the crossfire," the older male explained. "There's nothing we can do about that. We had to leave the house. They found us somehow. I don't know. It may have been his men, but we don't think so. We think it's the feds. They're on to us."

"And the money? Has he told you where it is?" Johnny asked.

"He'll never tell. He's taking that to the grave."

"Do whatever you can to find the money and then dispose of the body."

"Yes, sir."

In the Escalade, the captive thought of his wife and two children and how they would feel if he was no longer with them. He smiled at the thought of playing with his children, watching them play with their neighbors, or hearing them laugh at every silly thing. He knew his wife was strong and would be there for their kids, but she loved him so and would miss him. The thought comforted him. Throughout this ordeal, he pushed them out of his mind so he could stay focused and strong.

Now after being shot, he finally understood there was a slim chance he would make it out alive and the faction of the mafia family holding him was serious about their retribution. He knew he tempted fate in the past, living beyond his means and bullying others in the organization to bend them to his will. They cowered in his presence and surrendered to his demands because of who his father was. He realized taking advantage of his position and forgetting the ways his father taught him how to lead men under his charge put him in this situation. Never heeding the warnings, never seeing the signs, and disobeying his father resulted in his current situation which was more than he could handle. He knew he had one last chance to make it right and to save himself. He had to do it. Otherwise, he would never see his family again.

The door to the Escalade suddenly opened and startled the captive.

This time, the captive looked directly at his captors and said, "Alright, I'll take you to the money. But you have to promise to let me live. Or we don't have a deal."

They were shocked at his request but were skeptical.

"Look, no more lies. We heard you say all kinds of stuff before that never panned out. This time, if you refuse to take us to the money, then we have the go-ahead to off you. We'll do it," the older male responded.

His companion gave him a bewildered look and pulled him to the side.

"Before we go looking for the money, the guy

needs medical attention," the younger male said. "We need to take care of his wound or he won't make it and we'll never find the money."

"We can't take him to a hospital. They'll report his gunshot wound to the police and that will be the end of it. It's protocol."

"We have to do something."

The older male thought hard about a workable solution.

"Get a rag or something from the back and tie it around his wound to stop the bleeding. Real tight. It's the best we can do for now."

He then walked into the driver's seat of the Escalade to ready the vehicle for their mission to find the money.

Opening the hatchback, the younger male looked around and found something he believed could be used to wrap the wound. As he wrapped the captive's bloody kneecap, the captive screamed in anguish.

"There, that'll do. Much better," the younger guy grinned.

He was secretly pleased the captive was hurting. The older male was also pleased with the captive's response and started the vehicle.

"You give us a hard time and we'll make it hurt," the older male said as he turned and looked at his other kneecap. "We'll make that one hurt too."

The captive could do nothing but listen as he grimaced in pain.

## 43  INFORMED

San Juan, Puerto Rico
That Same Morning

After pouring some coffee into a mug, Mrs. Quintana sipped to not only warm her slightly chilled body but also to refresh her mind and awaken her soul. She took several small pieces of mozzarella cheese and then dropped them into her coffee mug. Taking a fork, she gently stirred the mixture so the cheese could melt faster. Clanging the fork on the mug's rim so any residual coffee would drip back into it, she then placed the utensil on the table and took another sip. It was her morning ritual. She was pleased and now would be ready to face the day.

"*Hola*, Mrs. Quintana," the maid said before wiping down the breakfast table where the lady of the house was eating breakfast along with her coffee.

She placed a newspaper on the table for her employer to read and ensured the other place setting was immaculate.

"*Gracias*, Matilda," she responded while grabbing the newspaper and reading the day's headline.

Flipping the newspaper open to the science and art section, she continued reading it when her husband sat down in a chair opposite her. He was uncharacteristically silent and avoided eye contact. She watched from the corner of her eye while he was served breakfast and also began eating.

Once she understood he wouldn't address her, she inquired, "So, Jose, what's on your mind you won't kiss and greet your wife? It must be serious."

She half-expected he would tell her about the prior days' events. Instead, he looked up at her dumbfounded and speechless. Then he continued eating his white rice and red beans as if he was dining alone. She was displeased by his lack of response but understood it as he was preoccupied with addressing something and hoped he would speak to her once he was ready to.

One of his men entered the breakfast room, whispered something to *Chango*, and immediately left. Mrs. Quintana watched like it was a choreographed routine she had seen many times before. Her husband was the head of the family, and she was used to interruptions at all hours of the day and night.

He stopped eating and looked up at his wife with a serious demeanor.

"I have bad news. Really bad news," *Chango* cautioned.

His wife put down the newspaper and listened. It was not often her husband told her bad news. When he did, it oftentimes was difficult for him to admit it to her. So, she always tried to use a measured response.

"Earlier this week, our son was spotted at the Regal Isabela resort," Chango revealed uncertain how she would respond.

"What? He never told me he was vacationing on the island," she exclaimed.

"He was supposed to stay here for a while when he arrived from the States, but he decided on his own not to. I don't know what got into him. It's not what we'd agreed to."

*Chango* scooped some more rice and stuffed his mouth. He took out his frustration by chewing the food with vigor almost like a crazed man detached from reality. His wife was increasingly concerned but knew when he was like this he would snap back eventually. She waited for him to finish eating and to collect his composure before inquiring further.

"What was he doing there? Why didn't he come home?" she asked.

The question puzzled him at first. His son was always deferential growing up and listened to both of his parents. But once he met his childhood sweetheart who he eventually married, he became more rebellious, more brutal, and uncontrollable. Knowing what eventually happened to his son, *Chango* was at a loss over what decisions his son made over the past few years, including this latest one.

"Relaxing. Hiding out. Who knows. Once I was told by the resort's attorney he was there, I had a few men go pick him up. But...but they betrayed me."

She looked on in despair given her husband's solemn voice. He was still unsettled by the unresolved, internal conflict in his organization which now was affecting his own family. In the past, he'd promised her he was strong enough to keep their discontent in check. It worked originally but apparently not as long as he'd hoped.

"He was kidnapped out of retribution for his theft

of Johnny's money and some other stuff he stole. Johnny's not happy. A lot of the family isn't happy about how I handled the situation. I should have done more but I couldn't," *Chango* admitted.

"What does Johnny want?"

"He was willing to give us back our son if I step down and hand over leadership to Johnny and Luis."

"Are you going to step down?"

"I'm not giving that fool control of my empire, of all my hard work. He's a pimp. He'll run it into the ground."

"But..."

"But what? I'm not going to be blackmailed by one of my longtime, childhood friends. I expect loyalty. Absolute loyalty. I know this is difficult to accept but I had my guys try to rescue him. They shot at the car he was in, but it got away. We think there was a good chance he was wounded. We don't know where he's at or what condition he's in. We have people checking emergency rooms and any doctor's office. We'll find him. It's only a matter of time."

*Chango* casually chewed on some beans as if he wasn't speaking about his own flesh and blood but some stranger who was abducted and possibly killed. His wife knew better. Their father-son relationship was unbreakable and had been since his birth despite their son's recent behavior. She knew her husband would give his life for his son. He was being detached and strong just for her; to keep her from becoming overwhelmed with fear for her son. She loved him even more for that.

Despite his efforts to downplay the situation and reassure her, Mrs. Quintana clenched the coffee mug so tightly she thought it would break even if it was only in her mind.

"My boy," she muttered.

Her husband stared at her realizing this time he caused her immeasurable pain. He instantly regretted it but there was nothing he could do about it. At least not yet. He stood up and quietly walked out of the room while his wife looked on.

Once his silhouette vanished in the distance, Mrs. Quintana took another sip of coffee. A string of cheese hung from her lips as she nervously wiped it free with a linen napkin. Tears dripped down her face and she wiped those as well. She was ashamed to let anyone see her like this but given the circumstances, she was willing to be vulnerable because she didn't know what had become of her son.

Another of her husband's men entered the breakfast room. He told her she had a guest wanting to speak with her. Luis entered.

"Mrs. Quintana, I'm sorry to disturb you so early in the morning. I just spoke with your husband. I'm not sure if he told you about your son."

He waited for her to process what he just said before continuing. She sat anxiously waiting for him to tell her anything new about her son.

"The men following the vehicle your son was in called to update me. I just told your husband they say he is dead but, to be honest, I have my doubts. I...I think he's still alive." Luis looked around to see if anyone was listening. "Johnny also called me and told me your son is still alive. I don't know whether to believe him but there isn't any reason for Johnny to deceive me."

Mrs. Quintana was hopeful given the latest development.

"Does he still want my husband to step down?"

"I don't know if that's enough anymore. He didn't exactly say. He's focused on getting the money back. He thinks if he can give back the money to the other members of the family then they'll owe him and will make him head of the family instead of *Chango*."

"He really thinks that?"

"I can't say for sure. He's mixed up these days. He's not like he used to be. Power is all he's thinking about right now. But if I have to guess, many in the family will see Johnny's ability to right this wrong as a strength, more strength than *Chango* has shown these past few years."

Placing her head on her heart, Mrs. Quintana felt like giving up. An inner strength urged her to go on.

"What will he do with my son?"

"Once Johnny has the money, then he no longer has need of him."

Understanding the implication, she asked, "Is there anything we can do to stop it?"

"I'm sorry but that's a foregone conclusion. I've tried talking sense into him but he's not listening to me, not anymore. I don't know if he ever listened to me."

"Tell him, I'm willing to negotiate."

"Certainly," Luis responded as he exited the breakfast room.

## 44 CHASE

### Cayey, Puerto Rico
### That Same Morning

Pamela walked to her rental car with Daniel in tow. She stopped midway from the house to the car and turned around toward George who was walking to his and Virginia's rental car.

"Hey George, can Alberto locate the Escalade like he did before?" she asked.

"I'm sure he can," George said while pulling out his cell phone.

George noticed he had a voicemail message and listened to it.

"*Mijo*, I saw that Escalade again. It's here two blocks from my house," the older neighborhood watch lady said in Spanish. "Come by and check it out. Oh, I have some *mondongo* for you and your lady friend. You'll love it."

Smiling, George contemplated eating the Puerto Rican stew. He wasn't sure if Virginia would appreciate the beef offal used in the soup. Most people didn't. He understood she wasn't as open-minded as he was when it came to eating exotic dishes. But at the very least, he would extend the invite because Virginia was specifically invited to enjoy the meal.

Realizing he needed to focus on the present and their desire to rescue the other captive, he told Pamela, "My local contact just told me where the Escalade is."

George was stoked and could see both Pamela and Daniel were just as excited to know they had a lead so quickly.

"Come on. Let's go then. Text me the location," Pamela requested as she eagerly entered her vehicle.

Seeing Daniel struggle to get into the vehicle, she exited it, walked around to the passenger door, and helped him get to the car. He would on occasion groan from the pain as he hobbled. She gently helped him into the vehicle and also had to physically move his right leg into the car. When he was situated and felt reasonably comfortable, she drove off.

———

Seated on a wooden rocking chair on the front porch of her home, the elderly woman grinned and waved to George as he approached in the rental car. The woman pointed in the direction of the Escalade with exuberance. Both he and Virginia waved back.

"She's a sweet ole lady. I'm so glad she trusts us and is willing to help. She's been a joy to work with," George admitted.

Virginia was pleasantly surprised at his gentleness at the moment.

*George is always so stoic and distant, trying to*

*exude strength all the time*, she contemplated. *He is a softie after all.*

Turning left onto the next street, their vehicle drove to the location where the Escalade was last spotted. They were ahead of Pamela's vehicle given her delay. George watched his rear-view mirror to ensure Pamela's vehicle also followed him by making the turn.

"There it is," Virginia said as she pointed toward its direction.

The Escalade was parked in an open area on the side of the road where no homes were built and only the native plants and trees were growing.

George slowed down the car to allow Pamela to catch up.

As they approached, the older captor was getting into the driver's seat. The younger one closed the hatchback, opened the rear passenger door, did something the others could not see from their vehicles a block or so away, and then entered the front passenger door. The Escalade then drove off.

"Don't let them get away, George," Pamela said even though he couldn't hear her from inside the rental car.

She was about to honk the horn when George's vehicle sped after the Escalade. Knowing there was going to be a chase, Daniel made sure his seat belt was on and secured tightly. He then turned toward Pamela to double-check that she was buckled in.

Sensing what he was doing and without turning her gaze away from the Escalade, Pamela said, "Yes, I'm wearing my seat belt. No need to worry. I'm not a novice at car chases."

Daniel was embarrassed but pleased, nonetheless.

———

When making a left turn in the direction the captive told him was the hidden money, the older captor saw two vehicles behind him. The vehicles were speeding in his direction.

"Hey, are those the same cars outside the house when we escaped?" the older captor asked the younger.

The younger captor turned around to look at the vehicles pursuing them.

"I think so. I think they're after us."

The older man floored it as the Escalade tore down the small residential street that led away from the center of the city.

Hearing the exchange, the captive also looked behind him and smirked.

*It's only a matter of time before they free me,* he thought.

He was unaware it was not his father's men pursuing the Escalade.

———

Seeing the Escalade speed off, the two rental cars made the turn without slowing down. Daniel gripped the grab handle so tightly that his knuckles whitened. His body writhed in pain from the centripetal forces pressing against him when the vehicle accelerated from the turn. As the overgrown trees lining the street swept passed Pamela's vehicle in a green blur, Daniel's body jostled up and down causing him excruciating pain.

He grimaced and tried to keep the pain to himself, but it was obvious to Pamela the chase was taking its toll on him. He wanted her to slow down but he felt the request would undermine their mission to rescue the captive.

Noticing the two vehicles were still behind the Escalade, the driver made a sudden right turn into a narrow street in hopes of evading his pursuers. The wide Escalade careened into a vehicle parked on the opposite side of the street scraping the sides of both vehicles. The sound of crunching metal and screeching tires reverberated throughout the neighborhood. Undeterred, the damaged Escalade continued swerving from side to side to avoid any other vehicles parked along both sides of the narrow street.

Daniel saw George's vehicle make the right turn with ease and barrel down the street toward the Escalade. He smiled initially and then realized Pamela's vehicle would have to make the same maneuver. He braced himself again for the inertia forces his body would experience.

Opening his mouth to warn Pamela about the consequences of a rapid turn, instead, his body tightened in anticipation. Pamela noticed his reaction but had to focus on the pursuit. She gently touched his hand with hers and quickly returned it to the steering wheel and floored the gas pedal to accelerate.

———

"They're gaining on us," the younger captor shouted at his older compatriot. "Do something?"

The older male gave him a dirty look and retorted, "You do something. You have the gun."

The younger male had a puzzled look on his face

until he finally understood what he was supposed to do. Lowering the passenger window, the younger captive grabbed his gun and wildly shot at the vehicles pursuing him.

———

The windshield of George's vehicle was pierced by a bullet narrowly missing both private investigators. George ducked lower into the driver's seat and swerved so his vehicle wouldn't become an easy target. Virginia did likewise. Her heart pumped rapidly as if it was going to tear out of her body.

"Shoot back!!" George exclaimed.

Virginia froze at the command.

Figuring she wasn't as adept in these situations, George grabbed his gun and shot twice. The Escalade was bullet-ridden but so huge it didn't make a difference to the driver.

Concerned he would hit the captive because he was shooting while driving which affected his aim, George looked at Virginia and said, "I need you to do this."

Virginia clenched her teeth and then shot out the window towards the younger captor having gained her courage.

———

"This is getting serious," Daniel gulped as he saw the younger captor shooting at them.

"Don't worry. We'll handle it," Pamela responded.

Their vehicle continued up the narrow street

when another vehicle drove through the intersection crossing in front of Pamela's vehicle.

"Look oooouuuttt!!" Daniel exclaimed.

Pamela's vehicle clipped the rear of the other vehicle, causing it to uncontrollably spin and collide into a home.

Pamela did not keep her eyes off of the Escalade but relentlessly pursued it. As they continued through the intersection, Daniel watched the spinning vehicle, hoping the occupants were okay.

———

The younger captive was shot in the shoulder by a bullet coming from Virginia's gun. She was a better aim than he was giving her experience at the gun range with George and on her own. Although wounded, the younger captor tried valiantly to continue shooting at his pursuers. But the pain became more unbearable causing him to drop his gun onto the street.

He quickly pulled his body back into the Escalade. The older captor was disappointed by his compatriot's inability to deter the pursuit. He understood it was up to him to evade them. His only solution was to go even faster in hopes the other vehicles would err while pursuing them. Instead, the older driver panicked while he was looking in his rearview mirror at his pursuers. The Escalade crashed into a parked vehicle facing the opposite direction.

# 45  CRASH

An Undisclosed Place in Puerto Rico
Moments Later

S team funneled upward from the front of the
Escalade. Its grill was smashed and entangled
with the vehicle it slammed into. The crash pushed
the parked vehicle backward into another one. The
loud banging sounds emanated through the streets,
causing the neighbors to look out of their windows
wondering what was happening.

The Escalade's driver-side door opened, and the
older captor stumbled out. He grimaced in pain,
blood dripping from his head. He looked at his
wounded compatriot on the opposite side of the Escalade and reasoned he couldn't assist him in his condition. He saw vehicles fast approaching him and
then limped up the street hoping to escape.

The first rental car stopped behind the Escalade.
George and Virginia exited their vehicle and strode
on opposite sides of the Escalade toward the front
while brandishing their weapons. Virginia looked into

the front passenger window and saw the young captor wounded from their previous encounter.

He turned toward her, raised his arms, and pleaded, "Please don't shoot me."

"Get out of the car," she ordered while waiving her weapon to indicate her request.

The younger captor struggled to exit the vehicle while Virginia watched. She directed him to sit down. He ached while lowering his body to straddle the curb.

Meanwhile, when George approached the opened driver-side door, he examined the inside confirming the driver's seat was empty but had droplets of blood. He was disappointed. He then checked the damaged parked vehicle and noticed it was completely empty. George was relieved no innocent bystanders were injured.

"No one's here," he said while watching the young captor sitting down on the sidewalk. Once he was assured the captor was secure and Virginia had things under control, he told her, "I'm going after the driver. I think he's injured."

Acknowledging his comment, Virginia nodded as she kept her weapon trained at the younger captor.

Moments later, Pamela's rental car came to a screeching halt and parked alongside the other rental vehicle. Pamela exited and immediately sussed out the situation. When she saw George running after the older captor, she intended on ordering him not to pursue him, but he was too far away for him to hear her voice. She holstered her weapon and turned toward Daniel who hobbled out of the vehicle.

"Looks like we got one and the other one is on foot. George is in pursuit," she explained to Daniel.

He was pleased and slowly walked toward the rear passenger door eager to find out if the captive was alive. Opening the door, he saw the restrained captive inside squirming in a vain effort to free himself. Finally able to see his face because on all previous occasions both captives had been blindfolded, Daniel believed he recognized the captive's him but couldn't place where from.

The captive grinned deviously and gestured to Daniel to remove his restraints.

"Not yet, buddy. Not until I know who you are. What's your name?"

The captive didn't say anything in response but looked dumbfounded at Daniel. Having heard his voice many times before while in captivity, Daniel knew what he sounded like but didn't want the captive to repeat one of his curse-filled rants. Although Daniel would have liked an answer to his question.

"It's only a matter of time before I find out," he added. "You might as well tell me. I might be able to help you."

The captive grinned again this time with the same obstinate defiance he gave his captors when they tortured him.

"If that's what you want?"

When Daniel closed the door to ensure the captive would stay inside the vehicle, he noticed Pamela was on her cell phone.

"Yes. Thanks, Cameron." He heard her say. "He's sending a team to pick up these guys," she told Daniel.

"Nice. He's been very helpful today," Daniel acknowledged while listlessly walking over to Virginia's position.

"Yes, he has," Pamela said.

She was beaming with pride for her older brother.

Before she could say another word, additional vehicles approached with members of Gerald Ravan's security detail. They introduced themselves to Pamela who let them take charge of the scene. She was relieved it was finally over.

The security detail dispersed the neighbors, tended to the two wounded men, and then cuffed them.

Daniel looked intently at the younger male finally being face-to-face with one of the individuals who captured him. Filled with emotion and regret, he had nothing to say to him. All Daniel could do was envision the adjacent casita and wonder if the same individual tortured the guest who was staying there or if the situation was totally unrelated.

*Why did they do this to me? They must have known we were on to them. What did they really want?* Daniel thought.

Pamela walked beside him and asked, "Do you know any of them?"

"I don't know this guy here but the one guy inside the Escalade, I've definitely seen him before. I just don't remember from where. He won't tell me his name, but I think I know him. I'm sure I do. I just have to rack my fuzzy brain to remember. It will come to me."

Daniel thought hard and fast, but nothing came to mind. He searched his memories for when he was inside the tossed casita and he rummaged through the belongings to find any clue about the guest they believed had been captured. The only thing he remembered was the airline ticket with the name "C. Quintana".

*Think! Think!*

When it dawned on him what who he was, Daniel was still uncertain.

———

Further down the road, a vehicle was parked just far away so that it was inconspicuous from the goings on that attracted everyone's attention. Inside was one of Luis' men. He used binoculars to observe the scene. He watched as several vehicles from the Puerto Rico police department arrived. The police sirens briefly sounded as the dark blue and white lights blinked alternatively. The officers were escorting both men into separate vehicles as Pamela and Daniel looked on.

Turning his binoculars further away, the man could see George bringing the older male back to the crash site and handing him to the police. Virginia slapped George on the shoulder pleased with his efforts. He could see her mouth words to George but could not hear what she was saying. George was definitely amused by her comment.

A local man was wailing in front of the damaged park vehicle upset it was severely damaged. He cursed in Spanish unconcerned about what others thought of his outburst. The man with the binoculars gleefully smiled at the spectacle.

He then watched as the police vehicles exited the scene followed by the vehicles used by Gerald Ravan's security detail. Neighbors looked on as the sirens blared and eventually faded away. The male continued watching Daniel and the others as they conversed before entering their rental cars and driving off.

He waited to see if any others approached the scene. Shortly after everyone was gone, two vehicles drove alongside the Escalade. Men exited the vehicles and frantically searched the Escalade. The man observing them couldn't tell what they were looking for or whether they found it. Given their dejected expressions, he assumed they did not. One of their crew was handed a car key and slowly drove the wrecked Escalade away. Screeching tires and burnt rubber filled the air as the tires scraped the wheel well while it was driven away.

A tow truck eventually appeared and stopped where the Escalade previously rested. The driver looked around in despair as the whereabouts of the missing vehicle were unknown. The tow truck driver radioed headquarters and apprised them of the situation.

Once the area was cleared and no one was interested in what previously transpired, the man with the binoculars made a phone call.

"Yes."

"The police took him away. All of them."

"Thank you, *hermano*. Good job."

———

When Luis ended the call, he was pleased with himself. He knew his skill as a self-proclaimed mediator would be needed again and perhaps he would be rewarded beyond his expectation.

"Mrs. Quintana," he said after his next call was placed. "We have some good news."

She listened, anxious to hear about her son.

"Johnny's men no longer have him," he added.

He heard her sigh in relief.

"But I'm afraid there is a little bad news. Not something we won't be able to handle, but bad news nevertheless."

"Tell me," she anxiously demanded.

"He's with the police. Battered and bruised but he's alive."

"*Gracias, Señor*," she said while crossing herself.

"I can have my men look into where he's being held. We can try to get him out, but it may require that we...that you call in a couple of favors," Luis suggested.

"Whatever it takes. I want my boy home as soon as possible."

"Understood. Do you still want me to arrange a meeting with Johnny?" Luis asked after remembering his initial charge from Mrs. Quintana.

"I do. I know he no longer has his bargaining chip, but I think there is something else we can discuss. He might be interested given his current position."

"Yes, ma'am."

———

As Pamela and Daniel traveled back to San Juan, Puerto Rico in the rental car, Daniel was pleased he was not only rescued but the captive who had been tortured for information was finally free. A heavy weight was taken off his shoulder and the fear of impending death now seemed a distant memory only to resurface again someday once the normal routines of life returned and Daniel would wonder about his future.

He looked at Pamela who was still focused on their mission to follow the police caravan to police headquarters where the men from the safe house and the men currently being transported would be processed and interviewed. A beaming smile came across his face. He couldn't hide it. He was happy beyond measure and Pamela noticed it but dismissed it temporarily.

Looking in the rearview mirror, Daniel saw George and Virginia conversing together in their rental car as they followed behind. He wasn't sure if it was a heated argument or just the typical banter between coworkers. He was happy just to experience normality again.

With the windows down, the mountain breeze filled the car. Daniel breathed deeply and surrendered to it. He slowly regained his peace until his thoughts became engrossed in one thing: *What will happen to him?*

"I need to take him with me to Phoenix," Daniel told Pamela.

"That's not a small task. I'm not sure they'll let you. He's a *mafioso's* son. Apparently, a high-ranking member himself. I wouldn't be surprised if he's wanted by the Puerto Rican police for crimes committed here and other places."

"We need to do something. It's important."

Pamela could tell by the expression on his face, he was serious. She hadn't seen him so concerned since the deaths of those individuals associated with the royalty case he litigated the previous year.

Acknowledging the significance of his request

even though she didn't completely understand why, she replied, "I have a couple of connections who owe me a favor. Maybe...just maybe I can pull it off."

"Are you talking about that Alberto guy Virginia mentioned to me? You should have seen her face when she spoke about him."

Pamela shook her head.

"So you mean Gerry then?" Daniel asked.

"Maybe? I know he can help us but let's just say I don't want to reveal who it is...who they are. Not just yet. It's not important who they are anyway so long as they get the job done."

She grinned at Daniel as she gripped the steering wheel tightly, looked away from him, and sped down the highway.

Sufficiently pleased by her response, Daniel grabbed his cell phone and called Marissa.

## 46 CONTINUANCE

Phoenix, Arizona
The Same Morning

"Ⓐll rise, the Honorable Jessica Furman presiding," the bailiff announced as everyone in the courtroom rose to their feet.

The jurors, however, were not in the courtroom yet.

"Ms. Robles, because of the juror's illness you were unable to complete your closing argument yesterday. Are you ready?" the judge asked.

"Your honor, we have a new development. If it pleases the court, we would like to request a one-day continuance," Marissa requested.

Doug Clarkson jumped to his feet and declared, "I object your honor. Defense counsel hasn't spoken to me about a continuance. This is the first I've heard of it. The jury has been empaneled for nearly two weeks now. Any further delays would prejudice my clients. My clients have been waiting for justice and are entitled to receive a verdict from the jury without any further delays. We would request that defense counsel finish their closing argument so the case can proceed."

"Sit down, Mr. Clarkson. Defense counsel hasn't even said what this new development is before you were quick to object. Let her speak so the court can know how to evaluate the request and rule upon it. But your objection is noted," the judge retorted with a stern look on her face.

Doug immediately sat down but with a slight feeling of defeat.

"Thank you, your honor," Marissa said as she turned to side-eye Doug before continuing. He ignored her glaring look. "I apologize. I'm not able to provide a lot of detail just yet as to the new development. Defendants have located a witness who I think will shed light on this whole affair and from whom the jury will want to hear testimony before closing arguments are completed. Because defendants will need to confirm the identity of the new witness who we intend to call, we are requesting a continuance."

"Your honor...," Doug said as he began standing up again.

The judge lifted her gavel and he stopped himself before she spoke.

"Is there a reason why defendants haven't disclosed this witness previously? You have an obligation to fully disclose witnesses before trial. This is unorthodox and seems to be a last-minute sandbag of the plaintiffs and their counsel," the judge inquisitively asked.

Doug nodded. He was clearly in agreement with the court's questioning and what he expected would be her likely ruling in their favor. He knew the judge was a stickler for the rules of civil procedure and rarely granted any exceptions.

"Your honor, suffice it to say that the defense counsel were totally surprised about the existence of this witness and were unaware of his whereabouts. Had we known, we certainly would have disclosed the witness earlier in the litigation and complied with this court's scheduling order. And frankly, had we learned of this sooner, it would have completely eliminated the need for this entire trial and saved the parties the time and expense as well as this court's invaluable judicial resources. At least in my opinion," Marissa said. "As an officer of the court, I avow on behalf of my clients, we are the ones who are in fact being sandbagged and it will become clear to this court once we can confirm the identity of the witness."

The judge was intrigued by Marissa's argument and contemplated her response.

"In light of this new potential evidence, I am inclined to grant a continuance, but I must say, Mr. Clarkson, is right. The trial has been going on for almost two weeks, which is longer than the average civil trial. The jurors have exhibited great patience with the process and have shown up every day to exercise their duty on behalf of the community. I'm surprised we have only lost one juror. That is highly unusual and illustrates the commitment and sacrifice of our jurors. I'm concerned that if I grant a continuance we may lose more jurors and it will result in a mistrial."

"I totally understand your honor's concern. We are only asking for a twenty-four-hour continuance, your honor. We assure you. We aren't asking for a substantial amount of time," Marissa explained.

"Mr. Clarkson, given this new evidence, I'm inclined to grant a short one-day continuance. I don't believe it will have a substantial impact on the jury. At least, I hope it doesn't. Do you object to that?'

Sensing the judge had made up her mind and not wanting to upset the judge even further, he replied, "Plaintiffs have no issue with a one-day continuance, your honor if that's what counsel avows she's representing to the court."

Selinda turned to her attorney and whispered in Danica's ear. She was obviously concerned about what was going on and why her attorneys weren't aware of it. Wanting answers, Danica had none for her client.

"Good, I will so rule and grant the one-day continuance," the judge said. "But there is one additional matter I need to bring to counsels' attention."

Counsel seated at both tables perked up and listened.

"Juror number six is in fact seriously ill and will not be returning to the jury. It means we are down one juror. We can sit an alternate juror as part of the jury panel now or the parties can agree to reduce the total number of jurors on the panel by one, so the number of alternates stays the same in case there are further delays."

The judge obviously conveyed she would be perturbed and would unlikely tolerate any future delays.

Mr. Clarkson stood to address the judge.

"Your honor, we appreciate the juror's service and also express our gratitude and concern. Hopefully, she will recover soon. I think we should keep the number of jurors the same. If for some reason there are any other new issues that arise, plaintiffs don't in-

tend on bringing any new issues to the court's attention, but if there are new issues, we can then address
the court's concern at that time and discuss reducing
the size of the jury. I think that's fair to my clients
which like I've said before having been waiting to receive their justice.'

He sat down knowing his argument was convincing and his response pleased his clients.

"Ms. Robles?" the judge said.

"Your honor, I have no issue with delaying this
discussion to a later date if needed. But, as I've explained before, hopefully, it won't come to that."

The judge stood up to exit the courtroom.

"All rise," the bailiff announced.

## 47 COURTROOM

### Phoenix, Arizona
### The Next Day

Daniel stood on the tarmac at Terminal One of the Phoenix Sky Harbor Airport. He smiled as the warmer, desert air swept around his body. It was a vast contrast to the cooler air in the mountainous regions of Puerto Rico. Normally, the cooler weather was a welcome reprieve from the dry heat in Arizona, but with his recent abduction and torture, Daniel felt differently.

*It's good to be home,* he reassured himself as he looked around the airport grounds to convince himself of the reality of the situation.

The darkness was gone both inwardly and outwardly. The only thing left was the strong light shining over every nook and cranny and everywhere he could see for miles on end. It pleased him in ways he would not fully understand until years later when he reflected on his experience.

Turning around towards the private jet owned by the Regal Wisteria corporation, Daniel watched as

Pamela walked down the portable stairs. She was pleasantly attractive in the way she took charge of rescuing him. He hadn't realized how seriously her military experience formed a big part of her life. To him, she was just a private investigator who did mundane jobs for his firm. Now she was something more. More than just a friend. More than just her sarcastic remarks and innocent flirtations, which made him uncomfortable at times but sometimes brought a smile to his face. She was now a force to be reckoned with which, in all honesty, brought a certain amount of concern or even fear he'd never associated with her.

Virginia and George followed her, both awkwardly holding carry-on bags. When they were on the tarmac, Cameron walked down the stairs. From afar, the siblings looked more like identical twins despite their age difference. His bright smile and dirty blonde hair contrasted with the aviator glasses to give him a sleek professional demeanor Daniel was surprised to learn he possessed after all those years of hearing about Cameron's antics from Pamela. Two members of the security detail were behind him carrying weapons.

Cameron walked over to his sister and said, "Dad's expecting me to come by the house now. I hope that is alright with you, sis."

He seemed in a rush which was unexpected.

Pleased they had been cordial with each other because of the harrowing circumstances the siblings experienced together but not yet having fully reconciled, Pamela gleefully replied, "Sure. I have some things to do before I head over. I'll see you there."

She handed him her house key and turned away.

Before she could take a few steps toward the terminal, Cameron joked, "Come on. You're not going to give me a hug goodbye after all I've done to save you? I've earned it."

Stopping in her tracks, Pamela contemplated her brother's request. She started walking away when, from behind her, Cameron gave her a bear hug. Her body relaxed as she allowed herself to enjoy it. She placed her right arm across her left shoulder and patted his shoulder. Her reaction pleased him.

Under her breath, she muttered, "I've missed you."

'I've missed you too."

She was surprised he heard her.

He squeezed her tightly one more time before letting her go.

"Let's go guys," he said after whistling to the security detail who then followed him into a limousine awaiting their arrival.

The vehicle drove away as if it would never return.

George and Virginia watched the whole spectacle. They were excited for their boss and what could lay ahead for her with a reconciliation with Cameron and the rest of the family. They knew it was what Pamela secretly longed for despite her past protestations to the contrary. When she was alone, they both approached.

Looking around and not seeing any limousine to whisk them away from the airport, George declared, "I'm exhausted. This whole ordeal wore me out."

He stretched his limbs to alleviate the soreness from the long flight and to rejuvenate his body.

305

"Me too. Both physically and emotionally," Virginia added.

"Take the next few days off," Pamela insisted. "We don't have anything planned anyway. If something comes up...never mind."

Pamela laughed. So did the others.

George and Virginia walked to the terminal leaving Daniel and Pamela alone.

Before long, another private jet taxied toward Terminal One. The ground crew rushed the portable stairs to the passenger door. It quickly opened. Walking down the portable stairs was a man wearing an orange jumpsuit, shackles, and a waist chain.

———

"Counsel, before we bring in the jury, I would like to discuss where we left off the last time the parties were in court," Judge Furman said as she gazed across the judge's bench inquisitively.

Both sets of attorneys were standing alongside their clients as the judge spoke. Selinda Hernandez and her children were eager to learn how the outcome of the continuance would affect them and who the mystery witness was. She tightly held each of their hands as they stood on either side of her.

Selinda held on to what her attorney, Doug Clarkson, told her two days ago when it was first brought up in court: "I think this is just a stall tactic to find something to help their case. They know they're in a bad position with the jury and hope the extra day will distract the jury somehow. I doubt it will work."

Although his words comforted her, his demeanor was more telling. Doug looked worried himself more so than her, perhaps due to the uncertainty of the situation. It was certainly out of character for him as a seasoned attorney to display doubt, especially in front of his client. Selinda could tell that her other attorney, Danica, was putting on a brave face as well while Doug discussed his take on the defense counsel's last-minute request.

While Selinda smiled in response to her attorney's conciliatory words, once home and away from the courtroom, her anxiety reawakened. Waiting an extra day for the revelation made her scour her thoughts of individuals at the scene who might have witnessed something, former disgruntled employees who could undermine her case, or even a medical provider who might have damning information about her husband's pre-accident medical condition. Her imagination was endless. Worrying only made her restless and lose sleep on each of the previous two nights. Now that she was in the courtroom again, her worrying only got the best of her.

"If I may your honor," Michelle said as she looked toward the back of the courtroom at the gallery for her expected visitor. When she realized he still was not in the courtroom, she continued, "I'm still waiting to confirm the witness's identity."

"Ms. Robles, I've given you more than ample time to do so. I can wait a few more minutes if need be, but my patience is wearing thin and the trial needs to proceed. We've taken enough of the jury's time and I don't want to delay things even further. Have I made myself clear?"

"Yes, your honor."

"Your honor, this is getting ridiculous," Doug interjected with his overly flamboyant display of disgust for opposing counsel he was known for while in court. "We've waited long enough...."

The main courtroom door creaked open making a louder noise than normal. The entire courtroom gazed toward the rear while Daniel Mendoza slowly entered. He looked worse for wear.

As he straggled in, wearing casual clothes rather than the typical double-breasted suit he wore while in court, Daniel spoke with a hoarse voice, "I apologize, your honor, for being late and missing most of the trial."

When the judge gave him an ornery look, Daniel added as he touched his clothes in acknowledgment of what the judge was going to say, "Yes, I understand and apologize for my attire as well. I just arrived on a late-night flight from the Caribbean and came straight here."

The judge's eyebrows furled.

"I hope you enjoyed yourself, Mr. Mendoza, but court decorum still requires you to dress appropriately notwithstanding your recent return from a vacation."

As Daniel limped toward the defense counsel's table, Judge Furman could recognize knots, bruises, and numerous lacerations on Daniel's face, neck, and the exposed parts of his arms. She gasped. So did Danica and Doug. Even John and Marissa were surprised at the obvious beating he had taken. Marissa placed her arm on Daniel's shoulder which only made him flinch. She quickly pulled it back worried she had needlessly caused her boss pain. He tried to dispel her concerns.

"Mr. Mendoza, are you alright?" the judge asked.

"I've had better days, your honor. Trust me, the Caribbean wasn't all cookies and cream," he joked.

Smiling only made the pain worse.

"I can only imagine," the judge added. "I take it your adventure is related to this case."

"Certainly, your honor. If we can discuss this in your chambers, I will be happy to fully explain."

The judge looked toward Mr. Clarkson for his response.

"I have no issues with discussing this privately in chambers," Doug agreed.

## 48  CHAMBERS

Phoenix, Arizona

When Doug walked toward the judge's chambers, Danica followed after him.

Doug stopped and turned to her, "Danica, stay here. This is going to be a waste of time and if it's not, then I need you to be here with the client, so she's reassured."

Danica wasn't pleased.

She gave Doug a perturbed look and said, "You need me, Doug. I know this case inside and out, frankly, better than you. If something weird comes up, I'm better able to address it. Let me take point on this."

"What about me?" Selinda asked. "I want to be there with you, Doug. I've waited so long. I deserve it."

Doug huffed in frustration.

"I'm pulling rank here. Ladies, sit down. I'll be right back."

Doug stormed into the judge's chambers and then tried to compose himself.

Huddled on the left side of the room facing the judge were Daniel, Marissa, and John. They looked on as Doug angrily walked into the judge's chambers. Even the judge was surprised by his entry.

"Counsel?" the judge directed at Doug.

"My apologies, your honor. It's been a long day."

"The day's just started," she added.

"Yes, it has. I guess I have no reason to complain compared to Mr. Mendoza," Doug admitted as he looked over to Daniel awaiting his disclosure.

Looking at him, the judge said, "No. No, you do not. I'm anxious to hear why Mr. Mendoza and his colleagues requested a continuance and if there is any merit to their representation that some star witness will be able to turn this whole thing around. I want to forewarn you, counsel. My courtroom is not a circus. If this isn't a legitimate issue then I will have no choice but to find you in contempt of court. Whether I refer the matter to the State bar is another matter. So, proceed."

"Thank you, your honor. As I previously stated, I've returned from the Caribbean. More specifically, Puerto Rico. Given the strange events that occurred at my hotel, suffice it to say, I was abducted."

The judge's ears perked up.

"I was recently recovered and barely escaped with my life. But the main thing, your honor, is that I wasn't the only one who was abducted. There was another gentleman who was abducted before me. In fact, he was abducted at the same hotel as I was. I and my private investigator were looking into this man's abduction which apparently resulted in my own ab-duction."

Daniel coughed as his voice struggled given its hoarseness.

The judge offered him some water, but he politely refused, not wanting to distract from his purpose.

"Fortunately, not only was I rescued, but the other gentleman was rescued too," he continued. "I was certain there was something about this man that was familiar, exceedingly familiar. I contacted Ms. Robles to alert her about this and to request a continuance so I could travel back to Arizona with the gentleman after confirming whether my suspicions are true."

"What suspicions, Mr. Mendoza?" the judge inquired.

"If it pleases the court, I think it will be better to have him tell you himself."

She nodded. Doug Clarkson was silent yet anxious to find out who he was.

Daniel stood up and exited the judge's chambers to the hallway behind the row of courtrooms on that floor. Within a minute or two he returned. Accompanying him was a prisoner in an orange jumpsuit escorted by two men wearing blue jackets with the words "FBI" on the front. The two FBI men directed the prisoner to sit down in a chair and then flanked him.

Once Daniel was situated, he said, "This is that gentleman, your honor. Can you tell the judge who you are?"

Originally squirming in his seat, the man finally admitted, "My name is Carlos Hernandez. I changed my name once I moved to Arizona. Previously, I went by the name of Carlos Quintana. My father is Jose Quintana. He is the head of *La Familia* which is a Puerto Rican mafia. I moved to Arizona to conduct business on behalf of *La Familia*. However, the business wasn't going well like I thought it would. I needed the money to pay back members of the family who I stole money from. With no way to pay them back, I arranged a scheme with the help of my father to stage an accident. We targeted the resort because we knew it was a profitable, international company with loads of money. To make the scheme work, I faked my death and fled to Puerto Rico to hide out."

The judge looked intently at Carlos.

"Despite your bruises and lacerations, you do look like the photograph of the decedent that's been on the easel in my courtroom the entire time these past two weeks," the judge said as she squinted her eyes to see him clearer. "Yes, I do believe you are Mr. Hernandez."

The judge sighed deeply at the revelation.

She then turned to Doug and asked, "Is this true, Mr. Clarkson? Is this your client who you've claimed this entire time to have died in the accident with the shuttle bus driven by Mr. Weaver?"

"Your honor, as God is my witness, I had no idea Mr. Hernandez was still alive. I've been just as deceived as the court and the rest of the individuals involved in this case. I dare say even Selinda must have been unaware of his machinations. I assure you she and her children have been grieving tremendously at the loss of their husband and father. I've seen it myself numerous times and it's been genuine."

Marissa and John had doubts about Doug's sincerity but thought it better not to voice them to the judge.

———

"Mrs. Quintana, this is Luis. I'm so sorry to disturb you at your home but I have some bad news," he spoke into his cell phone.

She walked to a secluded area of the mansion away from any servants or anyone else who could overhear the conversation and closed the door.

When she was finally alone, she asked, "What is it?"

"We were unable to use our connections to get your son out of federal custody. Before our connection arrived at the FBI building, Carlos had already been flown to the States. There was nothing we could do. I believe he's back in Arizona now. Again, my sincerest apologies."

"Ay, coño!!" she exclaimed in a loud voice.

She quickly restrained herself for fear her husband would hear and inquire about her outburst.

"How could this happen? You assured me you would get him out and bring him back home," she said.

"I know. I'm sorry. I told my men to do just that. They tried the best they could but...."

"But nothing. If Jose finds out his son is in federal custody and back in Arizona he will want blood. He will want someone to pay for that. All of them."

Luis sensed Mrs. Quintana was getting increasingly agitated as the phone call progressed.

Anxious to allay her concerns, he said, "We can try to get him from Arizona but our only connections there are Johnny's men. And I don't think he's willing to cooperate. Not after all that has transpired."

"You don't have any men of your own who you trust to get the job done?"

"I'm afraid not. Even if I could get men there, it won't be in time to prevent Carlos from doing whatever the feds have in store for him."

Luis wasn't sure if Mrs. Quintana was kept in the loop on whatever *Chango* had devised to get their son home. Concerned he may violate his boss's confidence, he opted not to tell her.

"Jose's going to be very disappointed. Very disappointed," she reiterated.

"I understand. I can speak to *Chango* later about it. He also asked me to recover Carlos' body and is expecting an update. I have to tell him Carlos is alive and what happened."

"Leave that to me," she commanded.

"Yes, Mrs. Quintana."

Once she ended the call, Luis had a devious smile. He was extremely proud of himself.

Clearly apprehensive about the latest news, Mrs. Quintana trudged to the other side of the room, grabbed a coffee mug on the table, and then chucked it against the wall, breaking it into pieces. She then gripped her hands tightly into fists in a vain effort to prepare herself for a mental altercation.

*Something went wrong*, she told herself. *I've been betrayed.*

She wondered if the betrayer was Johnny who staged the whole coup or if it was Luis with his swanky outfits and overbearing charm and charisma.

*It could be both. They both stand to gain with my son out of the picture.*

Not wanting to be outplayed by her husband's *copas*, Mrs. Quintana decided to devise her own scheme. Something that would benefit her even at the risk of alienating her husband or even her son. She walked to the other side of the mansion to speak with her husband.

"Jose...."

## 49  DISMISSED

### Phoenix, Arizona

"All rise," the bailiff announced as the jury filed into the courtroom into their assigned seats in the jury box.

They were eager to get the court day started having waited in the jury deliberations room most of the early morning without any understanding of what was going on between the attorneys. Hearing rumors that the trial was continued for a day because of a mystery witness piqued the jury's interest. Most were excited to find out who the witness was and what testimony the witness would bring to bear that could change the case or change the minds of the jurors. They had been previously admonished not to deliberate in the jury room unless all of the jurors were present. But, like most humans who were prone to inquisitiveness, despite the admonition, they secretly spoke amongst each other when certain testimony was salacious or the conflict between counsel was especially combative. Even when there were moments they believed the judge was being protective of the jury, it was a cause of celebration and gossip among the jurors.

But this morning, the bailiff seemed to be in the jury room most of the time, running in and out to speak with the judge or running any errand the judge requested. The jurors were reticent to speak to each other in front of the bailiff for fear it violated some court rule and they could be ousted from the trial. After giving so much of their time, it was the last thing any of the jurors wanted.

Walking to their seats, grabbing their jury notebooks and a pen, and listening to the judge once more was all they wanted now.

"Members of the jury, I apologize for the delay, but there has been a development that has taken up a considerable amount of my time this morning. I assure you, we were hard at work just as hard as you work every day on this case. And I want to personally thank you for that," the judge said as she faced the jury.

All of the jurors were beaming at the judge's pronouncement.

Facing counsel's table, the judge said, "Mr. Clarkson, earlier, you requested some time to speak with your clients about the latest development. Were you able to confer with your clients and make a decision?"

Doug stood up. He was obviously dejected but purposed to stay composed for the sake of his clients and his reputation as an attorney.

"Yes, your honor. I wanted to thank you for that opportunity. I've conferred with my clients and they all have agreed to voluntarily dismiss this case."

"Good," the judge replied. "I believe that is the right thing to do. Mrs. Robles?"

"Your honor, although we appreciate the plaintiffs' willingness to dismiss the case, which we do not oppose, there are other matters we will ultimately need the court to address. I presume it will be briefed before the court. But we believe this is a travesty of justice that my clients were needlessly forced to try this case and incur the expenses of attorneys' fees, expert fees, and the time and effort to attend trial. We believe there has been a Rule 11 violation for bringing this case to trial when the decedent was never actually dead," Marissa argued with pose and determination.

"Counsel, let me stop you there. I appreciate the arguments and agree that there may be some merit to them. But as you already acknowledged, I think this issue is more complicated and should be briefed. Besides, I do not want to take any more of the jury's precious time given that the parties have already agreed to dismiss the case. Do you agree?" the judge asked.

After looking at Daniel for tacit approval, Marissa said, "By all means, your honor, I certainly agree with dismissing the jury and allowing these good people whose service we appreciated to go back to their homes, their jobs, and their lives."

"Mr. Clarkson?" the judge said.

"Your honor, of course, my clients agree that the jury should be dismissed."

"Thank you, counsel. With that, I am dismissing the jury and thanking you all for your service. Have a pleasant day," the judge announced.

"All rise," the bailiff repeated for the last time.

The jurors dispersed confused by their sudden

and unexplained dismissal. Murmurs were heard among the jurors as they speculated upon themselves while they gathered their belongings.

"This was a great trial," the juror who was a college student declared.

Some of the jurors who heard his remark gave confounded looks given his lack of attention at times.

Before the jury exited the courtroom, the side door opened, and a prisoner was being escorted through the courtroom by the FBI. All eyes were transfixed on the prisoner. A couple of jurors pointed to the easel and also to the prisoner.

One juror said in a hushed voice, "It's him. It's Carlos."

The others gasped at the revelation and turned toward the defense counsel's table. John and Marissa gently smiled as the jury watched them. Carl and Robin were finally present in court after having been informed of the revelation. They seemed just as proud of the outcome given they had done a lot of work behind the scenes the jury wasn't aware of.

Selinda and her children watched in dismay as her husband exited the courtroom. She struggled to hold back tears, both of joy and relief as well as sadness. They exited shortly after him along with their attorneys.

———

When the courtroom was devoid of any jurors, court staff, and also their clients, only members of the Mendoza firm were present. Marissa finally gave out a deep sigh of relief.

"I'm glad it's over," she admitted.

"Me too," John said. "I can't believe Doug didn't say goodbye or anything like that. He didn't even acknowledge us. What a bad sport!"

"I'm sure he's devastated," Daniel said. "He doesn't take losses well and this was a big one for him. He may never get over it."

"I bet," John said.

Daniel grinned although he knew he shouldn't have. The rivalry between the two attorneys was unspoken but Daniel relished the win even though he wasn't actually involved in the trial.

"Marissa, if you don't mind, can we talk," Carl said as he grabbed her catalog case filled with her trial notebooks and started walking toward the door.

"Sure," she said as she waved goodbye to everyone else.

She was uncertain why Carl wanted to speak after a grueling trial, but he had been there for her during it and she wanted to return the favor.

*It could be good news about Samantha*, she thought as the two left the courtroom.

Robin was going to embrace Daniel, but he stopped her because of the pain. He didn't want to offend her, so he gave her an air hug instead. She returned the gesture with a smile.

"Robin, I'm really glad you're here. Sorry I wasn't a part of the trial, but we appreciate all of your efforts in helping John and Marissa," Daniel said.

"Yes, we do," John added. "You and Carl are an invaluable part of the team."

He decided not to go into all of the detail while in court but would speak to her about her contributions once they were back in the office.

"Next time, we will make sure you're in the courtroom playing a critical role," Daniel insisted.

John agreed.

"I'd like that," Robin said eager to finally get into the courtroom after all of her years at her prior job working solely in the office and reviewing documents.

She smiled as the trio walked out together.

———

As the trio exited the courthouse so they could walk to the adjacent parking lot, they saw Selinda Hernandez pacing the sidewalk with a cell phone in her hand. They ignored her and kept walking to their parked cars.

When Selinda saw the opposing counsel, she became serious and alert. She stopped talking so the intruders into her conversation couldn't hear it. She watched them intensely with feelings of repulsion. When they were out of earshot, she continued.

"Mr. Quintana, as I was saying, I had to agree to dismiss the case. I had no choice. There was nothing we could do about it. They found Carlos."

She listened as *Chango* spoke.

"I don't know how they did it. I'm surprised myself."

She looked around her to ensure no one else overheard her conversation.

"I wouldn't put it past Johnny to sell him out after you told me what he's done."

She became furious at the thought of her husband being tortured and shot. When he walked out of the courtroom, she could see the strength in his eyes

322

nonetheless and admired him for that. She knew he was a fighter and always would be.

"If there is anything you need, Mr. Quintana, please let me know. I have Johnny's contacts here in Arizona. I agree that is one way to get him back."

Selinda was pleased as the prospect *Chango* would seek revenge on behalf of her and her husband.

# 50 DISCUSSION

Scottsdale, Arizona
Later That Night

Daniel Mendoza parked his car along the street near Pamela Williams' house. He looked at her house and could see inside her front window. Inside, Milagros, Pamela's sister, was seated at the dining room table smiling at her father who was apparently telling her one of his numerous adventures when he was in the special forces. She certainly adored her father even more so than Pamela.

Daniel walked toward her house somewhat apprehensive. Social gatherings were not his forte. But Pamela mattered to him in a way he fully did not understand. Ringing the doorbell, Daniel waited as he heard footsteps approaching in the distance.

"Who's at the door?"

Daniel could hear Gavin's voice through the door and the clanging of utensils.

"Don't worry, dad. Pam will get it," the sister said.

As the door slowly opened, Pamela appeared smiling from whatever conversation she previously had. She became stoic when she realized who was at the door.

"Hey, Daniel. I'm surprised. What are you doing here?" she asked while closing the door behind her.

"I...I came to see your father," he nervously replied unsure how she would respond because he hadn't told her about any visit.

"You shouldn't be here. You should be at home resting. Isn't that what the doctor told you?"

"I made a promise and I always keep my promises."

He awkwardly smiled given that his last comment sounded like a cliche. However, Pamela knew how Daniel was and knew his last statement was true. She grinned.

"That's so sweet," she said as she gently touched his shoulder.

She walked to chairs on her porch. The chairs faced the dimly lit residential street she'd lived on for the past decade. She sat down on one of them. Staring at the empty one, Daniel gave a confused look and pointed toward the front door.

"It's alright. Sit down. They won't miss me for a while. Dad's preoccupied. So is Cameron."

As he approached the chair and painfully sat down, Daniel said, "Cameron's inside? That's great to hear you two are finally getting along again."

"I wouldn't say that. It's a start. One of many. But this time I'm hopeful we can make it work for the long haul. He seems sincere."

Daniel listened quietly without responding. He saw the joy and concern on Pamela's face and didn't want to interfere in what she was feeling or thinking.

He was simply pleased to see this softer side of her he hadn't seen before.

*Her father's health issues must have reawakened them*, he thought.

Not wanting to seem overly emotional in front of her client who was now slowly becoming a dear friend in recent years, Pamela restrained any sniffles and said, "Sorry, I couldn't make it to court. I would have loved to hear what happened and watched all their faces reacting to it, especially Doug's face."

Daniel smiled. He also wanted Pamela there but understood why she wasn't even though she played an intricate role in the initial investigation and apprehension of the captive and the other mafia members. During the flight back from Puerto Rico, she mentioned having to do other things in addition to seeing her father once they landed.

Wanting to fill her in, Daniel explained that the kidnapped resort guest owed money to some of the other mafia members and how he concocted a scheme to cause the car accident to sue Regal Wisteria. When his injuries weren't severe enough to collect enough money to pay off the debt, he faked his death and fled to Puerto Rico to avoid discovery.

"Wow, what nerve? I guess the forensic pathologist was in on it?" Pamela asked.

"You mean, Dr. Weimar. It most definitely seems that way. Looks like he may be prosecuted for his role in the scheme. I'm sure the medical board is going to investigate as well. He may end up losing his medical license."

"He should. It's despicable behavior."

Daniel was surprised at Pamela's comment. She normally refrained from making judgments about an individual's actions especially because she had seen so much as a private investigator nothing seemed to faze her. It was another slight change he'd recently noticed about Pamela.

"And plaintiff's counsel. Was he in on it too?" she inquired.

"That's the thing. We don't know at this time. He vehemently denied it in court today. But to be honest, I suspect he was. He was the one who called Dr. Weimar. There was no way Dr. Weimar could get to the accident scene so fast given the traffic that day unless he knew in advance to be there just in case."

Pamela shook her head in disbelief.

"I'm not surprised. I've seen far worse," she admitted. "I suppose if he's involved he'll lose his law license too."

"It's certainly a possibility," Daniel added. "After all these years he's been in the profession, I'm sure Doug will just retire if it comes to that. His wife has been asking him to retire for years, but he loves practicing law even at his age."

Contemplating a fellow attorney losing a law license concerned Daniel. The uncertainties of the legal practice combined with varying ethical issues consumed many attorneys over the years. Most who lost their license were blinded by greed or were unable to handle the unending stress accompanying their profession. Daniel counted himself lucky he hadn't fallen into the same conundrum.

"I spoke with Gerry today about what happened," Pamela tepidly admitted out of concern Daniel would think she overstepped her boundaries.

Instead, he perked up at the comment.

"What did he have to say about all this?"

"He told me that Mr. Hernandez, actually Mr. Quintana's father was arrested by the feds along with two of his top men. Someone high up in the organization is working with the feds and tipped them off about the kidnapping and their whereabouts. He's not sure who it was."

Daniel remembered all the terrifying exchanges he heard while sitting there in the darkness.

"It sounded like something was going on with this mafia family. I just don't know what it was. I heard they're one of the largest mafia families on the island. I can only imagine what will happen as a result of this new power vacuum."

"Gerry didn't seem concerned. He hinted that there was already another head of the family. He didn't know who, but I think it was the one who tipped off the feds. At least, that's my suspicion."

"I tell you, I went to Puerto Rico to relax. The last thing I wanted to do was get in the middle of some internal mafia dispute," Daniel regretfully expressed.

He then groaned as his body subconsciously tightened from the pain he endured over the past few days. The topic was a subtle reminder of it.

"Are you alright?" Pamela asked while she watched his body writhe.

"I'm okay. The doctor said I'll be in pain for a few days possibly a week or two with my bruised ribs. But I can't take it," he said while smirking so he could come across as more manly in front of her.

Pamela decided not to reply with her typical snarky remark. She just smiled in response.

Daniel's cell phone rang interrupting what he was going to sarcastically say to express appreciation for her restraint. He glanced at the caller id and said, "I have to take this."

"Okay. I'll leave you alone."

Pamela entered her house and rejoined the festivities with her family. The aroma of food and drinks wafted onto the porch before she closed the door.

"Hey, Ed. How are you doing?"

Daniel lowered his voice so he could have some privacy.

"Bro, I'm fine. How are you?"

"It's a long story, but I'm okay. What's going on that you're calling me today?"

"I just got a call from Gerald Ravan. He told me your firm is counsel for his company. I've just got a new case from him. There was an explosion at one of the luxury villas at the Regal Wailea resort in Maui just south of where I live. Gerry wants you to help me on this one."

"Really? I'd love to work with you on this one. It'll be the first time we've worked on a lawsuit together since we graduated from law school."

"Let me get the paperwork together so you can get temporarily admitted into the court here in Hawaii."

"Thanks, bro," Daniel said with a beaming smile.

"Hey, I have to get to this inspection right now. It's last minute. I'll talk with you later."

"Sure. Call me tomorrow."

"Will do," Ed replied.

Daniel was extremely pleased he heard from his fraternity brother from college. They had slowly drifted apart once Ed Steinmann moved from the Los Angeles area to Hawaii after he graduated from law school.

*This new case we'll definitely give us the chance to reconnect.*

Daniel painfully stood up and walked to the front door.

Opening the door, Daniel asked, "Hey, what's for dinner?"

All eyes focused on him when he entered as the ongoing boisterous discussion continued.

## THE END

## ABOUT THE AUTHOR

 Mr. Maldonado is an attorney in the Phoenix area that has practiced insurance coverage and employment discrimination law. He is a co-author/editor of Couch on Insurance, a multi-volume treatise on insurance law. Mr. Maldonado is also a contributing author on CAT Claims: Insurance Coverage for Natural and Man-Made Disasters. Mr. Maldonado also wrote the employment chapter for the Arizona Tort Law Handbook. He has contributed to various law reviews and other articles. Now, Mr. Maldonado takes his hand to an area of personal satisfaction: relationships and emotional experiences.

———

To learn more about Daniel Maldonado and discover more Next Chapter authors, visit our website at www.nextchapter.pub.

# BIBLIOGRAPHY

This is a list of books and short stories written and published by Daniel Maldonado:

## Daniel Mendoza Thriller Series

*May it Please the Court: Daniel Mendoza Thrillers Series, Book 1* – A realistic legal thriller involving the suspicious death of a civil plaintiff. Daniel Mendoza's legal team is hired to defend the hotel and determine what really happened and if foul play was involved. It made the Short List nomination for the 2020 Drunken Druid International Book Award.

*The Fleeing Felon: Daniel Mendoza Thrillers Series, Book 2* – After a fleeing felon is involved in a fatal crash, Daniel Mendoza's legal team defends the corporate entity whose truck was involved. But was the crash an accident or a murder?

*The Mendoza Memo: Daniel Mendoza Thrillers Series, Book 3* – During the deposition, a witness becomes fatally ill. Other individuals associated with the royalty lawsuit litigated by the Mendoza law firm also show up dead. Daniel Mendoza and his team don't know why but need to figure it out before one of them are next.

*Where Darkness Resides: Daniel Mendoza Thrillers Series, Book 4* – While vacationing at in Puerto Rico, Daniel Mendoza and his investigator witnesses an abduction of a hotel guest. While investigating the case, Daniel is missing. Is he still or the case or did something else happen to him?

## Chambers Lane Series

*From the Streets of Chambers Lane* - The intriguing story of the Mendoza family's unexpected loss of their youngest son and sibling, Michael. Dealing with spiritual struggles and disillusionment as well as familial rivalries and quirky social interactions, the novella introduces the reader to each diverse family member's perspective of the tragic event while personalizing their cultural past and fears of the unknown future.

*When Dreams Abound: A Return to Chambers Lane* - Fatherless, Daniel Mendoza learns from a myriad of male friends and neighbors who come into his life from childhood to adulthood about what it actually means to be a man.

*The Prodigal Son from Chambers Lane* - The oldest son, Jose Luis Mendoza, Junior, battles a haunting past secret that has hindered his growth even into his adult years. He must confront his unloving and hard-hearted mother and others who have betrayed his desire to be loved before he is able to escape it and embrace his future.

*Butterflies Blue: An Interlude in San Juan, Puerto Rico* - While vacationing on the tropical Caribbean island of Puerto Rico with her newest boyfriend, Layla unexpectedly encounters her former jealous boyfriend, Leon, who desperately wants her back.

*Collection of Short Stories*

*The Palace of Winds and Other Short Stories* - A collection of poignant short stories addressing romance, failures, intrigues, and beliefs from a male perspective.

*Through Thunder and Light* - A follow up to the original compilation "The Palace of Winds and Other Short Stories."

**Thank You**

Dear reader,

Thank you for spending your time reading *Where Darkness Resides* (*Daniel Mendoza Thrillers, Book 4*). I value your word of mouth and appreciate any efforts you can expend to let others know about my books. If you enjoyed this book, please consider supporting me by doing any of the following:

- Please leave a book review on Amazon.com (also for your country's version of Amazon if different), Goodreads, BookBub, and any other book site that you use to help market and promote this book.
- Please tell your family, friends, coworkers, and colleagues about this author and his books.
- Please share brief posts on your social media platforms and tag the book (#ChambersLane) and/or the author (#DanielMalAuthor) on Twitter, Facebook, Instagram, WordPress, etc.
- Please suggest the book for book clubs, book stores, schools, or any local libraries that you know.

Again, thank you in advance for your support. I look forward to reading your review and hope you enjoy the rest of the series and my other books.

Where Darkness Resides
ISBN: 978-4-82416-653-1
Mass Market

Published by
Next Chapter
2-5-6 SANNO
SANNO BRIDGE
143-0023 Ota-Ku, Tokyo
+818035793528

23rd January 2023

Printed in the USA
CPSIA information can be obtained
at www.ICGtesting.com
CBHW010955080224
4120CB00051B/1304